My Life with a Few Fabrications

by

Ken Gray

RoseDog Books

PITTSBURGH, PENNSYLVANIA 15222

The contents of this work including, but not limited to, the accuracy of events, people, and placed are depicted; opinions expressed; permission to use previously published materials included; and any advice given or actions advocated are solely the responsibility of the author, who assumes all liability for said work and indemnifies the publisher against any claims stemming from publication of the work.

ISBN: 978-0-0859-8725-6
Library of Congress Control Number: 2007921219
Printed in the United States of America

First Printing

For more information or to order additional books, please contact:
RoseDog Books
701 Smithfield Street
Third Floor
Pittsburgh, Pennsylvania 15222
U.S.A.
1-800-834-1803
www.rosedogbookstore.com

Chapter I

Smokey opened the smelter for the final pour with a large, pointed rod. Gerry moved the bucket into position. The men stood around waiting to shake out the mouldings. This was the final day that these men would sweat ten pounds of fluid each in a matter of three hours. The single meager exhaust fan rattled away like rocks shaken in a tin can. Bellwood Foundry was no more: it was to be shut down. Smokey finished the last pour and headed to the basement. His cheque and pink slip were in the time-slot box. He checked the amounts, looked at the burns all over his arms, and shook his head. He thought, I did this job for one year, while some of these men have worked this piece of Hell for thirty years. *But most had died at around age forty-five after twenty years or so.*

I consider myself lucky, he thought. The place should have been closed down years ago for health and safety reasons. The air quality was so poor in the winter, the men often had lung, throat, and eye infections. Some men even had open sores on their skin. How could a place like this operate in 1985 with all the government health and safety regulations? At first he couldn't understand, it but gradually things became clear. Governments purchased the end products-sewer grates and catch basins were always being made for municipal government. And after all, Bellwood was the only foundry in southern Saskatchewan. The health and safety inspectors would come, peek their heads in through the door, and sign a sheet giving Bellwood the green light.

Ah, well, Smokey thought, *it's over. I got my layoff notice and can collect UI for awhile.* It would be hard work trying to get another job. Jobs were like small miracles in Saskatchewan, even in the government town of Regina. He had been trapped into working for Bellwood. His UIC had run out,and there were no other prospects in sight. He thought he would just do the job for awhile till something else came along, but.nothing else had come along in a whole year and he was in a bind now again. A year had gone by and he had gone from accounting manager to foundry worker. The problem was, he couldn't get his CMA designation. He had tried to get through Quantitative Methods three times and failed each time. His career as an accountant was essentially over, and labour jobs had dried up. He really didn't know which way to turn in terms of a decent career. He still felt he possessed both management skills and analytical ability, but there were no takers.

Smokey sat down in the Foundry basement, too tired to wash his hands. Holding his paycheck, he gazed at the floor. Willy came in. "What am I going to do now?" he cried.

Willy was a long-term survivor. He had spent twenty-five years in the foundry as a moulder and was now sixty-seven years old. Willy had helped him catch on to moulding. He knew the politics of hourly wages and piece work. He had seen men broken in only a few years, men badly burnt. He had taught Smokey how to pace himself through an eight-hour day.

Smokey looked at Willy and said, "It's time to retire, Willy. Thanks for all your help." There was no one else Smokey wanted to talk to, so he climbed the stairs and headed out the door. The sun hurt his eyes after every pour. He made his way to his car.

It wasn't just any car. It was a baby-blue '67 Ford Fairlane 289 two-door hardtop. He had rebuilt the motor in it back in '74 when he was still in high school. It had lasted all these years. He remembered he had worked the whole summer to pay for the new pistons and rings and the bore job at his uncle's trucking terminal. He had spent most of the summer working with a mechanic rebuilding a 230 Cummins diesel for a tractor trailer. It was all excellent experience if you wanted to be a mechanic, but that just didn't interest Smokey. He believed even back then that he was management material of some nature. Years had passed, and he had been given plenty of opportunities.

Smokey started the Fairlane and pulled out into traffic. He headed straight down Dewdney Avenue on the way to Ellis Street where his shack was situated. On the way he thought about the job opportunities he had had and how much more difficult the jobs were to get. He had worked for an agricultural firm for three years and had moved up the ladder quickly, but he wasn't satisfied with that. A few years later he found himself working as the accounting manager for a small retail cooperative in eastern Saskatchewan. The pressure had gotten to him in that job; small town politics had played havoc with him.

Despite all his experience, there were no takers back in Regina except for Bellwood. Now he had a few months' grace to search for opportunities. Smokey thought about unemployment and his father's experience with careers. His father had always wanted to be a doctor but ended up a commercial airline pilot. A glorified taxi driver, he had told his sons. His father was bright enough to be a doctor but couldn't get used to the sight of blood. Eventually he had failed his labs. He had also wanted to be a writer and completed two novels, never published, His second book was all about life-failures and depression and was filled with references to suicide. In the end, his father had backed his Volkswagen onto the highway in front of a three-ton truck, and that was his end. Was it an accident? It was a question Smokey had struggled with for years. But Smokey was in a similar situation as his father had been trapped in-taking unfulfilling jobs in order to survive, or worse on Pogy.

Smokey pulled into his driveway and turned off the key. He was home. Home was a small one-bedroom bungalow. It had been built from an old railway car initially and expanded gradually with additions. It had cedar siding and a tar roof. It wasn't much, but it was definitely home. It was 3:30 P.M. He had just enough time for a bath and half an hour to snooze before Red would call.

Red and Smokey had been friends for ten years, and now they were canoeing partners. They had been practicing every day since early March, and the first marathon canoe race was just days away, June sixteenth. It was to be held on an old creek between Lumsden and Craven in Saskatchewan. It was a difficult creek to race with several dead-heads and objects in the water. There was also current that flowed in channels that one had to learn. Home teams definitely had an advantage. Red and Smokey knew the course well and had every intention of surprising everyone as rookies.

Red had purchased a Mega Tuck racing shell from a racer in Saskatoon. The boat was designed for a heavier bow man and a lighter sternsman. That was perfect for them. Smokey was down to 176 pounds, but his ideal weight was 185. Red was about 140 pounds. They had been practicing in that shell now for well over a month.

Smokey ran the bath water and sat on the can thinking. He had been a bit of a disappointment to Red already. It wasn't that he wasn't committed. He was, but with the physical demands of the foundry, paddling a canoe ten miles every night was just beyond his capacity. He had been chubby at 216 pounds eight months ago. Now he was 176 pounds at six feet one-inch. That just wasn't enough meat on the bones. Things would be different now that the foundry was shut down. He could commit fully to a summer of marathon canoe races. The way he figured it, they were already pretty good. They hadn't raced anybody yet, but he knew they could really move. People often watched them from the shores of Wascana Lake, where they practiced every day.

Smokey jumped in the tub and watched the water turn black. He closed his eyes and relaxed. He was too tired to think anymore, and in less than ten minutes he was fast asleep, dreaming about being the provincial champions in marathon canoeing.

The phone rang; it was Red. "I'll meet you at the lake in twenty minutes," he said.

Smokey looked at his watch. He had slept for an hour in the tub. He dressed and headed out the door with his paddle in his hand. It was a Grey Owl Marathon blade with a bend in the shaft. He wanted to get a graphite blade, but they were just too expensive.

When he reached the lake, Red had the boat in the water and was sitting on the dock waiting. "Hi. How are you feeling tonight?" Red asked.

"Okay, I guess. Tired," Smokey said. Smokey got into the bow of the canoe and adjusted the seat. He checked his bottle for water. It was full. He put the hose which ran from the jug of water into his mouth.

Red got into the stern and said, "Draw out." Smokey did a draw with his paddle until the bow of the canoe was facing open water. He started with a slow stroke-rate of about sixty-five strokes a minute. The paddlers would switch sides every seven or eight strokes at Red's command. Some paddlers called out "Beep" to signify changes, but most, like Red, called out "Hut."

The logic behind switching sides is twofold. First, it helps with direction of the canoe, and second (and more important), muscle efficiency drops off to about sixty percent after seven or eight strokes, so switching to the other side uses another set of muscles, giving the first side a rest.

The first couple of miles always seemed to hurt. No matter what you did, you just had to break the threshold of pain and move on. Smokey felt the burning in his arms and abdominals. He knew he was dragging his butt. It would only be a matter of time before Red would want to pick up the pace. It seemed like the canoe was a bit out of trim, so Smokey adjusted the seat again. They had almost completed the first lap of the three-mile lake when Red said, "Let's pick up the pace." Smokey groaned but picked up the pace to about seventy strokes a minute.

They cruised the lake a second time around. Some people were yelling out, "Stroke, stroke, stroke," on the shoreline. They finished the second lap of the lake, and once again Red said, "Let's pick up the pace."

Smokey tried, but his muscles burned terribly and he was having trouble breathing. He had developed a cough and congestion a day or two ago. Smokey finally said, "I just haven't got any more in me tonight. Sorry." They cruised the lake a third time, but that was it. Smokey was wasted.

Red said, "Tomorrow after we finish work, we should do one last trip down Lumsden to Craven to check the water levels and any new obstructions that may have formed."

Smokey agreed and they called it a night. Smokey went back to his Fairlane, and the front tire was flat. He was sure somebody had let the air out of it. He took out the spare and jacked the front end up. When he took off the front tire, he saw the nail in it. He thought, *I guess I was a little paranoid, but you just can't trust anybody these days.*

Smokey drove home slowly because the spare tire was a winter-grip and on the front, it affected the steering. When he got home, he crawled up the steps. The front door was open...had he forgotten to lock the door or had someone broken in? He surveyed the room, checking for missing items. Everything seemed to be in place. He flaked out on the couch and took off his shoes. The nights were still cool, so he lit a fire in the pot-belly stove and put on the screen so he could watch the flames.

As the flames turned to embers, Smokey thought about the book he had read by Carlos Casteneda. He remembered how Don Juan, the sorcerer, had talked about finding power-spots in the home. Smokey wondered, "How do you know if a certain spot is powerful?" Then he remembered his friend Bill telling him about this vision he had had while working in Smokey's kitchen. Bill was an upholsterer part-time. He didn't have the strength to do the work full-time because he suffered from Becker's muscular dystrophy. Anyway, Bill had said that this vision he had was so real that it was like he was in another time-zone. He had seen himself as a farmer out on the prairie, not a tree in sight-just the scorching blaze of the summer sun. It was like he could really feel it. The vision had only lasted a few moments, but Bill had to tell Smokey about it. "It was no dream," he had said, "and some place it really happened." Could it be that Bill had found a power spot?

Smokey also remembered an experience his sister had when she came to visit and stayed overnight. He remembered she had left the house screaming in the middle of the night. She simply said, "I can't stay here. I just can't stay here." Later the next day, she explained that something had tried to pass through her body that night, some type of force she couldn't explain.

Smokey thought there was no doubt about it-his little home had special powers. So many people had had some sort of experience in his home.

The embers crackled and smoldered away in the stove. Smokey got up and went to the bedroom for a blanket. He wrapped a comforter around himself and curled up on the couch for the evening. Soon he was in dreamland. He dreamed of this beautiful woman in outer space. They were swimming between the stars together. Then suddenly, the woman changed into a pasty-white corpse and screamed into his mind, "Leave the dead alone."

Smokey woke up and felt his heart pounding in his chest. He felt prickly all over. He lay there in the dark listening to himself breathing. He drifted in and out of sleep, a very shallow sleep, the rest of the night.

The next morning, Smokey was up at 6:30. He headed for the bathroom for a morning shower. The water felt good running off his face. Breakfast. He knew he had to put on the pounds if he was going to be strong enough for the first race. He coughed for a few minutes trying to break the tightness in his chest. Five scrambled eggs and a cheese sandwich was a good start to breakfast. He munched his sandwich and thought about the day. He had to get the tire fixed on his car first thing. Then he had to take his pink slip down to the UIC office and register for unemployment insurance. Then he should have a short nap before he and Red headed out to Lumsden for a paddle.

When Smokey got to Freddy's Garage, he noticed the spare he had put on yesterday was low. He decided to invest in two new tires despite the fact that money was going to be tight. (He needed to be safe and bad front tires were just asking for an accident.) Freddy also mentioned that the muffler system needed replacing. Smokey knew it but he just couldn't afford everything right now, and Freddy had stopped giving credit a few years back after a bad experience.

The next stop was the UI shop. Smokey had hated the thought of having to go to that place, but he had to register anyway. Smokey opened the door to the UIC building and stepped inside. The air was thicker in here-thick with depression, thick with anxiety, and thick with judgment. One of the workers he recognized. She gave him that look that said, "You again." Smokey growled and went to the registration line-up.

After completing the forms, Smokey checked the boards just in case there was something up there, but the only recent job was a telephone sales job on commission. Not his cup of tea. He thought to himself, *There has to be a better way to get a job than coming to this piss-hole every day.* He knew from experience to keep records of every place he applied and every ad he answered. Before UIC ever paid, they would call you in and ask for a list of places where you had applied to for work. If you couldn't produce a worksheet, no UIC for you.

Smokey said to himself, "I'm not coming back here again. I'll start my door-to-door campaign again in a couple of weeks." He had plenty of time-it would be six to eight weeks before he got a penny out of the UIC offices.

On his way home he decided to fill out a few job applications at places he knew were hopeless unless you had connections. He could use the names for his list of potential employers in case the UIC office called early. So Smokey stopped in at the post office and filled out an application. He filled one out every year just for the hell of it. He knew that people like him never got those types of jobs. Next stop was the power company. He applied there every year too.

Finally he stopped at the provincial government offices and applied for casual or contract work. Another joke! Smokey knew at least forty companies that wouldn't hire, and he could fill out applications there to complete his list for UIC. But where was he going to find a real job? He hated playing these games, but there was little choice. He had been searching for a job for two years. He had spent a year on UIC and a year in the foundry actively looking for work. He had applied to over two hundred box numbers in the local paper with no response-not even one interview. He wondered to himself if possibly he was blacklisted as an employee from a previous job. It certainly would explain the lack of interviews and interest in his resumé.

If all went well, he would have at least another ten months to find work. But what was he qualified to do besides labour and a bit of bookkeeping?

Smokey made up his mind right there that he would need to retrain in some capacity. The right thing to do was to go back to the UIC building, as much as it hurt his pride, and analyze what type of jobs were on the market.

Smokey reached his little hut and checked his watch. It was only 2:00. Red wouldn't be off work till 5:30 that evening. He was tired but he couldn't sleep. He kept thinking about his unemployment situation, and he also thought about others who were struggling with unemployment.

Smokey sat down at the kitchen table and pulled out a lump of clay from his plastic bag. He had done a number of sculptures just for fun. He thought about the stress and anxiety before he was laid off. He remembered the lies. The manager had told him that if he could just produce a little more in the next few weeks, there would be a job for him in shipping and receiving when the foundry closed down. He had worked like a dog, believing he would have a job at the end of it all. Then the boys in the foundry gathered around him and clued him in. The manager had offered the same job to every employee who he thought could produce more. There was no shipping and receiving job available.

There was also pressure from the shop steward to produce as little as possible after the layoff notice came out. There were a lot of angry, depressed, short-fused men during the last few weeks.

Smokey thought about other people too who were laid off, even professionals. With the clay, soon he had created a hill or small mountain with cliffs and spikes and razor edges to represent the pressure before the layoff. At the tip of the mountain was the layoff notice and separation slip. Then down the mountain into a gully the clay went. He tried to mould what it felt like to be inside the UIC building. He tried to represent what it felt like trying to deal with a bank or a landlord while on UIC. Then he sculpted the essence of an unsuccessful employment search, including rejection letters. Finally he sculpted the trip to the welfare office and the humiliating experience. Smokey had also created other aspects in his sculpture, such as a hole in the center of it which represented suicide. It took him close to three hours to finish it, but when he was done, he felt it was an excellent, expressive piece of work. He would have it fired and then glaze it with colors.

It was 5:00. Red would be off work in half an hour. So Smokey decided to close his eyes for a couple of minutes, but he had another coughing fit and went to the bathroom to get rid of some phlegm. He noticed for the first time that his phlegm had brown flecks of dried blood in it. He was a little worried about that but thought that his lungs were just clearing themselves out. His chest was still tight and he was sweating quite a bit. Smokey really didn't feel up to a fifteen-mile practice this evening, but he knew he couldn't let his partner down.

At 5:30 on the dot, Red phoned and they decided to meet at Red's place in fifteen minutes. Smokey was sweating profusely now and wondered if it was tension. They took both cars so they could transfer the canoe at the end of the paddle since it was a one-way trip. They dropped off Smokey's car in Craven and then headed back to Lumsden. Red said, "Your sweating quite a bit from just sitting in a car."

"Don't worry, I'm just nervous about the race on Saturday," Smokey said. They got the canoe into the water and placed all the equipment inside. Smokey got in first while Red held the canoe. Bow man always gets in first.

They started their paddle, Red calling the "huts" every seven or eight strokes. They started off slowly and built up to seventy strokes a minute. Smokey just couldn't seem to get his second wind.. His chest was still really tight. They had paddled for about half an hour when Smokey tasted agricultural spray in his mouth. He thought, *Those damn farmers will poison us all!* He hoped it wasn't hopper spray. That stuff often killed gophers, burrowing owls, even cats and dogs. Smokey could feel his eyes stinging and his throat constricting. He looked up into the sky to see if he could see the spraying plane, but he saw nothing.

When they reached Craven, Smokey felt like he was trying to breath through a straw. He was sweating profusely, and his eyes were half swollen shut. Red seemed unaffected by what was in the air. They packed the canoe on Smokey's car and headed back to Lumsden to pick up Red's car. They talked about race day, about various strategies, and when to make their move.

When they got to Lumsden, Smokey turned to Red and said, "I feel really sick."

Red looked worried and said, "We'll take tomorrow off and rest before the race."

Smokey drove the Fairlane back to Regina and straight to a medical clinic. He sat in the waiting room for perhaps half an hour before a young woman said, "Hello, I'm Dr. Johns. Please come with me." Smokey started to cough. "That sounds real healthy," Doctor Johns said sarcastically. "We had better take a chest x-ray just to be sure we know what we are dealing with. What other symptoms do you have?"

"I'm hot and sweaty all the time," said Smokey. Dr. Johns stuck a thermometer in his mouth and began to read Smokey's past medical history.

"I see you were in a few months ago for an eye infection. Are you still employed as a foundry worker?"

"No, the place shut down last week."

"Good, you're too good for that life. You know, there is a real demand for male nurses. Just think about it. If you don't have the money, you could get a student loan."

Bed pans, needles, and pills-was that his calling? Smokey didn't know, but he would think about it.

Dr. Johns took the thermometer out of Smokey's mouth. "Hmm, 102 degrees," she said. "Let's get that x-ray done, then we'll talk."

After the x-ray, Smokey waited for what seemed like eternity before Dr. Johns came back. "Well, you have bronchial infection in both your lungs and a nasty fever. You have also been exposed to something that has irritated the linings of your throat and nasal passages. I'm going to give you an antibiotic to help fight the infection, and I want you to get a lot of rest for the next few days."

Smokey said thanks and headed to the pharmacy to get his prescription filled. When he got home, he took the antibiotic and curled up on the couch. After a few minutes, he got up and started a fire in the pot-bellied stove. He thought about race day Saturday. What could he do? It wasn't fair; they had planned this day for months, now what was he to do? Maybe if he rested all day tomorrow, he would be ready for the race. All he could do was hope and pray.

Smokey awoke the next morning at about 11:00. He had slept for nearly twelve hours. He was hot and clammy. The first thing he did was check his temperature. It was just under 102. At least it was going down slightly. He went to the kitchen and drank four or five glasses of water, then checked the refrigerator for contents. It would be a cheese omelet, toast, and hash browns today.

After breakfast, Smokey decided on a warm bath and lay in the tub for nearly an hour until he caught a bit of a chill and had to hop out and into a towel. He spent the rest of the day curled up in a comforter on the couch reading his book on sorcery. He thought, *There are so many things that happen on an unconscious level, including sickness.* How had he become so ill so quickly? Red remained in good health. What was his source of power?

After a big plate of pasta for supper that evening, Smokey decided he could use all the sleep he could get. After all, tomorrow was race day and he had to be ready. The phone rang. Smokey looked at the clock; it was 7:30. He was clammy and his chest was tight.

"Hello?"

"Ya, it's me. I'll be over to pick you up in twenty minutes. We can find a coffee shop and talk about the race, but I want to be there plenty early." Smokey said okay and hung up. The race didn't start until 10:00, but they needed time to prepare. Smokey hit the bathroom and grabbed the thermometer from the cupboard. His temperature was 101. It had gone down-not a lot, but enough, he thought.

Red was right on time, and they headed to a coffee shop on the north end of Regina. Red asked, "How are you feeling?"

"I'm sick," said Smokey. After that, there didn't seem to be much to say. Smokey had two cups of coffee. He would have had three if Red had let him, but Red wanted to get to Lumsden in plenty of time.

When they got to the river at Lumsden, there were already several boats there. Paddlers were busy making last-minute adjustments to their canoes and putting on spray covers. They pulled their canoe off the car. Soon everybody was lined up across the river and the count-down was underway. Smokey thought, *This is it. Give it everything I've got till we get to the end of the channel. Then set a stroke-rate.*

Chapter II

The gun went off and the water all around turned to foam as paddlers tried to bring their boats out of the hole. Smokey pulled as hard and fast as he could. The bow lifted. They were off. He looked sideways just in time to see the Lumsden team flip upside-down. That was one less team to worry about. Smokey was paddling close to eighty strokes a minute and his chest burned; halfway down the channel, he was gasping for air. Finally he had to slow down and let his lungs catch up with the rest of his body. Three boats had pulled out in front of them and were pulling away. When they reached the end of the channel, the other three boats had disappeared around the corner.

Smokey was stroking about seventy strokes a minute now. It was all he could do. He was desperately trying to get his second wind. They had paddled about two miles when they saw the third canoe in front of them. Smokey increased his stroke-rate. If they could get on this team's wake, they could get a pull downstream and gradually over time wear this team out.

It was only a matter of minutes and they had closed the gap. Smokey felt the tug of the other canoe and relaxed his stroke-rate. They were going for a ride at the expense of the other team. But this was a native team and seasoned paddlers. And it was only a few minutes and the team started sprinting away. Smokey increased his stroke-rate and hung on for dear life. They had managed to stay on the wash of this team now for several miles, and the team in front was beginning to slow down, Smokey thought.

Then Red guided the canoe onto the side-wash of the other boat, indicating to Smokey that it was time to try to pass these guys. Smokey started a sprinting stroke-rate as best he could, but he didn't have much left in him. They pulled even with the other canoe but couldn't get by them. Smokey tucked the canoe back in behind the stern-wash of the other boat. As he did this, the other canoe began to sprint away and Smokey was forced to pick up his stroke-rate just to stay on the wash. The two teams battled back and forth like this for several miles, neither team breaking free of the other.

Finally they came across the railway bridge which indicated that there was only one mile left in the race. Smokey and Red knew this, but the other team did not. It was time to give it everything they had. Red angled the canoe on the side-wash of the other boat and Smokey tried to step up the stroke-rate. But Smokey's lungs were burning with fire and he couldn't catch his breath. He had to reduce his stroke-rate. The other team sensed that they were in trouble and they sprinted ahead as hard as they could. Smokey and Red fell off the wash of the other canoe. It was all over-they had lost. As they rounded the finish line, the impact of their defeat hit him. Smokey knew it was his fault, but his body just wouldn't do what his mind wanted; his lungs had let him down. He had never really caught his second wind during the whole race.

They finished fourth overall. This certainly wasn't what they had planned on. They had dreamed of being a surprise number one team. It was obvious that they had a lot of work to do. They pulled their canoe out of the water and placed it on Red's car.

Red and Smokey went over to the native team, shook their hands, and said, "Good race." Smokey blurted out, "You're lucky I'm sick." They laughed, but it caused a lot of tension, and Smokey realized it hadn't been an appropriate thing to say.

Red said, "I think my partner was sandbagging it a bit today." Smokey hung his head.

They went back to the car and drank some fluid. Smokey had the shakes and felt weepy, but he knew that was just the fever. There was a race tomorrow in Saskatoon, but Smokey was cooked and he knew it. He was very ill and there was no way he would recover for tomorrow. He might as well let Red know now.

"I'm too sick to paddle tomorrow," Smokey said. Red nodded but didn't say anything. They drove back to Regina in silence, and Red dropped Smokey off at home. Smokey stumbled up the steps and headed for the kitchen. He drank six glasses of water, then went to the bathroom to get the thermometer. He stuck the thermometer in his mouth, but it was hard to keep his teeth from chattering. He pulled the thermometer out: 103. *The game is over*, he thought,. *Time to rest and get well.* He coughed up some phlegm streaked with blood. For the first time, Smokey accepted the fact that he was sick. He grabbed a blanket from the bedroom and curled up on the couch.

Smokey woke up Sunday at noon. He was drenched in sweat. He took his temperature: 102. He shoveled down the antibiotics and made himself some breakfast. Despite the fever, he hadn't lost his appetite. The day passed slowly. Smokey read for a couple of hours, but he was thinking of the race in Saskatoon. He wondered if Red had found a temporary partner. If only he hadn't been sick, they would have at least come n third, he thought.

That evening Red called and said he had found a partner and had raced. Smokey felt better about things. The only thing to do now was to get better. And prepare for the next race, which was a week away.

By Wednesday the following week, Smokey's fever was gone. He still had tightness in his chest, but he was feeling like it was time to get in a practice. Red had phoned every day to see how he was doing.

The next race was in North Battleford on the Battle River. Smokey and Red had done this race in a recreational capacity the previous year, and they knew how tough it was. The water was only about three feet deep in most spots, and the canoe felt like it was being sucked to the bottom when you paddled. It was often referred to by the paddlers as "suck water."

Red and Smokey met at Wascana Lake for a Wednesday practice. Red said, "We have an advantage over other paddlers in this race. We are used to suck water from paddling this sucky lake." Smokey agreed. He also knew that they were good cruiser class paddlers. There were no shells allowed at the Battle River, just cruisers and recreational boats.

Red and Smokey practiced for a couple of hours. They used a steady stroke-rate and then practiced a few short sprints. Smokey's lungs were loosening up quite a bit, and he was able to get his second wind that night. He was beginning to feel hopeful about the Battle River race.

He slept till Thursday noon after Wednesday's paddle but didn't feel too bad when he got up. It was another empty day with nothing scheduled, so he decided to take his unemployment sculpture in to be fired.

The lady at the ceramic shop said, "That looks pretty cool. What is it, a volcanic eruption?"

Smokey said, "Something like that."

On his way back, he stopped in at the UIC office just in case there was something there. There wasn't, but there was a woman handing out cards for professional résumé preparation. He took a card. Maybe it was the way he presented himself to employers that was part of the problem. He didn't think it was a problem, but he knew he needed every advantage he could get.

He picked up the paper at a corner store and took it home. The careers section of the paper was almost nonexistent, so he turned to the want ads. There were the usual telemarketing jobs on commission and Amway advertisements but nothing of real consequence in either the accounting section or the labour section. Smokey knew he would need to fill out a lot of applications before he met with any success, and he would have to start soon with a door-to-door search.

Five o'clock came quickly and Smokey met Red at the lake. Red had the cruiser on the car. When they lifted it off the car, Smokey groaned. It was three times the weight of the racing shell. They only practiced for about an hour. They wanted to conserve energy for the race on Saturday. The cruiser moved well in the sucky waters, but sprinting was difficult. After practice Smokey and Red went out for a large pasta dinner and talked about race strategy.

Friday morning Smokey woke feeling pretty darn good. He was still on antibiotics but he hadn't had a fever since Tuesday. He tried reading, but he was too excited about the race. *This time*, he said to himself, *things will be different*. Red picked him up at three o'clock and they headed for North Battleford. It was a long trip, so they would stop in Saskatoon for supper. Again it was a plate of pasta for supper-lots of carbohydrates. They pulled into the Battleford Hotel-Motel at about ten that evening. It had been a long drive, and both Red and Smokey were tired. They hit the hay right away so as to be well-rested for the race on Saturday.

Red woke early, as usual, and shortly after Smokey got up. They went to the nearest restaurant and had breakfast, just a light breakfast and coffee. After breakfast, they headed to the race site. When they got there, there were already some boats getting ready. The Craven team was there, so Smokey chatted with them for a while. Then it was time to get the boat ready. They taped their waterbottles into the canoe and did a last-minute check on the trim of the boat. Then it was time to line up again. The woodsman team from Saskatoon hadn't shown up for this race. They were the current provincial leaders in races.

Smokey thought about the competition. The only team they knew other than the Craven team was the Saskatoon Masters team, and he knew that they would be tough competition. They lined up for the gun and waited. Then they were off. The Saskatoon Masters team took the lead right off the start. Smokey and Red were a distant second. The Craven team were right on Smokey and Red's tail, trying to use the stern-wash of their boat, but things were difficult in this sucky water. There was no tow to be had from the stern-wash of Smokey and Red's canoe. In fact, being in the stern-wash was very difficult for the Craven bowman, and after a short time they fell behind. This left Smokey and Red in sole second place. They kept up a steady pace of seventy strokes a minute as Red analyzed the current and channels on the river.

After about an hour, they saw the Masters team ahead of them again. They seemed to be slowing down a little. Red said, "Let's go get them." Smokey picked up the stroke rate to above a cruising rate of seventy-five strokes per minute. It seemed like ages before they were within closing distance, but after fifteen or twenty minutes they were close enough. Red placed the bow of their boat on the side-wave of the Masters team's canoe, and Smokey felt a bit of a pull. They stayed there on the side-wave for as long as they could. The Masters team tried to sprint away, but Smokey clung to the side-wash like glue. The Masters team was showing little sign of fatigue, so Smokey made a move. He increased the stroke-rate and pulled even with the other boat.

They battled back and forth for several minutes with nobody the clear victor. Then Smokey decided, *This is it, time to sprint.* He increased his stroke-rate to a full sprint and held it for as long as he could. They had pulled ahead, and the Masters team was now on their side-wash. Smokey sprinted again for as long as he could hold it. This time they were all alone. The Masters team had fallen off their wash. They were in first place and headed for victory. Smokey kept up a steady stroke-rate of between seventy and seventy-five strokes a minute, and this seemed to be enough to put safe distance between them and the Masters team. It was another grueling hour before Red saw the finish-line. Smokey was so out of it he kept on paddling, not even noticing the finish line. They pulled their canoe up on shore and were surrounded by people congratulating them on their finish. Soon other canoers were onshore too, and everyone was talking about the race.

Smokey was so tired he lay down on the side of the highway and closed his eyes. The next thing he knew, Red was shaking him. "Get up. You can't sleep here; someone will run over you. Here, drink this and go over to the benches and rest there."

Smokey said thank you and went over to the benches. He realized he wasn't thinking straight and was obviously dehydrated. He drank the two liters of water Red gave him, and then he fell asleep while Red got a ride back to pick up the car.

When they got back to the hotel, there was just enough time for a shower and shave before the evening banquet and dance.

The announcer said their names, and Smokey and Red went to the podium with applause from the rest. Smokey clutched his trophy greedily and grinned from ear to ear. On their way home to Regina, Smokey said to Red, "This is just the beginning. There's going to be more like this, I know it."

Sunday they rested, and Smokey was once again reminded of his reality of unemployment. He picked up the weekend paper and searched through the ads. There was little there for him, but he applied to two box number for accounting assistant positions.

On Monday Smokey mailed his applications and picked up his fired sculpture. He now called it "Unemployment Manifestations." He bought several glazes to color his creation. He bought deep reds and bright reds to signify levels of pain, plus black, yellow, orange, green, and blue. Each colour represented emotions and conditions of unemployment. When he got home from the ceramic shop, he started to apply the glazes. At first there were warnings of layoffs, and Smokey glazed this part yellow. As the rumours were confirmed, this section was glazed orange. Then the layoff was glazed bright red. There were several aspects to the sculpture, such as dealings with banks and UIC officials as well as rejection letters. Smokey spent most of the day glazing his sculpture, and when he was done there was a black hole in the center of the sculpture. This was suicide.

The week passed slowly with canoeing practice being the highlight of each day. On the weekend, they raced in Saskatoon and were soundly beaten by the Saskatoon Masters team. It was Smokey and Red's first experience using sand shallows and often they found themselves stuck in ankle-deep water, but it was a learning experience for both of them. Despite this fact, there was a bit of tension between Smokey and Red.

Red was always the rational communicator, whereas Smokey tended to be emotional about things and to not always communicate well. When they finished the race, Adam, a world-class paddler from Cumberland House, invited them to a canoe race on the Reserve to celebrate Samuel Hearn Days next weekend. It was an opportunity to paddle against northern native teams and would be good competition.

Smokey and Red practiced hard all the next week, doing sprints and shorter, more intense paddling. During the weekdays Smokey looked for work and took his sculpture in to be fired.

When Thursday came, they packed up their tenting equipment and sleeping bags and loaded the car. Red tightened the racing shell down to the roof-racks and then they were off.

It was a long drive to Cumberland House, and the boys were very tired when they got there. They met with Adam and his family and talked about the next day's race. Adam said, "There are bank shallows that you should try to use, but it takes lots of practice."

The boys stayed with a big man named Abraham. They camped out on his front lawn. That evening they were a bit tense with tomorrow's race; also, if the truth be known, a little nervous about being white men on a reserve.

They sat around Abe's kitchen table. Abe had lots of good stories. He said, "I used to paddle those canoes when I was young too, except I didn't need a paddle. I just used my hands." He placed his hands on the table. They were like baseball gloves, absolutely huge. Smokey thought to himself, *One punch from this guy and your head would cave in. Good thing he's friendly.*" They passed the evening away chatting, then retired to their tent.

The race the next day didn't start till noon, and there were two classifications: pro and semi-pro. The boys had been advised that their best chances would be in semi-pro. The pro paddlers in Cumberland House were the best in the world and had proven it at international races. The next day at registration, they were encouraged to go pro class, but the boys knew better. They didn't come all this way to be humiliated. They weren't good enough yet for pro class. Maybe in a couple of years. They were still very much amateur paddlers. After all, this was their first year.

There had to be at least twenty boats registered for semi-pro class. They lined up at the river and waited for the sound of the gun. There was sprint money-first one to the bridge would make two hundred dollars. It was going to be fun. The gun went off and the paddlers headed for the nearby bridge. Smokey and Red sprinted as hard as they could to stay with the pack, and before they knew it, they found themselves in fourth place. It was easy paddling downstream in the current for the first eight miles, but when they turned to go upstream, they felt the impact of the current immediately. They headed to the bend and tried to get into the backwash and then use the bank shallows, but it was tough. They had trouble getting onto their own wave and staying on. After several attempts they gave up trying to use the bank shallows. It was something they would have to practice another time.

Smokey could see a team ahead that seemed to be slowing down. If they could pass them, they would be in third place. They stuck to the backwash and worked really hard—seventy-five strokes a minute for several minutes. They could see the bridge in the distance. Then they were on the wash of the other boat, and for a moment they relaxed. Later, at the bridge, they passed this boat with relative ease and finished the first day of the race in a solid third place.

After the race, they went to town and had dinner. Smokey was hoping he could get a moose-burger like his grandpa used to make when he was a kid, but the store just sold regular beef, much to Smokey's disappointment. They returned after dinner to Abe's and rested for the rest of the afternoon and evening. They both slept solidly and woke just in time to watch the pro race start. Smokey sat on the bank and ate a bag of oranges. Then it was their turn to race.

Red lowered the canoe into the water. He said to Smokey, "Let's be the first ones to the bridge today. We could use the money." The gun sounded and they were off. Smokey hit a stroke-rate of about eighty-five strokes a minute as they headed for the bridge. They were out in front, but as the bridge approached, two other teams came sizzling by on their right. One more team passed them as they headed downstream. They were in fourth place.

The course seemed longer than it had the day before but after half an hour they were at the first turnaround. On their way back up, one of the boats in front of them tipped. This put them back in third spot. As they reached the bridge, they were on the wash of the second-place boat. They clung there, waiting to make their move. When they reached the buoy to turn around, they tried to sneak by the other boat. They were unsuccessful and the other boat pulled away for good. Smokey shoveled some water at Red. He didn't know why he did it, he was just angry they hadn't passed that last boat. It was nobody's fault. Smokey felt guilty for the rest of the race.

They finished in third spot and were third overall for the two days. Red asked Smokey what the water in the face was for, and Smokey just shrugged his shoulder and said, "I was angry and you were the only person around."

"Anger without reason could mean you're suffering from oxygen debt," Red said, and that was the end of it.

It was a long trip home, so the boys skipped the ceremony. They picked up the trophies and the five hundred dollar cash prize for third place and headed back to Regina. Smokey looked at the trophy; it was absolutely beautiful. It had a solid oak base with a gold canoe on top. The plate read, "Third Place Semi-Pro Canoe Race, Samuel Hearn Days, Cumberland House." They had done well and they knew it.

Red dropped Smokey off at home and said, "No practice tomorrow." Smokey smiled and said, "Okay, sounds good to me."

Smokey was absolutely beat. He slept for twelve hours that night. The next day he was once again faced with the reality of unemployment. It was beginning to really get to him now.

He picked up his sculpture and brought it home. It had turned out perfectly. He cut a piece of plywood, placed the sculpture on it, then wrote on the plywood, "Unemployment Manifestation."

That evening, some friends came over to visit. One of them was an art teacher. He said, "What's this?" and Smokey explained all the facets of unemployment and the feelings that were expressed in his sculpture. The art teacher said he was going to show it to his students the next week.

Smokey smiled and said, "I'll be famous." They laughed, but unemployment was no laughing matter for Smokey. It was a frustrating fact of life. There was only one race left in Saskatoon, and then there would be nothing to distance him from the problem.

The last race was held on Blackstrap Lake near Saskatoon. Smokey and Red finished a disappointing third in that race. They both felt they should have been second, but at the end of the race they were invited to attend the Canadian Nationals, to be held in Peterborough, Ontario. Smokey wanted to go; he wanted to represent Saskatchewan along with other teams. Red didn't say much. The truth was, Red and Smokey weren't getting along that well at the end of the season. Sometimes a canoeing team was like a bad marriage, even worse. Each partner had such high expectations of the other. They talked about it over the next week and continued to practice. There were several obstacles. They didn't have a car that could make that type of distance, and Smokey had absolutely no money.

Chapter III

The next day, true to their form, the UIC office called and said they wanted to see him. Smokey took his list of employment applications with him; he knew the game. No employment search meant no UIC benefits. The procedure was short and sweet when he got to the UIC office. The employment search he submitted with 36 names would be accepted, but he would have to try much harder in the future. Smokey said he would be. He went home and waited. Three days later he received his first UIC cheque, for $382. He wondered how much it would take to get to the nationals in Peterborough. That evening after practice, he talked to Red. He told him that he had about $350 he could put towards the trip to the Nationals. Red said his boss would give them a company car to make the trip. They decided that evening they would go. They had an honest chance of doing quite well at the big race.

The rest of the week went slowly as they prepared for the trip. Smokey knew it was a big gamble. He was spending his rent money to go to Ontario. He would be in a lot of trouble when he got back, but some things you just have to do for yourself despite the costs.

The following day they prepared a list of the things they would need and set about getting them. That evening they packed sleeping bags and a tent plus personal clothing for a week. Smokey crashed at Red's place so they could get an early start. The alarm went off at 6:30, but Smokey noticed Red was already dressed and getting ready to batten down the hatches on his place. They went to the garage and pulled the racing shell down off the sawhorses where it had sat. They had the shell on the company car and everything packed in fifteen minutes. They drove to the nearest Robin's Doughnuts and had a morning coffee.

This is it, Smokey thought. *This is really it.* They were going to compete at the Canadian Nationals!

As they drove past the prairie wheat fields, Smokey couldn't help but day-dream. If they could get into the winner's circle with a bronze medal, that would look great on a personal résumé. It would show he had drive and discipline. It might make a difference if they could just put it all together for this one-time shot. Smokey hummed to himself as they drove along. Red never seemed to tire of driving, and Smokey enjoyed being a passenger.

It wasn't long before they were bypassing Winnipeg and discussing how far they should try to make it the first day. Smokey knew a little campsite on the far side of Kenora, and that seemed like the best spot to go for. When they arrived at the campsite, there were only two spots left down near the water's edge. One of them was absolutely perfect, so they set up their tent and started an evening fire. They spent a short time discussing possible race strategies, and then they sat in silence as the campfire dwindled down to embers. Smokey gazed into those embers, and in his mind's eye, he saw himself and Red standing on a podium with medals wound around their necks. Red said, "It's time to pack it in, Smokey. Iit's going to be a long day tomorrow." Smokey nodded, and they doused the embers with water and headed up to the tent. They fell asleep despite their excitement.

They awoke suddenly to the sounds of a large truck and several loud voices. "Let's burn their fuckin' tent down," one said. Another said, "This is our camp spot." "Fucking scabs come to take our jobs, that's what they are," another yelled.

Smokey and Red sat in the tent, eyes open, waiting. They heard the clinking of beer bottles and small stones being thrown against their tent. They waited in silence. They waited all night as the men got more and more drunk and the threats became more real.

Smokey and Red saw the sun come up through their tent. They quickly rolled up their sleeping bags and listened for the men. All was quiet. They got out of their tent and began to dismantle it. A couple of the men came staggering over. The fat one said, "There's no jobs here, boys. You better keep moving."

Red said, "We're not looking for work. We're on our way to the Canadian National Canoeing Championships."

The two men looked at the funny-shaped canoe on the roof. "Is that home made?" one asked.

"No," Red said, "it's a marathon boat." The two men looked around some more and then said, "Have a good race, guys." They went back to their campsite.

Smokey and Red packed up quickly and headed into town for an early-morning breakfast. They found a restaurant for early birds and sat down. Smokey pulled out the map. They had to make a lot of distance today and tomorrow in order to be in Peterborough on time. Smokey counted the miles and split it in two. They had to make it to a spot somewhere near Sault Ste. Marie by the end of the day. Smokey looked for the nearest campsite on the map given their objective and circled it. They ate breakfast in silence and then headed out to the highway. Soon Smokey was fast asleep. He didn't wake up till they were in Thunder Bay. Smokey asked if Red wanted a break from driving, but Red said no, he liked to drive. They reached their camp spot at dusk and, luckily, there was vacancy. They set up their tent in the dark. There would be no campfire tonight, just sleep.

Red was up at six looking eager to get underway, so Smokey crawled out of his sleeping bag and pulled on his jeans. "Peterborough, here we come." Smokey laughed and headed to the camp washrooms, stumbling along the trail.

They didn't stop for breakfast;.they had to make tracks. They bought some oranges at the camp store and headed for the highway and a day's travel. The day passed very quickly. Soon the scenery changed from fir and deciduous to open farms with deep red soil.

They arrived in Peterborough in the early afternoon and set up camp at a campsite in the city. The Saskatoon Masters team was there and so was the Craven team. They talked about the race, and then Smokey and Red decided to check out the course for tomorrow's race. They wouldn't do the whole course because they needed to save their energy, but it would be important to know the type of water with which they would be dealing. They had to know where the deep water was and where it became sucky. Also very important was how much current was in the channel.

Smokey and Red took their canoe down to the lake with a copy of the course in hand. They paddled at a relaxed pace at first but soon found themselves working up a sweat. They found deep spots on the lake course as well as some very sucky areas.

They were on their way back to shore when they noticed a large powerboat coming toward them and putting out a very large wave. Smokey kept paddling hard. The wave struck the bow of the canoe and poured over the sides. Smokey felt the canoe lean to the left and fill. There was no doubt about it, they were going over. He tried to put in a brace to keep them upright, but it was too late-over they went. The next thing Smokey knew, he was upside down in the water.

Smokey surfaced and looked around. Where was Red? He waited and waited and then began to panic, searching frantically for Red. Finally, Red surfaced.

"Are you okay?" Smokey asked. Red said no, but it looked like he was smiling—or was he gritting his teeth? Smokey couldn't tell. They pulled the canoe to shore and drained it. They got back in and headed across the lake to where their car was. It was time for supper anyway. They loaded up the canoe and headed into town to an Italian spaghetti palace. Pasta was the key before a race: lots of carbohydrates. Smokey had two pasta dinners and a large glass of milk.

They drove back to the camp and just sat around with the other Saskatchewan racing teams. Dusk fell and everyone retired early, but Red was restless and couldn't sleep. He got up and went to the car to listen to the radio.

When Smokey woke up, it was late. Red was up, but he didn't look rested at all. His face was ashen gray and he looked really nervous. Smokey thought, *Well, it's race day and a guy is entitled to be nervous and a little off.* but he was worried. It was now two hours till race time. They took the car over to the start area and waited for debriefing and general instructions about the race. The race organizer thanked all the sponsors and then began to describe the race course and rules. The boats were all measured for proper length and width.

One hour till race time. Smokey and Red sat in the shade of a large tree and watched other racers run about with nervous energy.

Then it was time to line up. Smokey looked at the course and said, "Left side" Red said, "Right on." It was a slightly shorter distance to the first turn if lined up on the left side. Any advantage they could see, they would take. They lined up.

Five minutes to the start.

Two minutes waiting.

The gun sounded, and the lake was filled with paddles and foam as each team sprinted for the first turn across the lake.

Smokey and Red were in the lead pack as they came to the first turn. Smokey immediately looked for a wash he could ride—the fastest canoe he could find. Four or five boats passed them and Smokey began to worry. Then they caught a wash on the back of an Ontario team. They paddled around the lake, working very hard. Smokey was gasping for air, but he wasn't going to let up. This was it, the Canadian Nationals. They had to give it all they had. After they paddled one lap around the lake, Red started to cough. The cough got worse and he seemed to be losing strength on one side. By the time they reached the channel Red had stopped coughing, but he had absolutely no strength on his left side. He could barely keep the boat straight—in fact, he started leaning the canoe in order to keep it straight. Smokey and Red fell further and further back, but each time a team would try to pass them, they would fight like dogs to keep them back. When they finally did pass, Red and Smokey would ride their wash for as long as they could—sometimes a mile or more.

Coming upstream, Smokey realized the boat was really losing power. It seemed like the canoe was bow- and stern-heavy at the same time. When they reached the lake again, Smokey was absolutely exhausted. He had never paddled this hard in his life before, and they weren't finished. They had to keep from losing any more positions. But as they headed south along the lake, another team came up behind them. Red steered them into the suckiest water they could find. Smokey wondered what the hell Red was doing, but the team behind them followed them in. If it was hard on the first team, it was clearly harder for the second team in this type of water. The team behind soon fell back, and Smokey and Red were free of them. One thing was for sure: Red might be hurt and barely able to paddle, but he was smart. He was always thinking.

Smokey and Red turned the corner—the final corner—and headed for the finish line. Smokey pulled as hard as he could, trying to make the best possible time. Then they were across the finish line and it was all over. They had finished twelfth. Smokey said, "I gave you everything I had."

Red said, "You did good." They pulled the boat up on shore and shook hands. "Thanks for the paddle," Red said.

Smokey smiled but he could see the disappointment and pain in Red's eyes. He looked away. There was physical pain and the pain of humiliation. They had finished twelfth-certainly a long way back from where they hoped they would be, but they could have ended up twenty-fifth and suffered double the humiliation. After all, you can't go from being a two-pack-a-day smoker and beer-drinking twat to a national-caliber athlete in one year. They had done their very best.

Smokey knew he was rationalizing. Deep in his heart he knew he had failed. He also knew the reason Red was hurt was from the spill they had taken the day before. It was all his fault. Smokey went and sat under a tree.

"Hello there!" Smokey looked up. It was his brother Ross and his wife, Kathryn, smiling at him. They had come all the way from Toronto to see him race. "You guys looked pretty good out there."

"We did our best," Smokey said. "We'd like you to come and visit with us for a couple of days."

"That would be great, but I'll have to talk to Red."

Smokey found Red and they talked about it, but Red was eager to go home. They agreed to separate at that point and go their separate ways. Smokey had a sinking feeling as he drove away with his brother. Should he have gone back with Red? Did they need to talk about the race, what went right and what went wrong? Smokey knew in the back of his mind that things weren't finished. Not quite. Red needed to know that Smokey thought he was a great paddler and they could be better next year if they really wanted, but right now the disappointment was too great to talk about anything.

Ross and Kathryn took Smokey to a restaurant in Toronto for supper. Smokey didn't feel hungry, but he drank seven glasses of water, driving the poor waitress crazy.

When they got back to Ross and Kathryn's place, they sat around the small, cozy living room and just talked about things. Smokey still felt a sinking inside. *What do I do with my life now?* He went to bed early.

Chapter IV

The next day Ross took Smokey for a drive in the country to see the old farmhouse where they had spent a year of their childhood before their father had died. As they drove along through the cornfields and open red soil, Smokey thought about his life. He was almost thirty years old, and he was penniless without a career. Spending his UIC cheque on a dream like the Canadian Nationals really wasn't such a smart plan. Now he would not be able to pay rent on his little place. But dreams are dreams, and Smokey knew he'd always been a dreamer. Driving along the gravel road toward the farmhouse, it looked small compared to his childhood memory of the place. One of the barns had been taken down and the other looked like it might fall over any time. Smokey thought back to his childhood. He remembered playing in that barn with his brother. Then he remembered his father shaking him and telling Smoky to smarten up or one day he would drive away and not come back. And essentially that's what had happened. His father drove away one morning and met that three-ton truck. *What a way to screw up a child's mind,* Smokey thought.

Then he remembered being inside the old brick house up in his bedroom and his father at his bedside singing an old German love song to him. "You, you, you are my true love, you, you are the one."

Smokey was filled with emotions as they stopped the car and walked through the pasture. "You know," Smokey said, "he was a real prick sometimes, but he loved us. And I know he wasn't well the last few years. You know, it might have been an accident. His death, that is."

Ross looked at him knowingly and said, "Yes, I suppose it's possible."

Smokey had had enough. If he was going to hold himself together, he couldn't spend time trying to understand something that had happened twenty years ago. Still, he couldn't help thinking. His father had had a career, a family, a wife, and many talents, and yet it wasn't enough to keep him alive. He had sought an end despite all that he had. Smokey had no wife, no children, and no career—not even a job to pay the rent and put food on the table. All *I have is broken dreams,* Smokey thought.

Ross and Smokey drove home in silence. There wasn't much to say—what could one say? Each man knew the other could feel the darkness of the past. There were no words sufficient to express the childhood memories of 1965. When they arrived back at the apartment, Kathryn had a homey dinner ready. Ross and Kathryn were vegetarians, so Smokey had no idea what he was eating sometimes, but it was certainly tasty.

Smokey spent one day in Toronto wandering the streets. He spent a couple of hours in a café called Dooney's drinking espressos. When he returned to the apartment that evening, he knew it was time to make his way back to Saskatchewan. The next day his brother dropped him off at the train station, and Smokey boarded the VIA for Regina. He found himself a seat by the window so he could watch the landscape change till dark. He slept reasonably well that night despite all the thoughts that were running through his head.

The next morning Smokey ate the old cheese and dill pickle sandwiches his brother had prepared for him. By noon he had found the coach that served alcohol. He didn't want to think anymore. He needed the numbness alcohol would bring.

As the day wore on, bottles gathered in front of him. By six o'clock that evening, Smokey had lost most of his coordination and went stumbling back to his seat. There was a young woman who had a guitar out and was singing. Smokey sang along, much to her irritation.

Soon Smokey was asleep again, and he slept for several hours. When he woke up, the conductor was calling out, "Winnipeg." His head felt like there was an ironworker inside pounding metal. He made his way to the washrooms. He would be home in six or seven hours, and what was his plan? He had twenty dollars left to his name, and a taxi home would cost him eight. Rent was due, along with power bills and food requirements.

Smokey returned to his seat and gazed out the window. Some of the farmers were harvesting already. The crops looked good from a distance, but up close one could see the effect of the grasshoppers. If the crops were poor, the farmers didn't buy, and if the farmers didn't buy, there would be more layoffs and job opportunities would be very hard to get. That's the way it was in an agriculture-based economy. There would always be government jobs for the lucky and the blessed, but for most there would be nothing till spring.

Smokey was beginning to panic inside. The fun was over. Reality was back, and he had no answers for a winter of poverty which lay ahead.

The train pulled into Regina, and Smokey got off with three other passengers, a huge lady with twins about five or six years old.

Smokey thought about walking home to save the money, but with a suitcase, four miles was too much, so he ordered a cab. He was right—it cost him eight dollars to get home.

Smokey stood at the door of his little house and reached into the mailbox to get his mail. He unlocked the door and went into the only home he knew.

Chapter V

Once inside his little home again, Smokey began to unpack. Then he began to take stock of his resources. He had twelve dollars plus a jar of change he hadn't counted. In the cupboards he found four cans of beans and three cans of pasta sauce, plus some pasta and a jar of instant coffee. In the refrigerator he found a dozen eggs.

Next Smokey filled out his UIC cards and walked to the corner store for a stamp. The UIC cheque, if it came without a problem, would take at least eight days, and it would cover the two-week period. The amount of the UIC cheque would be $382. Smokey's rent was $300 and his power bill was $64. This would leave him with $18 for the next two weeks if the cheque came on time and he could survive the next week on the $12 and the change he had.

Smokey realized he was going to have to sell something. The only two things he had were his car and the commercial saw he and Red used to build canoes. He decided he would sell the saw.

He gave Red a call, but there was no answer. He decided to take some change from his jar and do two loads of laundry. Smokey took eight quarters from the jar plus some dimes and nickels and headed out the door with a bundle of laundry. He would do just the basics–shorts, socks, and sweats.

He started up the old Fairlane. There was half a tank of gas in it. *Lucky,* thought Smokey.

Smokey watched his clothes drying in the machine and was reminded of his friend Bill. Bill had asked one time when they were doing laundry together where he thought odd socks went. Bill said, "I think they spin so fast in the dryer that they end up in hyperspace." Smokey had smiled and said, "I think you're probably right. It makes sense–where else could odd socks go?" Smokey thought, *I'll give Bill a call tonight and see what he's up to.*

That evening Bill came over with a couple of new records. A new Van Morrison record interested Smokey. He lit a fire in the potbellied stove and put the screen on so you could see the flames.

"Have you talked to Red?" asked Bill. "No, I haven't been able to get hold of him since I got back."

"Well, maybe I should tell you. Red had four broken ribs and a dislocated ribcage from when you guys flipped over the day before the race."

Smokey felt ill. He hadn't realized that Red's injuries were so serious. Red had driven all the way back home with four broken ribs pressing on his left lung. Bill said, "He doesn't blame anybody for the accident, but Smokey knew it had been his fault. He had charged that boat-wave like an animal, when all he had to do was put in a brace and steady the boat and things would have been okay. It was his fault and he knew it. He had seriously injured his partner and friend and had abandoned him when he needed him the most. None of this did he express to Bill, but Bill could tell that Smokey was upset.

They spent the evening listening to the new Van Morrison album and watching the fire glow in the stove. Smokey was deep in thought. What could he possibly say to Red to make up for what he had done? He had ruined their chances at the Nationals and left his partner, who was probably in shock, to make his own way hundreds of miles home. There was nothing he could say to Red. Nothing could change what had happened.

"Do you want to order a pizza?" Bill asked.

"No I'm sorry, but I'm on limited finances for a while now. The trip to the Nationals has cleaned me out. Can't even pay my rent on time."

Bill smiled and said, "I got twenty bucks I can spare. What do you want on it?" So they ordered a pizza and ate by firelight.

Bill told Smokey about making transitions in his life, how he no longer could do upholstery and had trouble doing cooking and kitchen work for long periods because of his muscular dystrophy. Bill said, "I'm working at being an artist," and he showed Smokey a picture he had done of a loon on a lake. Smokey was impressed. They watched the embers dwindle in the stove.

Then Bill said, "Don't worry, Smokey, Red is a forgiving type of guy." Smokey was silent. They listened to one more record; then Bill left for home. Smokey tried calling Red again but there was no answer.

Three days later, Smokey finally got hold of Red and they talked briefly, but it felt really strange to Smokey. So much needed to be said, and yet he found himself talking about nothing. In the end he told Red that he had to sell the commercial saw for rent money. Red said, "Okay, no problem."

Smokey sold the saw in two days and got the money to pay his rent and his power bills, but he also realized there would be no more canoe-building with Red this coming winter. He had sold the equipment, or a good portion of it.

The following week his UIC cheque came, so Smokey had a little bit of money, but he decided to save it for winter when the power bills would be higher. Smokey started his employment search once again. He went regularly to the UIC office and checked the papers every day, but there were few openings anywhere, and even when he went door to door, few managers had the time to see him. It was going to be a long, boring winter if things didn't change.

It was the end of September and Smokey and Red still hadn't talked about what had happened at the Nationals. As time went by, Smokey found it harder and harder to find words. Smokey wanted to confess his guilt, but his pride wouldn't let him. As the weeks passed, Red and Smokey saw less and less of each other, and they never got into a boat together after the Nationals. Each of the two partners used their solo boats to practice. Maybe it didn't need to be said that there would be no tandem team the next year. Maybe it was just understood. Smokey didn't know.

It was a late September day when Smokey opened the daily newspaper and found a new employment ad in the classified section. It said, "Wanted: Marketing Assistant. Send résumé to...." Smokey thought about it. He had taken a couple of marketing classes at the University of Regina. He would mention this in a cover letter, and he would have a new résumé prepared stating his trip to the Canadian Nationals under Personal Accomplishments. Nobody had to know they finished twelfth.

So that evening Smokey prepared a letter and résumé for the position of marketing assistant. He mailed them the next day. The rest of the week, Smokey did the old door-to-door search without getting a single interview. He was tired and frustrated by the end of the week, so he took his canoe out to the lake Friday night and paddled around the lake, blowing off some steam, then looking up at the stars and relaxing into a gentle paddle.

Tuesday morning the following week, Smokey received a call from the employer who had placed the ad for the marketing assistant. The man said, "We need people like you on our team. Come for an interview at six o'clock tonight." He gave Smokey the address. Smokey thought six was a bit late but thought no more about it. He went into his bedroom and pulled out a pair of dress pants and a good shirt. He had to make a good impression. Smokey was nervous. He spent most of the day practicing what he would say about his background, his past employment, and his education. At five o'clock, he dressed and headed out the door. He wanted to make sure he had plenty of time to find the place.

When he got there he was surprised to see it was a residential address. He waited till 5:55, and while he waited he saw four other people go to the door. Smokey was now a little suspicious. He walked up to the door and knocked. A short little man in a suit smiled and said, "Welcome. Come on in." Smokey stepped inside and was directed to the living room. There was a slide projector out and a screen set up, and half a dozen people sitting in front of the screen. Then Smokey saw the Amway kits in the corner. It was a scam. This little shit was going to try to get them to sell Amway. *It's very close to false advertising,* Smokey thought. *Very deceitful, anyway.*

Smokey left the room and headed for the door. The faster he walked away the angrier he got. When he reached his car he was steaming. "You fucking little cocksucker!" he screamed as he drove away, nearly ramming into an elderly woman crossing the street. *Damn,* Smokey muttered to himself. "After all this time looking for work, all I can attract is a fucking Amway salesman."

Smokey had heard the Amway pitch before. It was a lot like Jesus: if you just believe, everything will work out. What a pile of shit. Smokey headed for the LB store to pick up some beer. He had had enough of life today. He needed a little poison to smooth out the day.

Smokey sat in front of the potbellied stove with the screen open so he could see the fire burning. He sucked back the beer and began thinking about his financial situation.

He had UIC benefits till spring, but that was slim pickings as far as that went. There would be enough money to pay the bills, but that was all. He thought about those people who win the lotteries, those lucky suckers. Or were they really lucky? There is something very dark about the lottery systems, especially 6/49. Was it really luck? And if you won, was the price of winning really just a dollar? What would balance the winning of a million dollars? Would his mother suddenly be diagnosed with cancer and his brother killed in a car accident? The world was a matter of balance and imbalance. The real price of winning the lottery was unknown, but it certainly would bring as much pain as it brought pleasure. That was the way of life. It was the same with those people who got the post office jobs and other union jobs or the government positions. They had a guaranteed income, but what price did they pay for it? Did they say, "Thank you, Satan," or did they say, "Praise Jesus"? Who were these people anyway? Smokey looked at the empty beer bottles scattered around him. There were two more in the refrigerator—might as well drink them down. But as he attempted to go to the fridge, he realized he had had enough. Save it for tomorrow.

Chapter VI

The morning sun shone through the living room window. Smokey had slept on the couch. "Oh boy, what a head I've got—*ouch.*" He made his way to the shower.

After a long shower, Smokey made some scrambled eggs and toast for breakfast. He sat down at the table and picked at his food. *I don't feel like looking for work today. It's a good day for poetry." Did I think that thought or did someone else? Strange!*

But yes, it is a good day to spend creating poems. Smokey reached for a pen and paper pad on the table and began to write. After an hour or two he had created his first poem:

Lights refraction through prism glass
Moon's face on a still lake
Star sparkle in oceans of space
The twinkle in my eye

Deep water on a dark night
Lost in a void
Heavy are the entanglements of life
A bitter tear

Between a tear and a streetlamp's light
She comes to me, my image of comfort
My long-lost love imagined
And so she was created

Now I must set her free
And so all things must change

She was of my mind in the beginning
Now she is herself

Alone yet always among you I wander
I bend to gaze into a flower
But the flower is a starving child
Who will set us free

On this world all things are both
As time is space space is time
As mind is matter matter is mind
And the source of the river is the river

As all things are and all things change
As energy flows returns and changes
Is my purpose in motion
Why am I?

Lights refraction through prism glass
Moon's face on a still lake
Star sparkle in oceans of space
The search for meaning in my eye.

Smokey looked over his poem with both satisfaction and concern. It felt like someone else or something else inside of him had created the poem, yet intuitively he knew this poem was an expression of his future and an expression of life itself. He tried to do some more poetry but nothing else seemed to come, so he thought, *I'll bring out the clay and do some sculpture.*

Smokey thought about his poem as his hands began to mold the clay. The first thing that seemed to come through the clay was a distended belly. Then he moulded a ribcage, and gradually he moulded a complete child. A hungry child of clay. Then Smokey began to mould the petals of a flower around this starving child. It was beautiful; it was life.

A voice spoke inside his head: *Duality.*

Smokey was frightened. Something was wrong with his mind. Was there a spirit inside him? What other explanation could there be? He thought for a moment, then went to the refrigerator and pulled the last bottles of beer out. He opened them and dumped the contents down the sink. "No more," he said to himself.

Smokey went and lay down on the couch but his mind wouldn't let him rest. He thought about the starving child in the flower. *Yes*, he thought, *the voice is right. This is duality. But what is this voice that speaks inside of me? Is it the spirit of the dead come alive inside me, or is it too much booze?*

The week passed slowly and Smokey was less and less enthusiastic about doing a door-to-door search for employment. It was Friday morning and Smokey decided he would check out the UIC office just in case something had come in. People quite often got fired on paydays. He backed the Fairlane into a parking spot about three blocks away. It was getting cool out these days. Pretty soon it would be time to pull out the winter parka, Smokey thought. He reached the UIC office on Broad Street and took a deep breath before entering the building. The same clerks stared at him with disgust as he walked in. Smokey checked all the boards for employment. Respiratory technologists seemed to be in demand. Smokey wondered how long it would take to become one of those. The thought of something in the medical profession was very appealing, and he, being an ex-smoker and foundry worker, had something to say about healthy lungs. He would make some inquiries.

There was nothing else on the UIC boards of any interest or that suited his abilities, so he made a mental note of the respiratory technologist position and left for home. Just as he got in the door at home, the phone rang. It was his sister Janet. Janet said she was coming over in the evening for a chance to sit by the fire and have a good cup of coffee.

Smokey loaded up his solo boat on the Fairlane and headed for the lake. There was a thin sheet of ice on the edges of the lake, but it was open water further out. Yes, soon it would be winter. Smokey pushed the canoe over the thin sheet of ice and into the water and got in. His paddle broke the thin ice as he headed for open water. This would be his last paddle of the season—a time to reflect on the season and all that had transpired. He knew there would be no next year with Red, yet friendship was important and he made a mental note to call Red and see how he was doing. The paddle glided through the water and the cedar-strip canoe moved swift and fluid through the glass-like water.

Smokey paddled for about ten miles, drifting in and out of various thoughts from solo competition in the future to new career prospects. Nevertheless, it was going to be a long, hard winter. He decided that he should try to wax his skis in anticipation of an early snowfall.

After his paddle on the lake, Smokey, feeling much more relaxed, took a shower and prepared supper. His sister arrived just as the sun was setting. True to her word, she was there for an evening fire and a good cup of coffee, so Smokey threw a couple of logs into the potbellied stove and put the screen on so they could watch the flames lick the logs. They talked small-talk for several hours, and soon it was time to restock the potbellied stove. Janet asked about his work situation, and Smokey confessed the future didn't look too bright without some form of retraining. He said that he was interested in job postings in respiratory technology. Janet thought that was a good idea, but she also made it clear that he shouldn't waste time and should make inquiries right away. Out of the blue, Janet said, "I have a friend in Winnipeg who is looking for a pen-pal. Would you be interested in writing her?" Smokey said sure, he had nothing else to do this winter, by the looks of things. Janet left Smokey an address and name—Sherry—to which he could write.

Smokey spent the next day tarring his skis, and in the evening he sat down to paper and wrote a letter to this woman Sherry. He thought about what was interesting to him and shared his thoughts and issues. He talked about canoeing at night under the stars.

Two weeks passed uneventfully for the most part. Smokey spent the days sculpting a giant chess set. He loved the game of chess, though he really was only an average player. Each piece he worked at diligently, trying to bring life and character to every pawn. Then one day he opened the mailbox and along with his UIC cheque was a letter from Winnipeg. From Sherry.

He opened the letter first and hovered over every word she had written. Enclosed also was a picture. Sherry was a cute little redhead. She talked about her job in the grain marketing business and her other job as aerobics instructor. She liked chocolate and Tigers and all things orange. She was an Aries, the fire sign of the zodiac. Smokey liked her instantly. He knew that she was a very special person. He sat down to write, but he couldn't seem to get anywhere. Then, as though he was almost in a trance, he began to write a poem about a tiger and a bushman. He knew she was the tiger and he was the bushman who found the tiger swimming in the White Mouth River. The current was strong and was going to sweep the tiger away to her death, but the bushman in his canoe saved her.

Smokey sat back and looked at the poem. He could feel his heartbeat. This was no ordinary poem—this was a spell cast to catch a lover. He knew it but couldn't do anything about it except mail the poem the next day.

A week passed and the first snow fell. It was just enough to slide the skis across without scraping off the tar. The first snowfall in Saskatchewan is so beautiful; it covers the summer fallow and the barren ground. Smokey took his skis out and made a trek to the nearest open field. He skied about 10 kilometers in the morning and then had a shower and got ready to go to the UIC building. He needed to get more information on respiratory technology training.

At the UIC building, Smokey saw a counselor who seemed most pleased that Smokey would consider retraining. She gave him several lists of programs for which UIC would pay, but the bottom line was that UIC paid for one-year courses only, and respiratory technology was a two-year course. Smokey looked at all the one-year courses and shook his head: they were hopeless courses that would lead to further unemployment down the line. None of the one-year programs were substantial enough to offer even mediocre remuneration when employed either. He asked if UIC would pay for one year of the respiratory technology classes but UIC didn't sponsor partial completion of classes and refused to assist financially toward a two-year course.

Smokey left somewhat discouraged. Another problem was that there were no training centers for respiratory technology in Saskatchewan, but there was a center for training in Winnipeg and Edmonton. Smokey thought about the cost of a move and living in a strange city for two years. The barriers seemed insurmountable to regaining a livelihood without a lot of personal sacrifice.

When Smokey got home he opened the mailbox and was surprised to see another letter from Sherry. He had thought he had scared her off with his romantic poem, but to the contrary, Sherry was most impressed and talked about actually meeting sometime in the future. This cheered Smokey up considerably.

Smokey spent the rest of the day sculpting. At first nothing came to mind, but then he began to sculpt madly. In no time at all he had sculpted a tiger in the arms of a bushman. After it dried, he took it in to be fired. While he was there, he looked at the glazes. After a short search, Smokey found a suitable orange colour. When the sculpture was complete, he set it on the kitchen table and gazed at it. Was it good enough to send to her? He debated for a long time, then passed his left hand over the sculpture. He could feel the power of the spell flow into the sculpture. It was good enough to send to her for Christmas. If she didn't like it, she wasn't meant to be any more than a friend. He packed the sculpture in a box with paper and taped it shut. There were still two weeks till Christmas, so Smokey left the box on the table and began to sculpt other things. After a short time, he had sculpted a small Buddha. He decided that this would be an excellent gift for his brother, who had recently become a Buddhist. A few days later, Smokey mailed his sculpture, and in the next few days he received packages from family in the mail.

It was the day before Christmas and Smokey was at the back of the yard splitting logs for the fire he planned for Christmas Eve. The phone rang. It was his sister saying she was coming over for Christmas Eve. She said she had a surprise for him. Smokey finished cutting the wood and then waxed his skis. The day was long, but toward early evening, Smokey grabbed his skis and headed for the ski trail. The stars were just beginning to shine through early dusk. He skied a short 5K and then headed back to the house to await his sister.

Chapter VII

Smokey and his sister sat in front of the potbellied stove and watched the fire through the screen. Janet seemed terribly restless–even a little excited. Then she said, "Remember I told you I had a surprise? Well, Sherry is coming to visit for New Year's. And you can pick her up at the bus depot on the thirtieth.

Smokey smiled.

Christmas morning, Smokey unwrapped his presents. It wasn't like it was when he was a child, but it was still nice to be thought of. The best gift he got was from his brother. It was a little round meditation cushion. Smokey sat on the cushion and said, "Can you feel me, Sherry? Can you feel the power of the spell? This meeting is no accident." Smokey wondered if Sherry had received the package with the sculpture in it-the tiger and the bushman. He couldn't be sure.

The next day, Smokey went Boxing Day shopping. He was trying to find something small but appropriate to give Sherry when she came. He was about to give up when he looked into the window of a small shoe store. There in the window was a small pair of tiger-paw slippers. Smokey laughed. That was just perfect. He went in and made the purchase.

Smokey sat on a bench in the bus depot. She would be here in twenty minutes. What would he say? He had nothing romantic to say. He didn't even think he could make chitchat. The bus pulled into the station and one petite redhead hopped off the bus and bounced across the room. She stopped and looked around. Smokey's stomach was in a knot. Could she recognize him, never having seen him before? Then their eyes met and two old souls said hello in another state of consciousness. He could feel her when she moved–his chest was humming. He took her hand.

"Oh," she said, "let's not forget my bag," so they went out to the bus. Sherry said, "Guess which one is mine."

Smokey looked at all the bags and suitcases. He was about to say, "I give up," when the bus driver unloaded a small orange backpack. "That's it!" he said. She laughed. "Did you get my package in the mail?"

"No, not yet," she said. "But now I'll have something to look forward to when I go home."

He dropped her off at his sister's and said, "I will see you New Year's Eve." Sherry said, "We should all go dancing. Looking forward to it." Then she was gone.

Smokey's chest continued to feel warm as he thought of her. He could still see her orangey brown eyes flashing. She was a tiger. How to tame a tiger? No, no, never tame a tiger—the very spirit that is so appealing would be lost. A bushman knows that! The bushman went home and made a fire in the stove. He watched the flames. They were all orange tigers licking the logs. He went to bed early that night thinking of the next day.

Smokey woke very late and felt that he had been traveling all night. Where had he gone? And who had he been with? He stumbled into the shower and soaked. He thought about fire. Fire and water. Can water have flames? There was something about fire and water in Revelations. Strange thoughts. The oceans will boil over. Smokey could feel a poem coming on, but this poem would be about everlasting commitment, about continued existence in the flames of hell. Our right to imperfections. Very strange thoughts. Smokey finished his shower and made himself some eggs and toast.

He thought, The *flames in the fireplace-all little tigers, flames in hell.* There were pieces missing. It was too soon to write.

He grabbed his skis and went out the door to the ski trail. It was a crisp day, probably close to minus 20°, but it didn't take long to work up a sweat. It felt really good to be working his body. There is something about physical exercise for which there just isn't any substitute.

Smokey traveled along the Wascana trail towards the lake. He would reach the lake and make a circle and then head home again. It would take a couple of hours and would take his mind off Sherry. There were few people on the ski trail today. It was probably too cold for most. There were a pair of sundogs in the sky and it was bright.

The rest of the day passed slowly for Smokey. He listened to every Van Morrison record he had. Janet called at about 6:00 to let him know that they would pick him up about 8:00 to go dancing. Smokey had a long shower, then pressed his jeans and a rust colored shirt.

Soon Janet's car pulled up to the house. Smokey made his way to the car smiling. They went to a pop-rock joint and ordered drinks. Just coke for Smokey—he was committed to an alcohol-free life. The music was loud so it was difficult to carry on any conversation, but Smokey found himself gazing into Sherry's eyes on several occasions. The night progressed and Smokey danced with both of them. Toward the end of the evening, they were playing more and more waltzes. Smokey held the tiger close. She was dressed in a black leather shirt and orange stockings, and she wore red triangle earrings. The music continued. Smokey could feel her body so close, their legs brushed together. That first kiss is always so awkward. He had to bend down quite a ways to find her mouth. He gently kissed her. She pressed herself into him. They held each other for a moment. The song ended.

For the rest of the evening Smokey danced with her, and every waltz was more intimate than the one before. It was close to midnight, so Smokey and the tiger went and sat with Janet. New Year's held promise, Smokey thought.

"Happy New Year's, Tiger!"

"Happy New Year's, Bushman," she whispered.

They arrived back at Smokey's about 1:00. Smokey got out and said goodnight to the ladies, but Sherry got out of the car and said, "Good night, Janet." Janet looked a little embarrassed, but she said good night and slowly drove off. Sherry took his hand and they walked to the door. Smokey stopped and looked up. The stars were out in full force and the moon was about full. A perfect evening.

Once inside, Smokey took the tiger's coat and made a small fire in the pot-bellied stove. He put the screen on so they could watch the flames together. She curled up in his arms on the couch and purred. He stroked her head and kissed her gently again and again. Her eyes flashed. She moved his hands onto her breasts. He was as hard as a rock and dying to be in her. He took her hand and led her to the bedroom. Moments later, they were joined together. He was pressing into her hard. Her fingernails dug deep into his back–tiger claws. The passion was strong and they made love several times, catching only a few hours' sleep.

Smokey awoke suddenly to the smell of coffee and toast. *Oh my God, is this heaven?* he thought. They spent the morning talking over toast and coffee. About eleven o'clock, they decided they should phone Janet. Janet was just on her way out to walk her dog, Hobo, but she invited them over for coffee in the afternoon. Sherry was anxious to get a change of clothes and she wanted to do an aerobic workout. She thumbed through his records looking for something with a fast beat. She didn't find much that pleased her. "Do you suffer from depression?" she asked. "I mean, really, Gordon Lightfoot, Bruce Cockburn, Leonard Cohen! Do you play with razor blades for fun?" Smokey laughed. Then she found an Aretha Franklin record and put that on.

They met Janet at about 3:00. Sherry went to shower and get a change of clothes. Janet sat with Smokey over a cup of coffee. She was mostly silent. Then she said, "Are you sure you know what you're doing?" Smokey smiled weakly.

He had brought the slippers along to give Sherry and was looking forward to the moment. Sherry came into the room and Smokey handed her the parcel. "This is for you," he said. He couldn't help but grin. She was like a little kid tearing into the wrapping paper. As she opened the box, she squealed with delight. Even Janet couldn't help but smile. Sherry wore her tiger slippers for the rest of the afternoon.

That evening they all went out for pizza. They went to the Famous Chimney Restaurant. Smokey was enjoying every moment, but he also knew Sherry would be returning to Winnipeg tomorrow and his heart ached. It had just begun to work and it was going to be over tomorrow. His chest burned.

They sat at the bus depot and he held her hand lightly. They didn't speak. Then the announcer came on and said, "Winnipeg bus departing in five minutes." He grabbed her orange backpack and walked her to the bus. He looked into her eyes. They didn't kiss.

"Goodbye, Tiger."

"Goodbye, Bushman."

She hopped onto the bus. Smokey walked away. He had a lot to think about. Life could be complicated. The woman he liked lived in a different city. It was only a seven-hour drive away, but his old Fairlane was on its last legs.

Smokey pulled his fur hat over his ears and got into his Fairlane. The temperature was dropping. The radio said it would be minus 35 overnight with a high the next day of minus 28.

Smokey drove the Fairlane slowly down Dewdney Avenue. He thought about moving to Winnipeg. Life is a matter of choices. Some people get better choices than others, but we all have choices to make, and it seemed that employment opportunities in Regina, Saskatchewan, were almost nil. So the choice was simple. He could depend on welfare and live like a dog or perhaps worse, or he could pack his bags and try his luck elsewhere. Just as Smokey pulled the Fairlane into the driveway, there was a bang and a clunk and the engine was dead. Smokey lifted the hood, and there was number six cylinder right through the side of the block. That was it! The motor was finished. Smokey sighed and went into the house, turned the heat down, and threw a few logs into the potbellied stove.

This new development would further restrict his employment search. Smokey sat by the fire and looked into the flames. Sherry would be halfway home by now. He thought, *Could I move to Winnipeg? I would lose all the support of my friends, but it would be a chance to start again.* Every employer in Regina knew him by now, and there was absolutely no hope. Smokey put his thoughts into the back of his head. He watched the flames and he could hear her voice singing on the bus back to Winnipeg.

As the moon came up bright and beautiful on the wane, Smokey latched on his skis. He started slowly along the trail, building up speed as he went along. Smokey enjoyed skiing, but it was hard on his lower back and he found that a 10K ski was about all he could do.

The next day, Smokey woke up late. He showered and ate a small brunch. He put on a parka with hood and headed for the bus stop. The radio had said it was minus 31°. He would pick up a bus schedule as soon as he could. He reached the bus stop and stood in the shelter from the wind. The bus was just rounding the corner. "Now that's timing," Smokey thought. The bus went right by the UIC building, which meant he could undo his parka.

Smokey asked one of the workers in the UIC building if they had more information on respiratory technology. They gave him all the information they had including addresses to the Respiratory Institutes in Winnipeg and Edmonton. Smokey was only interested in the respiratory center in Winnipeg. After visiting the UIC center, Smokey went to the florist shop and ordered a dozen roses to be sent to Sherry at her work address. Inscription: "To the Tiger from the Bushman."

Smokey was going crazy with too much time on his hands. He hated soap operas and generally despised television, and he could only read for so long. He went skiing every day but found himself becoming angry with his limitations as a skier.

A week passed before that special phone call. Sherry called and said both the flowers and the sculpture were wonderful surprises. But did she feel the power? Was she caught in the spell? Smokey didn't know. After talking for several minutes, they decided together that he should come to Winnipeg for a visit and see if he liked it. They decided that Valentine's Day would be a good week to come. Sherry said she had a couple of days off coming to her. She said, "I'll meet you at the bus depot. It's right downtown. Goodbye for now, Bushman."

"Goodbye, Tiger."

Valentine's Day seemed an eternity away. Every day seemed to be minus 30 without any break. Smokey spent the time the best way he could, reading, listening to music, and going skiing.

He took a night bus to Winnipeg so he would be able to spend the whole day with Sherry. On the bus, he created a poem for her. He called her "The Golden Dragon of love and light dancing on a beam of light." He could see in his mind the swish of her tail and the gleam in her eyes. A powerful ally.

The bus seemed to stop every twenty miles, even though it was the express. Soon he could see the sunrise and it was one of hope and promise. Today is yesterday's future. The bus pulled into Portage La Prairie, a ten-minute stop for morning coffee. Smokey ordered a large black coffee and fixed the lid on tight. He sipped his morning coffee and looked out the window at the barren landscape.

It was only about an hour before he saw the sign for Winnipeg. His chest was burning with excitement. The bus traveled through the city at a slow pace. It seemed to take forever to reach the depot. They pulled into the depot at about nine o'clock. He saw her right away, her red hair blowing in the breeze. It was a short haircut but it seemed to suit her. They hugged each other and waited for the luggage to be unloaded. Smokey grabbed his bag and they headed for Sherry's car. He saw it before she could say anything—an orange VW rabbit. Smokey laughed when he saw it, it suited her so well.

Sherry took him to a place called the Bombay Bicycle Club for breakfast. Her golden eyes flashed at him as they chatted. He knew with certainty he would love this woman for the rest of his life. She was the tiger, the golden dragon of his imagination. Smokey pulled out a box of chocolates and the poem he had written for her. She read the poem and Smokey swore he saw a tear in her eye. She smiled and said, "You understand. I also love chocolates!" They sat there and ate chocolate and talked about the future. She was a competent woman and couldn't see how a man like Smokey couldn't find employment in a city as large as Winnipeg. He told her that he was considering retraining as a respiratory technologist but he had to be accepted as a student first. The next set of classes would start the following September. He would have to find work first, at least temporarily, and it seemed to Smokey that Winnipeg was as good a place as any to look for work. She said that she would send him the *Winnipeg Free Press* classified section in the mail every weekend.

Sherry took him to Osborn Village, a neat little trendy place, and they spent the day window-shopping. Smokey found some wonderful hand-painted cards he could send to his brother and his brother's wife. Sherry spent the time looking at fur coats and trying on clothes. It was a wonderful day, and despite the fact that the relationship was new, there seemed to be very little tension.

They spent that evening talking and developing a letter to send to the Respiratory Technology Centre along with a résumé. Sherry knew what she was doing. She could bring out all his positive qualities. She made him both intelligent and competent. She gave most generously of her time, and this Smokey remembered most of all.

That evening in bed, he watched her purr a soft, gentle snore. He wanted to stroke her head to feel her breath close to him. She was alive, not just his imagination. Who was she, really? What kind of woman could see his good side and all his potential in such a short time? What kind of woman would care?

Sherry was up early the next morning. Smokey groaned and then headed for the shower. She said, "You're not a morning person, I can tell." Smokey just smiled.

They spent the day visiting Sherry's favorite spots. On the way home, they were stopped at a red light and then suddenly there was a bang and Smokey's head flew back. It took a few moments to realize what had happened.

Smokey said, "Sherry, are you all right?"

She said, "No."

Smokey got out of the car. There was very little damage to the vehicles but he knew Sherry was hurt.

Smokey waved over a bus driver to phone the police. The fellow who was in the other vehicle could barely stand up, he was so drunk. His wife was saying, "Please, let's just go home, we'll pay any damages."

The police came and took a report, and then everybody did go home. Smokey couldn't remember if the man was charged or not. He was feeling strange already. His thoughts were confused. Sherry was holding her neck.

They both had a terrible sleep that night. The next day Smokey couldn't move his head to the right and Sherry was in terrible pain. They decided to consult a lawyer and a doctor both.

The visit to Winnipeg ended on a terrible note. Smokey kissed Sherry goodbye at the bus depot not knowing whether he would see her again. The bus ride home was awful. He could hardly keep he head up, the muscles in his neck were so sore. He wondered how Sherry was doing.

The day following his arrival home, Smokey went to the chiropractor and was given a neck brace. There was what they call soft-tissue damage to the trapezius and some notable restrictions. He learned from Sherry that her condition was much worse.

They spoke on the phone and talked about the future. They talked about a future together, at least dating. Smokey was in love; he would do anything to be with her. Finally, a few weeks after receiving Sherry's promised classified section in the mail, they had a long talk on the phone. She said he could stay at her place initially, until he found a place of his own, if he chose to move to Winnipeg.

In March the weather broke and there were even a few days when it was above zero. Smokey stepped out of his home and took one last look. It was a big move, but he was giving notice and moving on.

Smokey contacted Bill and asked when he might borrow his dad's truck for a move to Winnipeg. In a few weeks it was all arranged. Smokey had said goodbye to the Fairlane and called the auto wrecker.

Bill, because of his disability, wasn't able to help much loading the truck, but his companionship was appreciated. Smokey packed the stereo up front and then filled the rest with boxes of various things. It only took a couple of hours and they were loaded. Smokey's two budgies, Higgledy and Piggledy, were put into the cab. Bill let Smokey drive because he found the clutch on the truck hard to operate. The two of them were off to Winnipeg. Smokey's mind was on Sherry and Bill had little to say, but he had been encouraging despite the fact that they would be miles apart in the future.

As they drove along, Bill asked, "How much do you know about this woman?" Smokey thought about it before replying. He said, "I've known her before, maybe in a previous lifetime, but I know her."

Bill seemed to understand and said nothing further.

It seemed to take forever to arrive at Winnipeg, but after seven hours they reached the outskirts of the city. Both men were silent. There wasn't much to be said. It was a new beginning for Smokey, and Bill was helping make it a reality.

Smokey pulled up to Sherry's apartment and rang the bell. Sherry came out and Smokey introduced her to Bill. Bill rested while Smokey went to work at unloading the truck. The hardest thing was getting his solo canoe off safely. They finished unloading at about nine o'clock. Smokey and Bill shook hands as Bill pulled the truck out to head back. Smokey felt a moment of regret. Bill was his best friend and he would miss his sense of humor. But he could always send him a card from Osborn Village.

Chapter VIII

Sherry looked delighted to see him. They hugged and then sat together at the kitchen table. Sherry made some coffee. It had been a long day, but there was a need to talk about things. They discussed his strategy for employment and retraining and set out daily objectives. Sherry knew he could get a job. He just wondered if he could.

It was only about four days when Smokey got his first employment opportunity as a midnight street sweeper. It was cold and wet and hard work. He found that it was too hard on his back, but at least there seemed to be some hope here in Winnipeg. Each day he would buy the *Free Press* and search the classified section. He also found out where the UIC building was and made daily trips to check the boards. Sherry was as encouraging and supportive as she could be. She just didn't understand why a man with his talents had a hard time finding work. The truth was, she could only see his good side.

The weeks passed and the pressure was on. His UIC cheques would soon come to an end. Then there was only welfare!

On the following Monday, Smokey got a call for an interview for respiratory technology. This was a very exciting event. He had given up hope. The interview was on Wednesday, so Sherry drilled him with questions to prepare him for the interview.

Fear is a terrible thing, and deep down, Smokey had fears about being responsible for other people's lives. What if he did something wrong? Over the next two days that fear grew inside him. It was a matter of competency. The day of the interview arrived and Smokey was filled with dread. Finally, in the course of the interview, he expressed his fears openly. The interviewer smiled and said, "Don't worry. You will be well trained after two years of intensive study." The rest of the interview went well, but deep in the pit of his stomach Smokey knew he had failed himself again.

After the interview, he talked with Sherry. She seemed amazed at him, almost angry, that he had expressed these fears at an interview. "Where is your confidence?" she said.

Smokey returned to his daily employment search and also started an anatomy and physiology class at the University of Winnipeg in preparation for respiratory technology. He wanted to test his brainpower. It had been years since he had studied for exams.

Spring was in the air, and Smokey felt hopeful about the future. His fear of doing something wrong as a respiratory technologist had faded with the success of his university class. His final mark was 82 per cent. This was acceptable. Sherry said she was proud of him.

It was Friday afternoon and Smokey waited for the mail. He was expecting his final payment from UIC. It came, but also there was a letter for him. Probably just a registered letter. But he opened it up and stared at what he saw. It was an interview date set for the following Tuesday for a position as manager for a housing complex. Smokey couldn't believe it, he was so excited. He didn't believe he had a chance at the job.

When Sherry finished work, Smokey was right on top of her with his news. She smiled but she seemed fatigued, played out. Unemployment is a roller-coaster ride for both parties. It affects relationships and often destroys them.

Tuesday morning his stomach was in knots. He showered and shaved. He had to do it this time; he could not express fears. He had to be confident. Show no weakness. He took the bus to the location of the interview. It was a long, bumpy ride. He reached the door of a townhouse and knocked. A huge man answered. Smokey said he was here for the interview. The man smiled and said, "I'm the vice-president. Come in."

There were five interviewers waiting for him. They peppered him with questions for half an hour. Smokey was beginning to sweat. He had to exude confidence. When the vice-president asked about salary, he went for it. They seemed impressed by this. They wanted a man who could take control. They valued his accounting background, and he could learn about housing from other complex managers.

They shook hands and said they would be in touch with him shortly. On the way home, Smokey thought, "That's the best interview I've ever had. I believe I've done it. I believe I will get this job."

They phoned him later that same day and told him he had the job of complex manager. Smokey was in heaven. He would start the job Monday morning. He was to place an ad in the paper for a secretary and accounting clerk to assist him in the general operation. There was already a maintenance staff. He shared his excitement with Sherry but she seemed distant. In fact, she had seemed distant for over a week. Finally she said, "I want my space. I'm giving notice on this place at the end of the month. You'll have to find yourself your own place. I still want to date, but things have been too stressful around here."

Smokey couldn't believe it. He had just thought things were coming together. Now it looked like things were falling apart. Not only did he need to think about the job, he needed to find a place to live.

Saturday Smokey slept in, and then spent the day looking for a place downtown. He needed a place close to a bus route that would take him to work. He was just about finished looking for a place when he saw a sign on a big white house on Spence Street. He knocked on the door and a lady answered. "I'm here about the suite for rent," he said. She looked him up and down. Then she took him to see the suite.

Smokey liked it. It was roomy with hardwood floors. "How much is it?"

"For you," she said, "Four hundred a month."

Smokey said, "I'll take it. I'll move in at the end of this month." Then he quickly thought, "Maybe I could move in a couple of days before the end of the month." She said, "Okay, bring me a deposit of two hundred and you may move in."

The reason he wanted to move in early was that he and Sherry would need to work together to be out of the old place in time, and something told him he would need to inspect units at the housing complex. People would be leaving and new people would be coming in.

That evening he told Sherry he had found a place. He asked if he could use her car to move his stuff. She said, "Of course–you help me, I'll help you." She said again, "I still want to date you, you know. It's just this past month has been very stressful. You need to work on your problems and I need to work on mine."

Smokey could feel the pressure between them melt. Intellectually he understood the need for separation but emotionally he couldn't catch up. But that evening they made love and they seemed even closer than before. He didn't understand, but that didn't matter.

On Sunday they spent the day walking in the park and Smokey's mind was clearly focused on his new job.

Smokey arrived early Monday morning for work. The vice-president was there. The phones were all lit up and there was coffee on the counter. The VP said, "Fuck the phones today. We have to find out our financial position. We don't know where we are. Also we must confirm who's moving in and who's moving out. Place an advertisement for a secretary and she can answer some of the lines that are lit up."

The last time they had financial statements was over a year ago. A one write accounting system had been started, but monthly receipts did not balance with potential revenue and unpaid accounts. Things were a mess. He would need to reconcile the bank to the records and all other accounts. The VP said, "We want financial statements as soon as possible." This meant an end-of-the-month financial cutoff. He needed help, and he needed it fast. He placed an advertisement in the *Winnipeg Free Press* for a secretary accounting clerk. He would show her how to issue receipts and balance the account ledger.

From the records, he had to find out who was supposed to move in at the end of the month. It seemed simple enough, but information was missing. By the end of the day, Smokey realized a lot of information was missing. He knew there were going to be mistakes made, and he knew he would be held accountable for those mistakes.

By the end of the next week, Smokey was ready for month-end. He had hired a secretary and shown her how to do an accounts payable synoptic as well as record incoming money. They were prepared for month-end cut-off. but eleven people were moving out and another eleven were moving in. The units had to be inspected. It was going to be a busy weekend.

Smokey moved into his suite a few days early and then helped Sherry move to her new apartment. As Smokey expected, things were nonstop at the housing complex for the next five days. Smokey found some move-in forms and went through the checklist as well as he could for the eleven suites that were empty or soon to be empty, but the bottom line was, nobody was happy. The people leaving thought the place was clean enough, while those moving in found the place unacceptable. At least the financial cut-off was successful. Smokey closed the synoptics and cheque register and made journal entries to the general ledger.

A week had passed and the worst was over at the housing complex, so Sherry invited Smokey over for dinner. Dinner was wild duck,-one of Smokey's favorite dishes. They lit candles at the table and opened a bottle of red wine. She sat across from him and he gazed into her eyes. "I've missed you," he said. "Things got really busy there for about a week."

"I knew you would settle down," she said. "You were so tense there before we moved, I didn't think I could handle it."

After dinner, they did dishes together while listening to music. Smokey said, "How about a dance?"

She smiled and said, "As long as it's a waltz." At about midnight, he kissed her goodnight and left for his apartment.

Saturday morning at 7:30, the alarm clock sounded. Smokey stepped into the shower, then made himself a quick breakfast. Then he prepared some sandwiches for dinner and grabbed a bottle of water. He pulled his canoe out of the garage and threw his knapsack inside. He lifted the canoe onto his back and headed down the street. It was only two blocks to the river.

Smokey headed up the Red River into the current. He passed all the beautiful riverfront homes and soon was out of the city limits. It was so much quieter. He could really hear the birds now. The one thing Smokey could not seem to get used to was the noise of the big city. He lived for Saturdays and Sundays now that the river was flowing. He longed to be racing again, but he knew it would be some time before his neck healed completely from the auto accident. He also knew that working full-time and a canoeing training program did not go well together. Even amateur canoeing took a lot of dedication and training, but he planned on finding a partner next year if all went well. This year, he would be satisfied with weekend trips along the Red River.

Chapter IX

The summer passed quickly, and soon the river had ice around the edges again. Smokey had enjoyed the summer and early autumn. Canoeing and sculpting had helped keep his sanity during the evenings and weekends. It was the end of November when Sherry asked him to move in with her in a lovely little home in St. Vital. Smokey was truly excited about seeing more of Sherry. The relationship had been on and off for the last several months.

The winter months passed quickly. Smokey did some swimming to keep in shape. He also met a paddler from up north named George with whom he went skiing during the winter. They talked about teaming up in the spring and winning the Manitoba Provincials, but spring was still a long way away at the time. George talked like a professional paddler, and Smokey couldn't wait till spring to get in a boat and try a few strokes together.

Chapter X

The ice was breaking up on the river. Yes, it was finally spring and the paddling could begin. There was a stretch of open water on the north shoreline, and Smokey placed his solo canoe into the cool waters of the Red River. Those first strokes of the paddle were sheer ecstasy. He paddled back and forth in the open water for about one hour, trying to exercise muscles that hadn't been used since last fall. It was going to be a good year. He was employed and had a canoeing partner for the season as well. Smokey pulled the canoe out of the water and headed for home with Sherry.

Chapter XI

Smokey and George, his new partner, sat at the river's edge talking. Today would be their first paddle. George was very enthusiastic. The practice went reasonably well with neither partner expecting too much of the other.

"Well, George, what do you think? Can we win the Manitoba Provincials?" George just smiled.

During the next three weeks, Smokey and George practiced every evening on the mighty Red River.

Chapter XII

There were nine racing shells lined up across the Red River waiting for the flag to drop. Smokey was nervous. Perhaps he and George could catch some of these paddlers by surprise. The paddlers next to them didn't look like much, but you never couldn't tell. The flag dropped and they were off. It became obvious that the race was really between Smokey and George and one other team. The other team was good-they had more power and rhythm, but their technique was poor. Smokey pulled in behind them and tried to ride their wash, but they were a light team and the wash was small. They reached the Assiniboine River and headed upstream. The current was very strong. The other team gradually pulled away, and Smokey could feel George giving up. They pulled into the finish-line an hour later, completely exhausted.

"Good race, guys."

"Thanks."

"We tried to keep up with you for a while."

"I'm Jim. This is Iain."

Smokey introduced himself and George.

Smokey wasn't disappointed with second place, but he sure didn't like the way George gave up so quickly. But George was his new partner and he wasn't going to get on his case right away.

The next race was two weeks away in Snow Lake. Smokey felt they should practice every night for at least two hours. They had to try to beat this Jim and Iain. The next two weeks went quickly. The days were hectic at work and there was practice every evening for a couple of hours. Late in the evening, Smokey would pull out his bag of clay and begin to sculpt, but the figures he sculpted seemed dark, almost tortured in some ways. He could see the sculpted figures in his mind's eye throughout the day. Sometimes they spoke to him. Smokey wondered, *What have I created?*

George pulled up in his half-ton and they loaded the racing shell. They were off to Snow Lake, the biggest race in Western Canada. Their expectations were high but achievable, they felt. It was about a five hour drive from Winnipeg to Snow Lake, and the roads were potholed and rough most of the way.

They arrived in the early evening. The stars were just coming out, and there was a full moon. They registered for the race and set off to a restaurant for a late-night supper. It is always good to fill up on pasta the night before a race, and the restaurant owner must have been advised of this because there were three pasta specials on the menu. Smokey and George sat by a window, and the moon lit their faces as they waited to order. It seemed like ages, but finally the waitress came. Smokey felt very strange as she approached. He was getting a tingling in his hands and arms. There was something very odd about this woman.

George was discussing race strategy, but Smokey wasn't listening. He was still captivated by the presence of the waitress, her long dark hair, her mischievous smile and bright eyes. *Could it be she was more than just a woman?* Smokey wondered.

Their order came, and George dug in like it was his last meal on earth. Smokey looked at his meal. There were four tomato slices aligned perfectly to form a square. Smokey thought, *Four-what is significant about four?* Then he remembered that four was a significant number in Native spirituality. Was it possible that this waitress was a sorceress and that there was a spell on this food? He didn't want to believe it, but it would account for the tingling in his arms. He had to decide whether or not to eat the meal. If he didn't, he'd be hungry before the race even started. He decided that the meal was harmless if he held the cross in his pocket while he ate it.

After dinner Smokey and George set up their tents in the backyard of a friend of George's. There's nothing like trying to set up a tent in the dark, but the moonlight helped a lot and soon they finished. Smokey curled up in his sleeping bag but couldn't sleep. He couldn't get that woman out of his head. He could see her smiling in his mind's eye.

It seemed as if he had just closed his eyes, yet he could hear the morning birds singing in the trees. Smokey looked at his watch. It was 5:30- too early to get up, but the chances of more sleep were slim. He thought about Sherry and how he missed her on these trips, but she was a busy woman holding down her own cleaning business and two part-time jobs, and was going to university part-time also. He wondered if they would ever really connect on a personal level. He hoped so. He dreamed so, but life doesn't always work out the way you hope.

Six o'clock. Smokey thought again about that weird experience the night before with that waitress. He decided that whatever the spell was, it couldn't hurt him.

At seven o'clock, Smokey woke up George and they headed to town for breakfast. There were several other paddlers already there, including some American teams. They ate in silence, then headed down to the waterfront where the race course would be outlined for all the paddlers. George seemed agitated, which was unusual as he was normally very relaxed before a race, but this race was in George's hometown and he wanted to put on a good performance.

Smokey and George took their canoe off the car and brought it down to the waterfront. It was a beautiful day for the races. The sun was shining and there was a gentle breeze-just enough to ripple the waters. Smokey prepared the water bottles and placed them in the canoe with hoses for intake.

George said, "This is going to be our day."

"I hope so," said Smokey, but he had an eerie feeling that he just couldn't shake about the day.

Chapter XIII

At five minutes to race time, all the canoeists lined up on the shoreline. It would be a sprint around the first island, then around the perimeter of the lake. Smokey sat in the bow of the canoe waiting for the gun to sound. They had gained good position on the shore and were ready. The gun sounded and they were off to the island.

Smokey set a stroke-rate of eighty-five strokes a minute in order to stay with the pack. Once they had reached the island, he reduced the rate to seventy-five strokes a minute-a solid cruising pace. They circled the island and then started following the perimeter of the lake. It felt good to be working hard. Smokey could feel the muscles in his back tighten. Jim and Iain were just in front of them, within striking distance. Smokey picked up the pace again but they didn't gain much ground.

After an hour on the water, Smokey and George were still in good shape. They approached a buoy near shoreline to make a turn. Smokey stuck in a bow rudder, but as he did so, he could feel the boat rolling to the side. The next thing he knew, he was upside down and swimming to the surface. When he surfaced, there was George looking shocked but okay. They swam the canoe to shore. In waist-deep water, they emptied the canoe.

Smokey looked around. There she was, standing on the shore: the waitress who had cast the spell the night before. She waved at them and smiled. Smokey thought, *You rotten bitch.* He knew she was responsible for the upset. She had cast a spell on them, a bad-luck spell, and it had spelled disaster for them.

They climbed back into the canoe and finished the race with disappointment. George and Smokey packed their bags and equipment in silence. There wasn't much that could be said as far as Smokey was concerned. They had been victimized by a sorceress and there was little to be done among mere mortals.

As they drove home to Winnipeg, Smokey stopped the vehicle and picked some wild tiger lilies by the roadside for his tiger waiting at home. Just as he was getting into the vehicle, a moth flew at his face and into his mouth. Smokey coughed, but eventually he had to swallow, and down went the moth.

George was killing himself with laughter. "That will teach you to leave your mouth open," George said. Smokey smiled. "Yeah, I guess so."

Smokey thought about the moth in his stomach. He remembered how shamans sometimes changed themselves into insects like moths. Could Smokey have swallowed a shaman? A shaman who wanted a new body and would take control of Smokey's body and mind? This was nothing to laugh at.

Twice in one day Smokey had felt he was the victim of powers greater than his own. He got into the vehicle and drove silently home filled with worry. There must be some way to protect himself against the spiritually powerful. Those who would possess one or cause one harm. So far nothing serious had happened, but Smokey felt it was only a matter of time before something more serious happened.

They got back to Winnipeg late and both men were exhausted. George said, "I'm sorry about the upset. It was my fault."

"No, no!" Smokey said. "We were doomed from the start!"

Not realizing what Smokey meant, George smiled and said the next race would be better. He dropped Smokey at his door and left for home.

Smokey grabbed the flowers and went inside. Sherry was in the kitchen making scones. Smokey loved Sherry's homemade scones with old cheese and he had an appetite.

George was busy for most of the next week, so Smokey took his solo boat out on the Red River. He paddled fifteen kilometers every day, practicing sprints and other intervals after work at the housing complex. He thought to himself, *This move to Winnipeg turned out all right. I have a job. I don't like it, but it pays the bills. I can compete in canoeing, and I have a woman in my life.*

The last race of the season before the Nationals in Saskatoon was a short race in Souris River. George and Smokey thought they were ready for this race. Saturday morning they loaded up the racing shell and headed to Souris River, a two-hour drive from Winnipeg. Souris River was a trickly little river with lots of current.

On the way there, Smokey thought about the hood ornament of Chrysler Corporation. He couldn't remember whether it had five or six triangles. If it had six, it could be the Mark of the Beast. There are three sides to a triangle. Three times six equals 666, the number of the Beast. *Could Chrysler be the devil's own?*

They arrived at Souris River about fifteen minutes before race time, so there was little time to spare. Smokey took the racing shell off the vehicle and placed it on the ground. He filled the water bottles and put them in the shell. There was no time to put on a spray cover. They lined up along the river. The gun sounded and they were off. They got a good start and were right behind Jim and Iain. Smokey placed the bow of his canoe over the stern wave of Jim and Iain's boat. There was a little bit of pull, which allowed Smokey to reduce his pace just slightly. Still, the sweat was pouring off his back. They were in the current now, they couldn't help it, and it was tough going. Jim and Iain pulled away and Smokey felt George giving up. It made him angry, but he kept paddling, determined to put in a respectable showing. They came to the final bridge and turned towards the finish line. Jim and Iain had already finished. Smokey had to admit they were good. He and George finished second.

The next step for Smokey and George was the Nationals, and they were invited to attend. On the way home, Smokey thought about the Nationals in Saskatoon. It wasn't that far to go, and he could try his hand at solo paddling as well. As they returned to Winnipeg, Smokey asked George if he wanted to go to the Nationals to try to do better. Smokey honestly felt that Red had been a better paddler than George, but he was willing to see what George could do under pressure. George said yes. They had one week to practice and Smokey thought they should practice at least two hours every evening, but George was busy two nights. Smokey would paddle solo those nights.

Days at the housing complex were frustrating, but it was a paycheque. Smokey worked hard at the job, but there seemed to be no rewards except the time off he was able to get to go to the Nationals.

Sherry, in her bright-orange shorts, loaded the last of the equipment. She wouldn't miss the event. Smokey thought, *My own cheering section* as he threw the canoe on the roof of the little car. Sherry drove while Smokey stared out the window at passing wheat fields all in the process of harvest. They would meet George at the Bezborough Hotel in Saskatoon.

George was sitting on the steps of the Bezborough Hotel when Smokey and Sherry arrived. They registered and unpacked in their room overlooking the South Saskatchewan River. The three of them went out for a quick supper of pasta and beans. That evening George and Smokey talked about the coming race. They agreed that they didn't have the power to stay in front and that they would have to wash-ride, which would be difficult in the shallows.

They retired early. George was asleep in ten minutes or less. Smokey and Sherry sat on their bed and just held hands.

Smokey said, "We're not ready for this race."

Sherry smiled and said, "You'll do your best, and that will be good enough."

But in Smokey's mind, it wasn't good enough. They had to place, or come close, in his mind.

Chapter XIV

Smokey and George sat by the water's edge. Two hours till race time. There was a cross-breeze blowing across the river. Smokey said, "That wind is going to be tricky." "You've got that right," said George. "We're not ready, are we," he asked. Smokey shook his head.

They sat at the starting line, trying to keep a good line on the first buoy turn downstream. The canoe was all ready with the water bottles in and hoses attached. The gun sounded and the waters turned to foam as the canoeists headed downstream. Smokey was breathing hard after just a few minutes, and he knew they would have to find a boat's wash to which to cling. They turned at the buoy downstream and headed west up the South Saskatchewan River into the shallows. They found a team that was about their speed and rode their side-wake, which helped keep them out of the downstream current. They rode the wash as close to the bank as possible and the wave lifted their bow up.

George was now gasping for air and was missing hut calls, and Smokey knew that they would soon drop off the wash of the other team and fall behind. About ten miles into the race Smokey felt George giving up. "Don't give up on me, George. We need this race." But George was giving up slowly bit by bit and Smokey knew it.

It was a long race through the shallows upstream. They grounded out on a small sandbar and had to get out of the canoe and pull it through. By the time they turned and headed downstream again, Smokey was exhausted. The best he could tell was they were near the back pack of paddlers heading home.

A few more canoes passed them, and Smokey knew they were near dead last. His heart sank. He'd known they weren't ready, but he hadn't expected to be humiliated either. They crossed the finish line and George collapsed. Smokey shook George's hand and said, "Thanks for the paddle," which was the right thing to do no matter how poorly they had done. But Smokey felt angry. He knew they should have done better, and he had given everything to make it happen.

The solo races were tomorrow. Smokey and George both signed up. They headed back to the hotel. George said, "I'm going to kick your ass tomorrow."

Smokey laughed and said, "Maybe tomorrow will tell the story." They got Sherry and went to the nearest restaurant for pasta and steak.

That night, Smokey couldn't sleep. He knew they should have done better than they had. Could it be that someone had cast a spell against them? Maybe one of the native teams. It seemed at times that there was a force-field in front of him that he couldn't quite break through. There are so many possibilities, and we are just mortal men fighting on a moral plane against forces we have no hope of overcoming. Smokey closed his eyes and heard a voice in his head laughing. "They're laughing at me!" Smokey was filled with anger. Why should dark forces win over him? Why can't it be a fair fight? Smokey thought about tomorrow's race. What was the point if dark forces were conspiring against him? He said a halfhearted prayer to a God he no longer knew and hadn't since he was a child. He closed his eyes and again felt himself being sucked into a dark void. He slept.

Smokey opened one eye and looked at the alarm clock. It was 6:30. Race time was 11:00. He glanced over at Sherry. She was staring at the ceiling. "Do you want to go for a morning walk?" asked Smokey.

Sherry smiled and got out of bed. "I'll just brush my teeth and be out in five.

They walked quietly along the river edge. Smokey was deep in thought. Then Sherry spoke. "My spirit guides will be with you today. I know you're going to do well." Smokey always believed that Sherry had strong forces about her and he felt good that she was behind him in this race. She said, "Do you believe in God?"

Smokey looked at her and smiled. "Sometimes I do, and sometimes all I can see are dark forces; but if there is darkness, there must also be light."

Sherry said, "You'd better believe there is." They went back to the hotel for breakfast. Smokey had eggs, even though they can be hard on the stomach, and two cups of fresh coffee. They went back to their room. George was just getting up. "Good morning," he said.

"Breakfast is good in the hotel," Smokey said.

"Thanks," George said.

"There's a cross-wind again today. Should be lots of fun in those solo boats,"Smokey said.

"Yeah, I guess so," said George. But he looked tired and half-beat already.

The three of them met an hour before race time down by the starting line to sign up. Smokey looked at the race outline. It was a real tricky course, lots of shallows, current, plus a crosswind. Only sixteen paddlers showed up for the solo race, and they were all top-notch competitors.

Smokey pointed his canoe downstream toward the first turn. He could just see the buoy. He sat at the start line with five minutes to go. He could feel his heart pounding and he actually felt weak. The gun went off, and Smokey hit the water with his paddle, long, deep strokes propelling the canoe forward. He was right beside George, but it only took him a moment to cruise by him. He knew he was stronger than George, but he was surprised at his own power. He looked behind him. Three boats behind him—that meant twelve in front of him. Smokey knew this race would be a game of strategy and require skill, not just muscle. He hoped he would prove himself today. He thought about Sherry's force behind him and smiled.

He turned at the buoy and headed upstream. He had to stick close to the bank in the backwater because the current was strong. He saw the next paddler in front of him. In order to pass him, he would have to enter into the current. It would take all his power to paddle into the current and pass this paddler. Smokey rode the paddler's wash until he was fully rested. Then he made his move into the current. It was easier than he thought. Now eleven paddlers were in front of him. The next two, Smokey passed in the shallows by poling over sandbars just under the surface of the water. There were nine paddlers in front of him now, and he knew passing them wouldn't come so easy.

As he came out of the shallows, he saw the next paddler in the distance. *I'll get there,* Smokey thought, *Long, deep strokes.* He turned at the buoy and headed back downstream. The canoe seemed to just glide along. He passed the next paddler without much difficulty. There were eight in front of him. He was halfway there, but time was running out. Under the bridge, Smokey saw the next paddler. He knew how to use the current to his advantage and keep Smokey behind him. Smokey rode the stern wash of the paddler for a while, then made his move. The two canoes vied back and forth for the better part of a mile before he could feel that the other paddler was tiring. With a burst of speed, he was past the paddler and on his way. The other paddler rode his wash for a while, then fell behind for good.

The final turn was in sight, and there was one more paddler in his reach. He poured it on for all his worth, and soon he was right behind the next paddler. It would be a matter of who had the most left. Smokey picked up the pace and came even with the other canoe. They struggled there together for a few moments, and then Smokey sprinted home as hard as he could. It was close, but Smokey came in seventh, ahead of the other paddler by three seconds. Seventh place out of sixteen. It wasn't what he had hoped for, but it was a respectable showing. After all, these paddlers were the best in Canada. Smokey pulled up on shore and dragged the canoe up on his back, and there was Sherry, smiling at him. He smiled back. Her smile had always been contagious. They went back to the hotel together.

George joined them much later. He didn't say much. He had finished fifteenth. Smokey decided right there that he wanted to train for solo competition—no more partners next year. But how could he get the training time he needed and still hold down a full-time job?

This consumed his thoughts all the way home to Winnipeg. Finally he voiced his thoughts to Sherry. He said, "I need an easy job that keeps me active and will still allow me to train for canoeing next year."

Sherry said, "Well, you can join my cleaning company and make ten bucks an hour."

Smokey thought that job was made to fit the situation. The very next day when he returned to work, he gave his notice without further thought or discussion with Sherry. The last two weeks of work at the housing complex went by fast. They were sorry to see him go and offered him a substantial raise to stay on, but Smokey's mind was made up.

Chapter XV

The following week he met Sherry's cleaning partner, and it became clear that there would be a lot less work than Smokey anticipated. He'd never bothered to ask Sherry how many hours of work he could expect. He was going to earn less than three hundred dollars a month doing the cleaning, so he pressed them for more contracts. Sherry's partner began to distrust Smokey, claiming that he was trying to take over her business. This eventually caused a split in the company where Sherry and Smokey kept half the business. Now Smokey had to live on less than two hundred a month. Finally, as a last straw, Sherry decided that she was going back to university and didn't have time to run a cleaning business anymore. The business folded and Smokey found himself without any income at all.

At first Smokey was angry, but as time went by and he applied for UIC, he began to see it as an opportunity of a lifetime. He could collect UIC for a year and train for the canoeing nationals full time. With the first UIC cheque he received, he bought a weight set. He sat down and started to develop a training program. The weight program took quite a while to establish. He wasn't after bulk–it was more for muscle-tone through the winter months. In the beginning Smokey would do half an hour of weights, then go to the public pool and swim forty lengths of front crawl. He would do this three times a week along with a short jog and an hour of canoeing while there was open water. The winter months passed, and Smokey did some skiing.

When the following spring came, Smokey was swimming 120 laps of front crawl in fifty minutes. He was spending an hour a day on weights and doing a six-kilometer run. As soon as the ice was off the Red River, Smokey had his canoe in the water. This would be his season.

Through the winter months, Smokey continued with his art and sculpture, but the pieces came out ugly and deformed. No matter how hard he tried, they all seemed to have a dark spirit attached to them. Smokey was troubled by this and by a voice in his head that was trying to contact him. He could feel it. The voice just couldn't break the conscious barrier. Smokey thought, *Maybe it's my father trying to reach me from the other side.* He wondered if his father would be proud of him now or not. He was going to be the national canoeing champion if he had his way, but he still had no career at thirty-two years of age. He remembered his father saying his second son was going to be a garbage man, one hundred dollars a month and all you can eat, ha ha. He used to think this was funny but the truth was, garbage men made thirty thousand dollars a year and the city wouldn't hire Smokey.

In the early spring evenings, Smokey would walk down to where the two rivers met. It was a power spot. He could feel the power in his hands, sort of a tingling sensation. Smokey would often raise his hands to sense if there was a power about. He could also feel when certain people he met had power. Again his hands would tingle.

Smokey reached the Red River and sat by the bank. It had started to rain. It occurred to him that maybe he was responsible for the weather. He didn't know how, but he knew that he was more than a single human. He too had power, and other powerful people began to recognize him. He began to dance and the rain came down harder! It was true! He controlled storms.

That evening he heard about an earthquake in Japan and wondered if he was responsible for that also. How could he know? All these things-his dark sculptures, his father's voice in his head trying to reach him, and controlling the weather-all troubled Smokey greatly. But who would believe him and to whom could he talk? Sherry believed in a strong spirit, but could he confess to her that he had caused an earthquake in Japan? He wasn't sure how he felt about Sherry sometimes. Sometimes he felt she was hiding secrets of her own. After all, it had been sort of a spell that put them together in the first place. Maybe Sherry had a dark side that he couldn't see.

As he walked along the river's edge, he listened to the birds. They seemed to be trying to tell him something. Then he thought he saw a group of people dancing in his mind's eye. There was a fire and there was chanting. When he got home, he took out a pen and wrote about his experience of the day.

> I place the paddle across the gunwales
> and step into my cedar-strip canoe.
> I begin the motion of the paddle,
> and soon I am in the current
> of the Red River.
> Reaching the Assiniboine River connection,
> I stop and pull the canoe up onshore.
> There is the song of many birds
> over the dull roar of Winnipeg traffic.
> I sit under a small tree near the shore.
> I close my eyes.
> Soon I hear other voices-

voices I do not understand.
I see a foot move swiftly,
then many feet dancing.
There is an evening fire glowing.
A hand gently touches my shoulder.
I open my eyes, no one is there.
I return to my canoe and
The motion of the paddle.

Smokey looked at the poem and decided he would send it to his mother in a card for her birthday, which was in early May.

Despite all efforts to improve his relationship with Sherry, the situation was difficult, especially with his being unemployed and not actively looking for work. He knew they were in for a rocky road, but he was not prepared to give up his dream of the Nationals one more time.

Smokey sat by the bank of the Red. It was the first race of the season. He had sized up the competition. This would be his first test to see if the winter training had paid off. The race course was rather simple—downstream ten kilometers and then back up, no portage. All the boats lined up at the start-line, tandem and solo boats together. Smokey was nervous but ready. The one man he knew would be really tough to beat-Big Mac from Flin Flon-hadn't made it down for the race. Smokey knew he could win this race, and that was the first step to being provincial champion.

The gun sounded and Smokey took off like a bat out of hell. In a matter of moments he was out in front of the other solo boats and was on the wash of a tandem team. As they headed downstream Smokey thought, "I can beat this tandem team and maybe some others." With deep strokes and rhythm, Smokey passed three tandem boats during the race and, at the finish, was five minutes in front of the next solo boat. He held the trophy in his hands and said to himself, *I'm going to get a lot of these.*

The next race would be Smokey's biggest challenge. It was a 4-day race from the U.S. border with Manitoba to the city of Winnipeg, about 165 kilometres. He had two weeks to prepare for the race. That evening, after another fight with Sherry, Smokey set out a two-week training schedule for distance paddling.

Smokey's neighbor used some herbicide-pesticide on his lawn the next day, and two days later Smokey had lung infection and a high fever. He spent the next three days in bed. In fact, before the next week was out he had to get some antibiotics from the doctor to help him fight the infection. With one week till the race and still with a fever, unable to practice, Smokey knew he was in trouble, but all he could do was rest. Three days before the race was to begin, Smokey's fever broke, The next day he went for a short paddle on the river, but over the past two weeks he had lost nearly ten pounds and this wasn't good.

Smokey also knew he was competing against demonic forces-forces that wanted to keep him ill, maybe even kill him. He could hear them talking in his head. He didn't know what they were saying, but he knew it was to his detriment.

Smokey wondered, *Why has God given me the gift to hear these evil forces? It must be to warn me of coming events. Will God protect me from these forces, or has something changed inside me that has separated me from Him? Am I becoming a demon too?*

Chapter XVI

Smokey loaded Sherry's little car up and put the canoe on the roof. It was race day, and he knew it was going to be the biggest race of the season. Big Mac from Flin Flon would be down for the race, plus a professional boat-builder from the U.S.-and many more.

Smokey drove along the highway toward the border. His thoughts drifted back to employment. He could race throughout the summer, but when the summer was over, so would be his UIC. He didn't know what to do. Perhaps he should go back to university and obtain an admin degree if he could, but that involved student loans and Smokey knew that that was high-risk. Debts build up fast, and if you can't pay, then what? Will debtors' prison become a reality once again? It was possible. Who knew? It wasn't worth the risk.

Smokey arrived at the U.S. border with about an hour to spare. It was deadly hot out and the antibiotics he was on made him sweat all the more. He filled his water bottle to the brim and attached the hose. He would have to paddle nearly fifty kilometers the first day in extreme heat on antibiotics when the doctor had told him to get plenty of rest.

Chapter XVII

Two minutes till start time. The solo canoes were lined up across the river. Big Mac looked over at Smokey and said, "See you at the finish line." The gun sounded and the canoes surged forward.

They paddled together for the first hour, staying in a pack. Everyone knew that this would be a long paddle, and nobody wanted to make the mistake of breaking from the pack too soon. After about an hour, Smokey decided to try to pull out in front. He picked his stroke rate up to seventy beats a minute and gradually pulled a hundred feet in front of the pack, but he was followed by the boat-builder from the U.S. Smokey was surprised by this man's power. He had to be close to sixty but he was fast-really fast. They paddled together for half an hour, trying to put distance between them and the pack, but the pack was strong and kept on coming.

About two hours into the race Smokey sucked in his last mouthful of water. This wasn't a good thing to be out of water so soon. He needed water to cool himself down. They came to a small set of rapids in the river. Smokey tried to determine the best path, but as he entered the rapids, he could feel the stern of his canoe taking on water. He got through the rapids, but he had about two gallons of water in the stern, which threw his canoe out of trim. It was slowing him down a lot, The boat-builder passed him, and then the pack was right on Smokey's heels. Big Mac passed him along with another paddler from Saskatchewan. He kept them in his sights for a long time, but then he was alone.

The sun beat down on Smokey and he could feel himself burning up. He began coughing, and soon he had run out of sweat and was dry. He wondered if he could finish the race-he knew his fever was high. Then he saw the finish line. He paddled as hard as he could and arrived just two minutes behind Big Mac. Smokey was disappointed in his performance, but he thought to himself, *This is a four-day race. Anything can happen.*

They were shuttled back to get their cars in an old bus. When they arrived, Smokey hopped in his car and headed for the nearest restaurant. There was a little Italian restaurant in the town on the border. Smokey ordered a big plate of pasta and a jug of water. He contemplated his strategy for the race. Tomorrow was only a fifteen kilometer race and the paddlers would be going all out. Smokey thought, *The best I can do tomorrow is try to stay with the pack as long as possible.* He drove back to his canoe and set up camp for the night in the park that was provided for the canoeists. The moon was almost full. Smokey made small fire and set his coffee pot on the stones. He gazed up at the moon. He could feel its pull on his chest and arms. *Lunar power,* Smokey thought. That's *what I have, I have lunar power.* He remembered a woman he had been talking to at the department store. Maybe she was a lunar goddess and was giving him power too. Smokey knew that he just had to hang on tomorrow and things would eventually go his way. Around eleven o'clock Smokey said goodnight to the moon and curled up in his tent.

During the night Smokey felt another body beside him, and he realized that it was the moon goddess come to share her power with him. There was an old crow calling this morning-was it calling out a warning or was it laughing? *I think it's laughing at me,* Smokey thought. What did the crow know that he didn't?

They lined up across the river, the sun was already beating down and it was near 30°Celsius. Smokey knew he had the power of a moon goddess to help him in the race and a warning from a crow to be careful. The gun sounded, and they were off.

Everyone was going full power, as fast as they could sprint. Smokey latched onto Big Mac's wash and hung on for dear life. In fact, Smokey managed to stay on Mac's wash up till the last two kilometers. During those last kilometers, Big Mac gained two minutes on Smokey. Smokey said to himself, *Tomorrow's my day.*

Smokey went into town and found a restaurant. He had an omelet with an extra order of toast. Not exactly a racer's dinner, but it would do. He decided that he didn't want to set up camp, so he booked a room in the hotel. He had a hot shower, then phoned Sherry. She sounded distant, not really happy either. Smokey wondered if he should go home and spend the night with Sherry, but he decided against it. He had to concentrate on the race. He went to bed at about nine o'clock and fell into a deep sleep. He dreamed he was swimming in space. Then suddenly he felt himself falling into a void. He saw a red eye watching him from above. All around him he heard moans and groans. He could feel entities trying to touch his body. He realized that these were souls wanting to be born. *Is this hell?* Smokey asked himself. *Why am I here?* He drifted deeper into the void till all thoughts became difficult and he felt as if he was bound somehow by the essence which surrounded him. Then there was no thought, only feelings, some of pleasure, some of pain. Then there was nothing, and he rested.

When Smokey awoke he felt really rested. There were still two hours till race time, so Smokey decided to have a light breakfast. Despite the warm summer day, Smokey couldn't shake the feeling that that cold red eye was watching him. A shiver went through his spine. The red eye was in his mind, hearing his thoughts, maybe even controlling some of his thoughts.

They lined up across the river for the third time in three days. Smokey was in fourth place overall, but he knew today was his day to shine. He could feel it in his bones. The gun sounded, and they were off. The boat-builder and Big Mac led the pack. Smokey and a guy from Saskatchewan followed close behind. The sun beat down on them. It was 30° again already. They stayed together for about an hour, and then the guy from Saskatchewan dropped behind and Smokey was left on his own. He picked up his stroke rate to seventy beats a minute and soon found himself on Big Mac's wake. The boat-builder was right beside Big Mac but began to pull away. Smokey thought to himself, *I have to sprint after the boat-builder*, so he picked up his stroke rate to eighty beats a minute. The next thing he knew, he was leading, but the boat-builder was close behind him. The two of them began to pull away from Big Mac. Smokey knew he was four minutes behind Big Mac overall and he needed to make up this time today, so he stayed in sprint mode for several minutes before relaxing his stroke rate to about seventy-five strokes a minute. The boat-builder and Smokey began to put lots of distance between them and the other solo paddlers. About four hours into the race the boat-builder became ill and vomited. Smokey took this opportunity to sprint away from the boat-builder, but the finish line was only a few yards ahead, so he didn't gain much ground on him. Smokey knew at this point that the boat-builder had won the race even though there was one more day to go. When he checked his time later that evening with the race officials, he found that he was now in second place. He had made six and a half minutes on Big Mac that day. Smokey thought *Second place isn't bad; it pays five hundred dollars. No trophy, though*"

On the last day of the race, every one of the paddlers was so tired that nobody had the energy to make a break for it. They all paddled together for the full fifty kilometers. At the finish line, Smokey congratulated the U.S. boat-builder on his victory. The media wanted to know how a sixty-year-old man could beat all these men in their prime. Some of the paddlers said it was his boat, but Smokey knew differently. The man was just plain tough as nails and had the experience of a seasoned paddler.

Smokey loaded his canoe on the car and headed for home. When he got there, he unloaded the boat and put it in the garage. He walked up the steps to the house.

Sherry met him at the door. She said, "Keys to my car, please." Smokey handed her the keys. She walked to the car, turned and looked at him for just a moment, then said, "Goodbye." She hopped in the car and drove away.

Smokey went back to the house and opened the door. He looked in. The place was half-empty. All her things were gone. Smokey sat on the floor trying to gather his thoughts. This changed everything. He had thought he had support, but he was alone in this dream of being the national champion. He was alone. And now he had no vehicle to get him to the races. It looked like his season was over. He began to feel really angry, not just at Sherry but at life itself. In other countries, they paid their athletes to compete. They didn't have to work full-time too; they could concentrate on their goal.

Smokey decided he needed some support so he phoned his friend Bill in Saskatchewan. Bill had been busy trying to make a living as an artist. They talked for awhile, then Bill said, "How about I come for a visit?"

Smokey said, "That sounds great."

Bill arrived two days later with samples of his artwork. Smokey fell in love with one piece. It was four loons guarding a nest in outer space. Smokey said, "I have to have that picture," so they settled on a price and went and had it framed. Later that evening, after Bill had retired for the evening, Smokey took out pen and paper and began to write his thoughts about loons. Soon he came up with a poem.

Kiss From a Loon My Eternal Death

Kiss from a loon
My eternal death.
Gently she engulfs my thought,
My consciousness softens,
A different light.

I am the northern lake-feel me
Swimming through me.
Through my mind and into space
Her laugh-her cry-silence.

Her motion more real than the waves that lap your feet.
Her essence a whisper of ages past.
Her being a touch of now.
Her spirit a kiss of eternal death.

My love of the loon-
It is a reflection.
Who else would feed me?
Secrets about the fallacies of linear time.

All of life is outside the moment,
Yet none exists past the moment,
I am dead.
I always have been.

Then it came to him—the red eye had been the eye of a loon, a spirit guide. Smokey said to himself, *I have a spirit guide that symbolizes past, present, and future, a bird of all time!*

The next day, Smokey suggested they go on a short camping trip. They packed their bags and headed to Dog Tooth Lake near Kenora. It was a pleasant drive through the Cambrian shield to the lake. When they got there, they had just enough time to set up camp before dark and light a fire.

Smokey and Bill sat by the fire they had made and began to update each other on their lives. Bill had recently fallen out with the Baptist church, but the big thing Bill indicated was that he needed to expand on his spiritual life and conventional religion fell short by miles.

Smokey said, "I gave up on Christianity years ago, but sometimes when I'm frightened, I still cling to the old beliefs. I can't help it; they're engrained in me since birth." Smokey was about to expand his thoughts on some of the experiences he had been having and share them with Bill, but then he felt maybe he should keep them to himself for now. Smokey could hear Bill talking but he could no longer make out the words—he was drifting in his own thoughts and gazing into the fire.

He knew Bill was a powerful spirit and an ally. They had talked about other religions many times, and Smokey remembered Bill saying, "We can exclude nothing from the realm of possibility." He wondered too if Bill could sometimes read his mind. It was possible.

The next day Smokey and Bill rented a canoe and headed out on the lake. Smokey did most of the paddling while Bill took pictures with his new camera. It was a calm day so Smokey had no trouble controlling the boat. They reached a small island and there on the far side was a loon. Bill adjusted his telephoto lens and then got two lively shots of the loon just about to take flight. They didn't talk much, they just enjoyed nature to its fullest.

That evening they started a camp fire and did some star-gazing. Smokey talked to Bill about his relationship with Sherry. "I just can't believe it's over," Smokey said. "I thought we were meant to be, like our names were written in the stars."

Bill was silent for awhile. Then he said, "I thought so too."

Smokey knew that Bill wanted to say something else but just couldn't. Maybe it was because even out in the wilderness, Big Brother, our government, was always listening. He thought that Bill was trying to communicate telepathically but he couldn't hear the words clearly. "Yes," Smokey said, "Big Brother is always listening, even out here."

Bill smiled and said, "You're probably right."

Smokey said, "They even have satellites that can take pictures of you anywhere you go."

Bill just smiled and said, "Uh huh." They watched a few satellites go by, then crawled into their tents for the night.

The next morning they headed back to Winnipeg. Smokey was busy trying to think about moving to a cheaper place and buying a car so he could continue his season paddling. When they reached Smokey's house, Bill said, "I'm not staying over. I'm going to try to get to Brandon tonight."

Suddenly Smokey was alone again with nothing but his tortuous thoughts. He decided to phone Jim and talk to him. Jim listened to all Smokey had to say. "Don't worry," Jim said, "We'll help you move to a cheaper place, and you can travel with Iain and I for the balance of the canoeing season." This was more than Smokey could have hoped. It was good to have friends.

Chapter XVIII

Two weeks later Smokey moved back to the rooming house on Spence Street, where he took the top suite for three hundred dollars a month. He also finished the canoeing season doing exceptionally well, however, Big Mac gave him a sound thrashing in Snow Lake. But Smokey had expected a tough time there.

It was now two weeks before the Nationals, and Jim couldn't take him. He planned to make the trip with his wife as sort of a holiday. The Nationals were a long way away this year, in St. George, New Brunswick. Smokey was at a loss as to how he could get there.

He was ready to give up and call it a season when Ben, a flat-water sprinter, said, "I'd like to go and see the races myself."

Smokey said, "I can pay for the gas."

Ben smiled and said, "It's a deal."

One week before the Nationals were to start, Smokey and Ben loaded their canoes on Ben's van and headed toward New Brunswick. Each day they stopped along the way and practiced, Smokey on distance and Ben on speed. There always seemed to be a lake somewhere where they could paddle.

They arrived in St. George the day before the Nationals were to start. Smokey was nervous already. This was the dream. He had trained for over a year. He couldn't be any stronger. He was ready to be Canadian National Champion.

That afternoon they went out and cruised the course outline. It was a tricky course with suck water and depth both. Smokey thought it was perfect. That evening, Jim, Ben, and Smokey went out for dinner-pasta as usual. They talked nervously about their expectations, but really, Smokey had only one expectation: to finish first.

That evening Ben and Smokey set up their tents as the sun was setting. Smokey asked, "Do you think I can do it?

Ben smiled and said, "Have confidence."

"But Big Mac is here with a brand new canoe that weighs less than thirty pounds."

"Doesn't matter, you're the best." Smokey paced back and forth for an hour, then, finally tired out, hit the hay.

Chapter XIX

The sun was up and the birds were chirping. Smokey felt stiff and did some morning stretches to loosen up. "This is the only day that matters," Smokey said to himself. The race was set for ten o'clock. This gave Smokey just enough time to have a light breakfast and let his stomach settle. At 9:45 Smokey brought his canoe to the start line and checked his water bottle and drinking line. His spare paddle was tucked in behind the seat. Thirty canoes lined up at the start line from all across Canada, the best from each province. This was going to be a hell of a race. The gun cracked the cool air like a whip and the canoeists were off. Smokey took three strokes to the right, then suddenly he felt his boat being pushed sideways. The next thing he knew he was under water and coming up for air. *Damn! Damn! Damn*!

He swam his canoe to shore and emptied out the water in it. He had to work fast so he could catch the back of the pack. It took him less than two minutes to get ready to go again, but two minutes is a long time to make up in the water. Smokey said to himself, *I may be last now but I won't be when I finish.* He started a stroke rate of about seventy-five strokes a minute and kept up this pace for several minutes. Smokey knew that long deep strokes were the answer to winning, and after a short time he began to pass some of the stragglers.

As he began to pass canoes, he heard his father's voice telling him the story of the little engine that could. *I think I can. I think I can! I think I can! I know I can*! Smokey found himself saying it over and over-*I know I can, I know I can!*

About an hour into the race he met up with Jim. Jim nodded and said, "What happened to you?"

Smokey said, "I flipped at the start line."

"Bad luck," said Jim.

They paddled together for a short time, then Smokey made his move and sprinted ahead. He found himself alone for awhile, and his mind began to wonder. Suddenly he had an image in his mind of himself when he was eight years old.

He was lying on the bed with his pants down and his father was standing over him with the leather belt in his hand. "No, Daddy, no!"

Damn, I have to concentrate. I can't be thinking of these things. I have a thou - sand good memories, why remember this? Smokey felt like he was coming unglued. He picked up the stroke rate to eighty strokes a minute and held it for as long as he could. This helped him focus his thoughts on the race. *This is my day of glory*, Smokey said to himself, *This is my day of glory.*

He caught up to four more canoeists who were riding each others' washes to try to gain some more speed. Smokey tacked his canoe in behind them and rested for a few minutes, reducing his stroke rate to about seventy strokes a minute. He couldn't rest long and he knew it, so after about two minutes, he pulled out and increased his stroke rate to about eighty strokes a minute. He passed all four canoes without much difficulty and soon found himself alone again. *On the trail to victory*, he thought. His legs were going numb and he knew this wasn't good because he still had to run a short portage. In fact he could see the portage coming up in the distance. He stumbled out of his boat as he gained the portage and his legs wobbled a little. He hoisted the canoe onto his shoulders and began to jog up the hill.

On the plain he was able to pick up some speed, but running wasn't his specialty. Soon he was gasping for air and could feel his legs begin to weaken, but the river was just ahead and he could make it, he knew he could. He did, dropping the canoe back into the water and climbing in. There, the worst was over. He saw two more canoes in front of him, but he decided not to push it just yet. He set a stroke rate of about seventy-five strokes a minutes. Even at that rate he was able to catch up to the two other canoes and begin riding their wash. He was tired now beyond belief. His muscles were beginning to ache, but they were still functioning okay and that was the main thing. He rode wash for a good five minutes with the other two canoeists, then he made his break for it. One of the other canoeists stayed with him for awhile, then fell behind, and Smokey was on his own again. He knew that time was running out and he had to give it 110 per cent from here to the finish line, so he stepped up his stroke rate to almost eighty strokes a minute and held it there. He could see another paddler in the distance, and he was making distance on the paddler too. It was a matter of time. *Deep strokes*, Smokey thought to himself, *long, deep strokes.* He was almost on the paddler's wash-just another few yards and he would be there. But the paddler sprinted ahead again, leaving Smokey behind. He tried again to get on this paddler's wash but couldn't quite get enough speed to get there. Then the paddler in front of him seemed to give up, and Smokey was on his wash.

They turned the last turn out of the channel and onto the lake. The water was shallow–too shallow. The paddler in front of him made it through to deeper water. Smokey did not. His canoe struck a sand bar and stopped. Quickly, he got out of his canoe and pulled it to deeper water, but that allowed the paddler in front just enough time to get away. Smokey sprinted after him. The finish line was in sight. Smokey gave it his all but it wasn't enough. He ended up five seconds behind the other paddler.

Smokey counted the boats that had crossed the finish line. There were five. That meant he had finished sixth. Smokey hung his head. "No victory. I have failed," he said. It didn't matter that there were twenty-four boats behind him—it was the five in front of him that were the cause of his failure. He pulled his boat to shore.

Ben was there and said, "You did great."

Smokey smiled thinly and said nothing. *A whole year's work finished and I'm not the national champion, and I never will be. The dream is over,"* Smokey thought to himself. The dream was over!

Smokey said to Ben, "That's it for me. I'm done racing. I'm not good enough for financial assistance, not good enough to turn pro. I'm finished." A young kid overheard Smokey talking and said, "Do you want to sell your boat?"

Smokey thought for a moment, and then he said, eight hundred and fifty and it's yours."

The kid said, "Can I try it out?"

Smokey said, "Sure, give it a try." Smokey had to laugh when he saw the kid paddle but he was selling the dream and that's all that mattered.

When the kid came in Smokey said, "You can have it for eight hundred." The kid agreed and went to get the money.

Smokey felt a rush of pain come over him. He had sold his dream. But he really didn't have a choice-he needed the money and besides, he still had a recreational canoe at home for exercise. Still, it was hard to let go so quickly. It had been his dream for over a year. He had lived and breathed canoeing for several years now. The kid came back with the money, cash, and Smokey said goodbye to his racing canoe. He thought to himself, "I can always buy another one if I win the lottery or something."

The trip home was hard for Smokey. He had to watch Ben practice in his canoe when they stopped by a lake or stream. But Smokey had greater concerns now that the Nationals were over. He only had about 2 weeks left of UIC premiums. The future did not look bright. He thought about what to do. Should he go back to school, and if so, what should he take? He hadn't been accepted into Respiratory Technology, and he had no other ideas where there was employment to be found. The ideal situation would be to find part-time work and go to university the rest of the time.

Ben said to him as they approached the city limits of Winnipeg, "Don't worry, you'll get work and you'll be paddling again next year."

Smokey unpacked his things and then had a long hot bath. *Tomorrow I go job hunting,* he said to himself, *Starting at the UIC office.*

The next morning came early. Smokey showered and went to a nearby café for breakfast. He was thinking of the eight hundred dollars and what to do with it. His first stop after breakfast was the UIC building where they posted job opportunities. Smokey checked the boards but there was nothing there that he could do. The only jobs that paid above minimum wage were the professional sections.

Smokey knew at that moment that he had to go back to school and get a degree. He headed straight to the University of Winnipeg and checked out their calendar. He registered and selected two classes which he paid for from his eight hundred. The only problem was, it was too late to apply for a student loan. He had to find part-time work somewhere.

His last stop of the day was a large department store on Portage Avenue. He submitted a résumé there and talked to Personnel about his aspirations. He was honest. He said, "I just need a part-time job to help pay my way through university. I can't get a student loan." They asked him for references and said they would let him know if anything came up. Smokey was hopeful.

The week went by quickly and every morning Smokey was out looking for work. On the last day of the week, the department store called him in for an interview. Smokey wore dress pants and a shirt and tie to the meeting. He was told there was an opening in the shoe department, someone was needed to stock the shelves and check inventory. This suited Smokey fairly well as he had inventory background from previous employment. They introduced him to the head of the shoe department, a tall, gray-haired gentleman. They seemed to hit it off right away, and Smokey was hired three days a week-Monday, Wednesday, and Friday. With his university classes on Tuesdays and Thursdays, it was a job made to fit.

The following week Smokey started his job. It wasn't much of a challenge stocking shoes, but he would earn about six hundred a month, enough to pay his rent of three hundred, and the rest would be for food and utilities.

It felt good to be back at university. He had two classes—one in sociology, "Understanding the Disabled," and an administration class. Smokey sat at the university library with his first assignment. He had to do a fifty-page paper on government administration. Smokey decided to do his paper on crown corporations. He had completed an introduction into the value of crown corporations and their relationship to the public and the taxpayer. Smokey thought the body of his essay should illustrate the pros and cons of crown corporations. He searched the library for books and reports supporting crowns—it wasn't hard to do, there were plenty of them. He spent the next several hours reading reports on crown corporations.

He was putting one book back when he noticed a new report on the shelf. He began to read it. It was all about an American shyster who hoodwinked the Manitoba government into building a massive lumber mill which had no potential for profit and how it became Manitoba's biggest money-losing crown corporation. The American's name was Alexander Kazzer and he made the Manitoba government look like country bumpkins. The more Smokey read, the more he realized that this was exactly what he needed to show government waste in the public sector and support the disadvantages to crown corporations. Smokey made about twenty pages of notes on this particular crown corporation and then made his references. It was eleven o'clock at night by the time he had finished. He had put in a ten-hour day at school.

Smokey walked home alone, and he felt lonely. He missed Sherry terribly. The nights were empty. Even if it was only an hour or two before bedtime, he felt the loneliness intensely. But he knew he wasn't entirely alone. There were people listening and watching him-he knew this. He didn't know who they were,but he could feel them listening to him so he couldn't talk to himself. He had to be careful what he said out loud. They could be government operatives of some kind listening to him through microphones or watching him through video cameras of some kind. He wondered too if his landlord could be trusted. Smokey eventually fell asleep and slept till about 8:30 the next morning—just enough time to get to work.

He showed his employee card at the doors of the department store and was let in. He had lots of stock work to do. There was a big sale on Saturday of Bellotti shoes and also Nunn Bush shoes. Smokey wanted a pair of the Bellottis for himself, but even on sale they were ninety dollars. He just couldn't afford that. As he worked, a voice came over the intercom reminding sales staff of their procedures, and then they announced any employee theft over the intercom as well. They seemed to take great pleasure in announcing employee theft and the consequences, prosecution. They made it sound like every employee would steal given the opportunity, as if they were all dishonest thieves. Smokey tried not to think about it, to tune the intercom out. Finally they played "Don't Worry, Be Happy" over the intercom, which signaled store opening to the public.

Smokey learned something very early on in his days as a stock clerk. There could be three sales staff standing around. but people always went to the person who was busy, usually the stock clerk. After awhile, Smokey just serviced the customers like a salesperson even though it put him behind in his own work.

The day passed slowly and Smokey's mind was on canoeing. He planned to take out his recreational canoe and spend the day on the Red River before freeze-up came.

That evening he wrote a letter to the Manitoba Addictions Clinic to request a practicum for his class in sociology. He would work with addicted youth for six months and try to illustrate in a report that addictions are a form of disability. Smokey at one point in his life had drank so heavily that he almost considered himself an alcoholic, so he had personal experience with addictions which he hoped to be able to relate to some of the youth. This was his plan, anyway.

It was only 8:30 at night and he had done everything he planned for the day, so he pulled out a lump of clay and began to sculpt. First he formed the body of one being, then another. Soon he had a multi-character of sorts with two heads each facing in the opposite direction. He called it "Brothers."

Smokey looked at all the sculptures in his room. He could hear them talking to one another. Suddenly a cold chill ran through his body. He realized for the first time that these sculptures had souls, souls trapped inside clay. He had somehow extracted these souls from hell. It frightened Smokey to think he had acquired such power over the spirit world. He began to tremble; then he began to weep. Finally he decided he must destroy all his sculptures and return these spirits to hell where they belonged. He got a hammer from his tool kit and began smashing each sculpture to bits. He threw the pieces into a garbage bag and took them out to the garbage. "Never again," he said to himself, "never again."

It was like his grandma used to always say to him, "Idle hands make the devil's work." It was certainly true. His hands had created the forms to hold dark spirits, evil spirits! That evening before bed he prayed a prayer for redemption that his own soul might be free of the devil's wicked hand.

He slept soundly and woke late in the morning. Smokey made himself a cup of coffee and some scrambled eggs, then headed to the canoe club where his recreational canoe was stored. It was a nice crisp morning, fresh, and the sun was shining! It usually was about a forty-minute walk to the canoe club, but this morning Smokey was clipping right along. He arrived at the canoe club in less than thirty minutes. He opened the doors to the boathouse and pulled down his canoe from the rack. It was a cedar strip boat-not really heavy, but much heavier than Kevlar. He threw his paddle in the canoe and lifted the canoe up on his shoulders. At the water's edge he dropped the canoe and said a little prayer to the Red River. He began a slow stoke rate-fifty to sixty strokes a minute. The cedar strip canoe responded well, and soon he was miles from the canoe club. For a moment he thought again of competition–maybe if he had new equipment he would stand a better chance. No! No! It was time to get on with life. Enjoy the canoe for the physical exercise it brings and enjoy the nature one often sees in a canoe like the beavers that make their homes along the banks and the birds in the trees along the shoreline.

Smokey took the canoe out of Winnipeg city limits headed south to the U.S. The exercise felt really good, but he couldn't shake the intense feeling of loneliness. He knew he had to start dating again soon or he never would. It was too easy to give up and say, "I was meant to be alone." But Smokey still had strong feelings for Sherry. It had been magical at first. He sent her his feelings in a form of energy from his heart to hers. That was all he could do. He whispered to the trees, "I still love her."

Smokey paddled for thirty kilometers, then headed home. The sun was going down. He realized he had been paddling for ten hours. As he reached the shoreline by the boathouse he looked up and saw a figure standing there.

"Hi, Smokey." It was Sherry.

"Hi there. I've missed you."

"I've missed you too" Can we talk?"

"Sure. Let's go get a cup of coffee," Smokey said.

She still turned him on and Smokey realized that she probably always would. He took her tiger paw in his hand and led her to her car.

"I smell," he said.

"It's forgivable," she said.

"Could we get some dinner," he asked.

She smiled and said, "Sure."

They went to a little restaurant on the corner of Smokey's block. It was quiet and they lit an evening candle. Smokey ordered the salmon and Sherry had the chicken. They talked on and off for nearly three hours. about their relationship-what was right and what was wrong. In the end they decided they would date like in the beginning. It would be fresh and new. They would learn a lot about each other all over again. In a way this was good for Smokey, because he had come to realize something about Sherry. Maybe it was coincidence and maybe it was her dark side, but every time he slept with her there would be a fire in the city. It happened nearly every time. She was Aries, the flame, a true fire sign. Perhaps she couldn't control her power. Anyway, Smokey didn't want to be responsible for fires in the city, so he wouldn't sleep with her anymore. They could make love but not sleep together–it was too dangerous.

Sherry dropped Smokey off at his apartment and she gave him a good night kiss. Smokey could feel things starting to come together again. He had a job, was going to school, and had some sort of relationship going again. Things were taking shape. He climbed the stairs to his apartment and turned on the lights. It was too quiet in the place. He turned on the stereo. He couldn't help thinking that somehow, some way, people were listening to him in his apartment.

It was Monday morning. Smokey had spent all of Sunday over the toilet. It was the fish he had eaten-they had poisoned it. It was the first time that Smokey realized that people were trying to harm him. He would miss a day's work getting over the symptoms of food poisoning. They had probably used rat poison. He realized that he would have to be very careful where he ate in the future. These Satanists were everywhere trying to kill innocent people. That's how they got their power-through killing.

Smokey sat at the kitchen table and looked out the window. It was a beautiful fall day outside. The leaves were in piles on the ground in the front yard, and he imagined himself crunching through them in his boots. As he gazed out the window he saw the postman coming down the street. He wondered whether government agencies were reading his mail. The post office was like one big electronic eye exposing people. The postman came up his steps and stopped. Suddenly Smokey felt his chest tighten. It felt like the postman had his hands around Smokey's heart. What telekinetic powers! It was clear to Smokey that the postman was trying to stop his heart. This is how Satanists got their power. Fear filled Smokey's thoughts. *How do I defend myself against these people?* The postman went down the steps and over to the next house, and Smokey felt his chest loosen.

It was clear to Smokey he was in trouble. First they'd tried to poison him; then they'd tried to stop his heart. Smokey lay down on the bed and tried to think of what to do. He couldn't hide from the world, but he realized he couldn't eat in restaurants anymore. It was just to risky. The problem was, he didn't know how to combat people with telekinetic powers like the postman, and he was sure he was going to meet more of them. He shuddered at the thought.

Sometimes Satanists tipped their hands, like the woman that wore red triangle earrings. Men were more difficult to figure out. The bottom line was that Smokey was entering a new world of terror and he had to be strong and smart.

Chapter XX

The next day Smokey went to school. He had completed his essay on crown corporations. He felt it was one of the best essays he had ever produced, but he was beginning to think that perhaps he shouldn't have been so critical of crown corporations, and he wondered whether he should have talked about the Manitoba lumber mill. Who knew what kind of connections that Kazzer fellow had and what he would do if he ever heard about Smokey's essay.

He sat in the back row and tried to listen to the professor, but there was too much noise in his head. He could hear people talking in his head, especially the Chinese students, who were all telepathic. He just couldn't seem to concentrate on what the professor was saying, so he read his textbook instead.

It was late November when the first little crisis appeared in Smokey's plan. He hadn't heard from the Manitoba Addictions Clinic, and he had to have a practicum established quickly. He decided he couldn't wait any longer and went to the teacher with the problem. The teacher suggested a new practicum dealing with MS patients one on one. Smokey thought about it for a moment, then realized he really didn't have any choice; he would contact the MS Society immediately.

The next four weeks passed quickly for Smokey, and it was December before he knew it. He had had a conversation with Sherry about Christmas, and they had decided to travel to Saskatchewan to visit with his friend Bill and then spend Christmas with his parents. Smokey was already thinking about Christmas presents for Sherry and his family. He really liked to see people's eyes light up. Smokey spoke with his boss about getting a week off for Christmas, and his boss seemed more than willing to allow Smokey the time. Everything was falling into place nicely.

Chapter XXI

It was December 20, and Smokey helped Sherry load the car for Saskatchewan. It would be a nice drive, a chance for them to catch up on one another. Both of them had been so busy with work and exams. Smokey said to Sherry when the car was loaded, "Let's not rush this. We can stop for coffee on the way out of the city." Sherry agreed this was a good idea.

They sat with their coffee and talked. Sherry said, "I don't want you to panic, but I think we might make better friends than lovers." Smokey knew what she was saying, and he knew this would be the last Christmas that they would spend together. Smokey's heart was pounding in his chest. How could he lose her after all they had been through? He realized that part of the problem was that there weren't enough good times. There was just too much struggle over the differences. They ended up driving most of the way to Regina in silence. There just wasn't anything left to say. All the pleading in the world wouldn't change anything. They were very different people, and what Smokey was beginning to see for the first time in his life was, love sometimes just isn't enough. But it was painful to let go after struggling so hard.

They reached Bill's house late that evening, and he had a nice fire going in the hearth. They sat around the fire and talked about everything under the sun. Bill was living with a guy named Barrie, a shaman by trade. Barrie talked about art and life and how the two were the same. Bill seemed to thrive in this conversation. They were a good match as friends.

As the evening drew to a close, Sherry took Smokey's hand and said, "It's nights like these, my bushman, that keep me hopeful."

Smokey said, "The tiger still rules my heart." She smiled.

Barrie presented Smokey with a gift of a picture. It was a picture of a phoenix rising from the flames and ashes of another world. It was gorgeous. Barrie said, "Sometimes that bird will fly back to visit me, but it's yours. Take care of it. Feed it good things." Smokey felt a little bit strange about the picture—it almost seemed as if it was alive for real.

They left feeling refreshed and went to the hotel in the south end of Regina. The moon was three quarters full and the stars seemed to be everywhere. They stood outside the hotel door and gazed up into the sky, but Smokey didn't see the sky-he saw the wings and talons of the phoenix in his mind's eye and he heard a lonely cry of a carnivore or a raptor of sorts. It sent a chill through his bones, and he wondered if accepting the gift of the phoenix may have been a mistake. They curled up in bed and Smokey could hear the tiger purring gently through the night. He didn't sleep. He wanted to remember what she felt like, the rhythm of her breath, the gentle movements through the night.

The phoenix seemed to be expanding inside his head. He realized that he had no control over it. It was a spirit-entity of its own making. It was just like his sculptures. It was a demon from hell and he had accepted it as a gift. As he lay in bed he wondered how he could have been so foolish. What could he do? He could feel the entity growing inside of him. He got out of bed and went to where he had placed the picture. He turned on the light and stared at the picture. It seemed to be harmless on the surface, and really, how could a picture harm him? *It was just plain silly*, Smokey thought. And he went to bed.

They spent Christmas in Weyburn, Saskatchewan, with Smokey's parents and returned to Winnipeg for New Year's. It was a great vacation except for the bird, which continued to grow in Smokey's mind. There were times when Smokey would look up expecting to see the bird over his head. At other times he would feel the bird's talons in his left shoulder.

Smokey returned to work, but he found that his thoughts were often confused and he had a tightness in his chest and sometimes some pain. He was worried about his heart. He would often take his pulse throughout the day. He wondered if the postman was trying to kill him again or whether the phoenix's talons were causing the pain in his chest. Or could it be the Satanists were poisoning his food? When Smokey finished work that night he went home and put a piece of tape at the bottom of his refrigerator. If someone was tampering with his food he would find out about it.

That week Smokey met with the manager of the MS Society to do his practicum. The interview was short and the manager gave him some pamphlets about MS. On the way home, Smokey started reading the pamphlets. MS was a mysterious disease. Nobody had a clue what caused it. There were all kinds of theories, but basically nobody knew anything. *Or at least that's what we were led to believe*, Smokey thought. Why had his teacher suggested the MS practicum? Something seemed fishy to Smokey. He knew his teacher didn't like him, and blonds could be vindictive. Was she trying to set him up? Was she trying to give him the disease? Did the government and doctors really know what caused the disease or at least how it spread? It was possible that the government had information about MS and was withholding it from the public. One thing was for sure-Smokey was in the prime age category to get the disease and he was Caucasian.

Smokey could smell a rat. Something was rotten in Denmark. He decided that he wouldn't do the practicum on MS. He remembered that people were trying to kill him and they may be very devious about how they accomplish their task. But why were people trying to kill him? He couldn't understand this. *Why not just leave me alone*, Smokey wondered.

A few weeks had passed and it was getting toward February and Valentine's day. Did he still have a tiger or was he a lonely bushman? He thought about Sherry every day but only phoned her occasionally. She always seemed pleased to hear from him, but they got together less and less.

It was March before Smokey knew it, time to prepare for exams, but he still had to work to see his way through school. He was busy stocking shoes, but his thoughts became confused throughout the day and there was a burning in his chest. Smokey wondered if there was a leak in the spray booth next door where they sprayed solvents and paints. He went to the spray booth door and found it open; there was a mist of spray leaving the area and entering the stock room. Smokey wondered how long this had been going on. How long had he been ingesting toxic fumes, and what had it done to his heart and lungs and maybe even his liver? Smokey went to the company nurse and complained of dizziness, thought confusion, and chest pain. The nurse sent him to the company doctor the same day.

The doctor spoke with Smokey for some time and scheduled lung tests and an EEG for the brain. He said, "I want you to see a neurologist tomorrow." Unfortunately, it couldn't be scheduled till three days later.

That night, Smokey sat at home and worried. His chest would burn and he would feel dizzy at times. He took his pulse–140. That was high for Smokey. Suddenly he felt a sharp pain in his chest and as he felt the pain he lost the pulse in his arm. Smokey panicked and dialed 911. An ambulance was there in five minutes. They took him to the hospital. Pulse 142, blood pressure 164 / 90. They hooked him up to a cardiogram and monitored him for twelve hours. He was released the next morning.

Smokey decided to walk home. He was confused about a lot of things. Was it the spray booth that caused the burning in his chest, or was it the postman trying to kill him, or was it a type of poison in his food that caused it? Had it been planted by Alexander Kazzer? He walked along the sidewalk on this cold March day and tried to think clearly about what was happening to him.

Suddenly the pain returned to his chest. He sank to his knees, and there before him was this large gray cat. The cat climbed up on Smokey's shoulder and laid its paws over his chest. The pain stopped.

"Thank you," Smokey said. "Thank you for saving my life."

Smokey had heard about the powers of a cat. The Egyptians used the cat in battle, but this was the first time Smokey had discovered the healing powers of a cat. That night as Smokey slept, the gray cat came to him in a dream. It transformed itself into a beautiful Egyptian woman. The woman bent down and whispered in his ear. She said, "I couldn't watch you die!"

The next day Smokey stayed home and wrote a letter to Bill explaining to him how his life had been spared by an Egyptian woman. When the postman came by, Smokey grabbed his cross and held on tight.

Smokey sat in the waiting room of the neurologist's office. He still felt confused and he hadn't trusted the company doctor who had sent him here. They were already trying to cover things up-Smokey knew it. Big companies never pay the price for negligence. The door opened, and the doctor said good morning to those waiting, then left. The office receptionist called Smokey's name and instructed him to go to the first door on the right and have a chair. He did so and he waited. The doctor came in a few minutes later.

"So you've had some exposure to solvent and paint fumes, have you?"

"Yes sir."

"Fine. I'm going to talk with you this morning and we're going to do a few tests. Before we get going I'd like you to remember three things for me. They are a ball, blue, and a tree. Can you remember those things for me? Say them for me first so we are absolutely clear."

Smokey said, "A ball, blue, and a tree."

"Good!" They talked for a few minutes about current events. Then the doctor asked if he had read today's paper. Smokey said that he had.

"What were the headlines?" the doctor asked.

Smokey thought long and hard but he couldn't remember.

The doctor said, "What do you remember about the paper this morning?"

Smokey realized after considerable effort that he could remember nothing about the morning paper.

"Don't worry," the doctor said, "lots of people forget what they have read in the paper. No big deal. Do you remember the three things I asked you to remember?"

"Oh shit," Smokey said. Then he thought. "A ball!"

"Good. What else?"

"A tree!"

"Good. One to go."

Smokey thought as hard as he could *What was the third thing? Damn! Damn! Damn!* "Blue! It's blue!" "Very good," the doctor said. "Now I'd like you to start at 100 and subtract 7 and keep going."

Smokey thought, "93 .... 85 .... 79 .... 72 .... 66 .... 58 .... 51 ...."

"Okay, that's enough, thank you," the doctor said. He then asked Smokey several more questions, then abruptly said that would be all.

Smokey did not return to work. He had already made a decision about going to school and working at the same time. It didn't work. Classes would end in April, so he really only needed one month's rent and food money to finish his classes. Or should he say, class? He would have to withdraw from the Disabilities class because he didn't have a practicum. He could use ill health as an excuse to withdraw. Smokey knew that if he had worked with MS patients, he would have mysteriously contracted the disease himself. It was really a self-preservation move-there were no other choices.

Smokey spent the next week at the campus studying for his Administration exams. He had done well on his essay-an A+. This gave Smokey encouragement for the future. He decided he would go to school full-time through the summer. He would apply for a student loan. In his heart he was terribly afraid of student loan debt, but he realized that if he wanted to go to school he had to pay the price like everyone else.

Smokey sat in the welfare office. He would meet a worker shortly. Smokey had never felt so dejected. Here he was in a welfare office. He couldn't believe it had come to this. Asking for money for food and rent. He had always managed before. This was a first.

The worker came in and they talked for about half an hour about what had caused Smokey's need for assistance. The worker said that it was probably a case of worker's compensation but that they would pay for one month's rent and food. After that, he would be on his own. Social Services wasn't in the business of paying for people's schooling costs. Smokey received a cheque for $425 to cover rent and food for April, $300 for rent, $125 for food and clothing. Smokey realized that before he applied for a student loan, he would have to find a cheaper place to live.

The journey to the Social Services Department really took its toll on Smokey. It went against everything he was taught to believe in, like, "Work hard and you will get ahead." The place was depressing. Shields of Plexiglas protected the workers from their clients, and the people he saw in the building looked as though they had been through hell.

Smokey sat at home and tried to write a letter to Bill. He wanted to describe his feelings while in the welfare office. The overpowering feeling of suffocation in the air. The judgment that came with being there. All of society judged you and the verdict was loser. At least that's how it felt. It seemed as though 30 per cent of the people in the place were intoxicated. Smokey wrote to Bill:

> Dear Bill,
>
> I finally experienced the welfare office. I never thought it would come to this, but it did. I think I finally understand how you felt when you had to go there. You go into the place thinking that you are going to receive something, but more is taken from you than you actually receive. I mean, they might as well do a rectal exam to see if you are hiding any spare change up there. You lose your dignity for a few hundred dollars—basically food money. I just wanted you to know that now I understand.

Smokey began his search for cheaper housing. A lot of the places had signs out so you could just go up to the door and inquire. He searched the district closest to the university but found nothing affordable. He would check the papers that evening. At home, Smokey put on some music. It felt like he had his own radio station. He was broadcasting to the world, he knew he was being heard. His apartment must have microphones hidden in it. It was a good thing he was leaving this place. Also, he was sure that the landlord was tampering with his food. That evening, he saw the phoenix in his mind's eye. It was trying to speak to him, but Smokey couldn't hear the words it spoke. He only got a feeling that the bird was hungry. How do you feed a spirit bird? Or will it feed itself?

The next day Smokey found an apartment just two blocks from the university for only $225 a month. It was a shared bath, but that was okay. Smokey gave the man a deposit and went on to school for the day. Smokey had three weeks to study for his final in Administration, but he would have to move during that time-period. He studied hard over the next few weeks. Although his short-term memory was poor, things came back to him after a couple of days.

Two weeks later Smokey was settled in his new apartment. Jim had helped him move. The apartment was small and furnished already, so Smokey put most of his things in a storage locker. When you considered the cost of the storage plus his current rent, he wasn't saving much over his previous rent, but it felt good to move-he didn't trust his previous landlord.

Smokey would start four summer classes on the first day of May and they would continue till the middle of July. Smokey had received his student loan of over $2000 but most of the money was for tuition and rent. There was very little money for food, clothing, and transportation—less than $150 a month. It was like living on welfare or even on a little bit less, but there was one big difference, and that was dignity. There was dignity in going to school and trying to better yourself. There was no shame in returning to school to get a better education. He knew his parents would be proud of him if he were able to finally get a degree of some kind he would use in a career.

The ice floes on the Red River had broken, and soon there would be nothing but open water. Smokey thought about how he would miss the racing season. It would be hard to concentrate on classes in the heat when he could be on the water paddling out of the city into the countryside. It would take willpower to resist the temptation to spend all his weekends in his canoe.

Chapter XXII

It was May 1—the first day of classes at the University of Winnipeg, and Smokey was up extra early to get to morning class. He had a class in Administration, two political science classes, and finally a sociology class. It was a long day.

As he walked down the street he happened to turn his head and see a black limo following him up the street. Then it turned in front of him and was gone. Smokey thought, *Who could that be?* Was it Alexander Kazzer coming to get him, or was it the department store management coming to check up on him? A government operative? Who was it and what did they want with him? He reached the university feeling a little bit spooked.

Smokey spent the day in classes but couldn't concentrate. He kept thinking about the black limo. He realized once again that he was in danger, but from whom he didn't know. He returned home late that evening and spent a few hours reading class material. The classes would be intense as they had to cover in three months what would normally take about eight months.

As he lay in bed he smelled something funny in the air. It smelled like gas or something, so he opened up all the windows and started the fan to exhaust the fumes. He noted that the smell was definitely coming from the vent in his room. Could it be that the landlord was trying to gas him? The last landlord tampered with his food, so maybe this one was trying to kill him in a new way. Soon there was fresh air in the place and Smokey could sleep, but he didn't. He tried to think of why people were trying to kill him. Not everyone was a Satanist. There had to be a reason why people were after him.

The next day Smokey met Sherry at her place after school. Smokey knew that this was goodbye. He could feel it in his heart. Finally she said the words. Smokey sat there in silence—there was nothing he could say. He looked into her eyes but they gave nothing back. She wanted her freedom, at least freedom from him. He took a picture from his pocket. It was a picture of him paddling his canoe across the finish line at the Canadian nationals. He said, "I want you to have this," and he gave it to her. They talked for a few moments about school and still being friends and all that meaningless bullshit. Then Smokey got up and made his way to the door. There was no kiss goodbye.

That night Smokey wrote the final verse about the tiger and the bushman. A tiger free to roam the forests again and a bushman who must someday hunt new game was the essence of the final verse. Smokey lay in bed thinking about things. He had lost his job and his love. He was living in poverty trying to get an education in a city where he had made few friends. The next few months he could wrap himself up in school, but late at night his heart would ache and he knew it.

He drifted off to sleep. As he was drifting through space and time he came across a large muscular man. Suddenly he realized the man was ejaculating. He was ejaculating on Smokey's picture, the one he had given to Sherry. The man was laughing. Then Smokey heard Sherry's laugh. He awoke to the darkness of his room. He whispered in the dark, "Sherry, what have you done? What have you done?"

The next day Smokey got up late, missing his first class. The smell was in the air again. He showered and took off to university, trying to catch his second class. As he walked down the street he noticed the black limo come up behind him.

Smokey studied and wrote essays for fourteen hours a day for the next few weeks. The limo continued to follow him regularly to school but never did anything to him. But the landlord was definitely putting something in the ventilation system at his apartment.

It was mid-June before Smokey knew it. He was shaving in the mirror at home one evening when he stopped suddenly and looked closely in the mirror. It couldn't be! But the moustache in it was a little shorter and his jaw line was similar. The eyes, the nose–it all fit. He didn't want it to be true, but he knew in an instant that it was. He was the reincarnation of Adolf Hitler.

It made sense. That's why people were trying to kill him. He should go to a synagogue and confess. No! No! It could be the Jews who were trying to kill him. What should he do? He could feel the panic setting in. He knew he couldn't stay in his apartment anymore. The stuff in the vents was probably killing him very slowly. He began to pack his knapsack with spare clothes. Where could he go? He couldn't afford another place. There was no one he could trust. There were just four weeks of classes left. He had to finish university.

Smokey took his stuffed knapsack and books and headed out the door. He found himself in the central park just after dusk. He placed his sack on a park bench and curled up on the other half of the bench. An hour later it was pouring rain. Smokey made his way through the rain to a bus shelter. He lay his pack on the cement for a pillow and curled up on the ground. He was soaked to the bone and he began to shiver. What else could he do? There was nowhere to go. He lay there shivering in the cold trying to think of his alternatives. If he returned to his apartment they could gas him in his sleep. If he stayed here he would undoubtedly be ill by the next day. It came to him at 1 A.M. that the bus depot was open all night long and it would be warm and dry. He made his way though the rain to the bus depot. He sat in the departure section all night and his pants began to dry. He drifted off a few times and dreamed of Sherry. He still couldn't believe that she would give his picture to that man to do what he did and laugh, but he believed in the power of the mind's eye and the power of visions and dreams. At seven o'clock in the morning, Smokey walked to the university front doors and waited for them to be opened. He had survived the first night of living on the street, so to speak.

Smokey didn't feel very good, but he knew that being outside in the park was safer then in his apartment. He realized, however, that he would have to return to his apartment in order to feed his two birds. He wondered if he should set them free. They wouldn't live long, but at least they would be free. That's what they always wanted.

It was hard to concentrate on school that day because he had so little sleep, and he was itchy for some reason. The day passed and Smokey was finished classes. He made his way to the student lounge in order to find a resting spot. He could stay in the University till 11:45 and could return at 7 00 A.M.

That evening, as he sat in a lounge chair, he thought about everything that had happened to him. He asked himself if the solvent exposure at the department store was really an accident-or was it planned? Most important, he wondered if Sherry had ever loved him, or was he just her toy to play with? So many things had happened: poisoned food, the plan to expose him to MS, realizing he was the reincarnation of Adolph Hitler, the limo that followed him, and the phoenix and its power of darkness enclosing over his mind. It was so overwhelming that he momentarily forgot about the postman who had tried to stop his heart.

At ten o'clock Smokey went to his locker to get his thick jacket for the night. He then made his way to the apartment to feed his birds if they were still alive. When he got to his apartment door he could smell the fumes, and as he opened the door the birds began to squeak. They were still alive! He opened a window for them and fed them some seeds. He really hoped the birds would survive until he could find another place to live, but he didn't hold out much hope. He returned to Central Park and found his park bench for the night. It had been a warm day, so the first few hours of the night were pleasant. The night sky was clear, and it seemed that there were a million stars in sight.

For the next two weeks Smokey made his home on the park bench, going to the apartment to feed the birds after a long day at school. School was difficult but manageable; he had a B+ average at midterm. But after two weeks in the park he realized he couldn't live in Winnipeg anymore. Too many things were set against him there. He had to start over. He phoned his parents from a pay phone so the government wouldn't be able to trace the call. He asked if he could come home for the long weekend in July. They were pleased by this and welcomed the visit.

Smokey rode the bus down the Red Coat Trail from Winnipeg to Weyburn. He was looking forward to seeing his parents. His mom always had a smile and his stepdad was friendly.

Weyburn Saskatchewan was a small town of mostly agricultural support with a little bit of oil. It was a Christian Conservative stronghold in the province. There was money in this town. As the bus rounded the last turn before the depot,

Smokey let out a sigh. He felt like he had come home, though he knew that it wasn't really home. He didn't really know where home was anymore. It wasn't Winnipeg, and it wasn't Weyburn, and there were no jobs in Regina. Where would home be after he left Winnipeg? And he was determined to leave Winnipeg.

His mom smiled brightly at him and said, "We've been worried about you. We haven't been able to reach you for weeks."

"Well, I'm home now," Smokey said as he shook his stepdad's hand.

That evening after dinner Smokey sat a bit on the back step. There was no din from the big city. Not a single car drove by. The only sound that broke the silence was the gentle coo of the morning dove sitting in a nearby tree. Smokey thought to himself, *This is where I need to be, if only for a short time.* Smokey needed to come home to rest for just a while and let some of his wounds heal. He had lost his job and his girlfriend. He needed to heal from those losses and get his mind straight about the future. But coming home was not an easy thing to do. He was in his thirties and supposed to be a man. How could he come home to live with his parents-even if they would have him? Smokey felt the shame burn inside him, yet he knew he was in over his head in Winnipeg. He had nowhere else to go. How could he broach the subject with his parents?

Smokey's mother came out and sat on the back porch with him. He talked to her about some of the things that had happened to him in Winnipeg, like the solvent exposure at the department store and Sherry saying goodbye for good.

His mother said, "You have had some serious losses, I think. If you like, it would be okay if you come home for a while till you can pick up the pieces."

Smokey thanked her but was filled with shame at the thought of having to live with his parents. There was no other choice at the moment, and as he listened to the morning dove he knew in his heart it was the right thing to do. Later that evening his stepdad came up to him and said it was okay. "We have a three-story house and it's just the two of us. You are more than welcome to stay for a while."

Smokey had a deep sleep that night. He couldn't remember any dreams, but when he woke the next day he felt rested. He had to prepare himself for the return to Winnipeg. How would he manage for the next two weeks until his exams were written? His parents decided to give him their second car to pack up his things and come home. This solved another problem for Smokey, though he didn't reveal it to his parents. He didn't have to sleep on a park bench; he could sleep in the car.

Monday morning, bright and early, Smokey sat on the back porch. It was quiet; only the hum of the few grasshoppers prevented complete silent. He had to return to Winnipeg, and he didn't want to go. He felt safe here. His mother cooked healthy meals, and he didn't have to worry about poison in the food. It was peaceful here, no stress.

After breakfast Smokey said, "It's time I was off."

His mother gave him a big hug and said "Don't worry if you can't write your exams. Just pack your things and come home."

Smokey smiled and said, "I'll write them, and I'll get A's-all A's." He hopped into the Dodge Dart and started it up. It was a good old car, and it had roof racks for a canoe. He couldn't ask for more.

As he drove along the Red Coat Trail he thought about the last paper he had handed in on the Meech Lake Accord. He wondered if he had done it justice. It was a complicated subject. He wanted Canada to stay together but at what price? What price was too high? The country needed a strong federal state, not a weaker one. Provincial governments were too small to negotiate agreements with other countries like the United States. And then there was the issue of Distinct Society for Quebec and the charter of rights and freedoms. At what point does promotion of one culture infringe on the rights of others, such as the French language laws currently in Quebec? Finally, Smokey thought about what had been said about the decision-making process. Why should ten middle-class men decide the fate of the country? The process was unfair. Smokey thought that he could do a master's thesis on participatory democracy as an alternative for Canada. He realized then that he was caught up in politics and constitutional law. He knew then that he would drop the administration degree in favor of a political science degree and then a law degree. He had a new course, a new plan, and there was hope.

He arrived back in Winnipeg early that evening, so he went to the university to study for a few hours. After stopping in to pick up his birds at the apartment and putting them in the car, he walked to school and studied at school till late, then returned to the car for the night.

When he got there, a big fat cat was sitting on the windshield starring in at the birds. Smokey said "Sorry, old chap, but these birds are my buddies, not your dinner. Take a hike." He pushed the cat off the car. He crawled into the back seat. It was a lot more comfortable than the park bench and he was soon fast asleep.

Smokey woke to the sounds of his two birds chattering in the morning sunlight. He looked at his watch. It was 6:30 A.M., and the university opened at 7:00. He had half an hour to kill before he could begin the day. He went to a little pizza and breakfast place at Portage Avenue and had a couple of cups of coffee.

He could feel the presence of the phoenix in his mind today. It was very strong and dark, foreboding. He could feel the talons of the bird sinking into his left shoulder and down his chest-at least he felt something strange on the left side of his chest. Maybe he wore the mark of the beast. He checked and he couldn't see anything, but he could feel it. Maybe this phoenix was a form of the beast. Maybe that was it!

Smokey cleared his head and tried to think of more positive thoughts, like who he would be ten years from now. He imagined himself as a constitutional lawyer fighting for the little guy with the charter of rights and freedoms. He would fight against the governments that tapped phones, bugged people's homes or allied themselves with big business and committees. He would make a difference!

Smokey looked at his watch. It was 9:30, He had been daydreaming in the coffee shop for two hours. Time to go to school. He paid his bill and headed for the university. As he walked along Portage Avenue, he saw a black limo coming up the street. He ducked inside a shop that was just opening. It passed by. Smokey knew it was the department store management or Alexander Kazzer who was after him. He waited a few minutes before continuing on his way. Arriving at the university, Smokey had some time to study.

Smokey studied hard, and he had a good idea what questions would be on the final exams. As he sat on the lounge sofa reading, two Muslim girls came and sat beside him. Smokey knew all about Muslim women. They were the devil's children. They wore those veils so they could suck your blood without you realizing it. He got up and moved away. There were so many things that he had to watch out for, like eating a meal. He could only buy previously prepared foods like sandwiches in the cafeteria. Most important, he had to control his thoughts because there were those who could read minds and listen in.

The day of final exams came quicker than Smokey realized, but he had studied hard and was prepared. As he sat at his desk, writing his last exam, he knew that he had done well. He wasn't sure whether he had an A average or not, but it didn't matter. It was over and he could go home.

As soon as he was finished he was out the door of the school and back at his apartment packing everything he could into his car. Then he went to the storage depot and got the rest of his things. His final stop was the canoe club where he stored his cedar-strip canoe. He loaded it on the roof rack and tightened it down for the trip. Smokey left Winnipeg that evening and he didn't look back, not once! The old Dodge cruised along at sixty-five mph no problem. Smokey turned on the radio low and tapped his fingers on the steering wheel. He had a lot to think about while he drove home. He thought about the past four years; it seemed like he had achieved almost nothing. He was four years older and still meaningful employment eluded him. He asked himself what he would do in Weyburn.

He reached the Souris River outskirts and pulled the car over to take a break. He got out of the car and headed for the ditch. It was near sunset, but Smokey could make out a small tiger lily in the ditch. He thought of Sherry. He walked over to it, then stopped. He stood straight, lifted his foot, and ground the flower into the earth. He then unzippered his fly and urinated on the spot. It was too early for true bitterness to set in but not too soon to feel the pain of emptiness at the end of a relationship. He wiped a tear from his cheek and got back in the car. He turned the radio off and sat in silence. He heard his father's voice in his mind singing "We're on the homeward trail," and soon he was humming it too.

He reached his parents' house late that evening. It was too late to unpack, so he locked the car and took the birds into the house. He set them on the kitchen table and put their cover on.

His mother was just brushing her teeth before bed. She said "There is a bed upstairs," but Smokey said that he preferred the basement where it would be cool. She said "Good night and welcome home."

Smokey stepped out on the back porch and looked up into the sky. He found the Big Dipper then the Little Dipper, but that's about all he knew. His friend Bill knew the stars like the back of his hand. Smokey thought, *I'm only seventy miles away from Regina. I can visit Bill again. He is a good friend, and good friends are what I need right now*! He closed the back door and headed for the basement.

The whiskey and liquor bottles were stacked in the basement. They had sat there for years and nobody had touched them. It was odd being there again. The last time had been when he returned from Eastern Saskatchewan virtually a drunk. He had been consuming a twenty-six ounce bottle of rum every night. He had spent a month in his parent's basement trying to dry out facing those same whiskey bottles over and over again. He remembered the emptiness in the pit of his stomach and felt it again now, but the battle of the bottle is not so difficult as battling the demons. They are real, and they can hurt you. *If you don't drink from the bottle the worst will soon be over, but demons and evil spirits can attack you anywhere,* Smokey thought. Then he remembered that the demons of the bottle were once alive in him too, very real. He remembered how he would take a whiskey bottle out of the carton and take it in his hands and his hands trembled and shook, he was so afraid he would drop the bottle. It hadn't been easy, but he had stopped the hard liquor. He still drank beer, but it didn't seem to affect him the same way. He would only have one or two, and for four years he hadn't had anything. He remembered the dreams he had of drinking a bottle of whiskey and waking up feeling guilty.

Yes, it had been a real struggle, but now he faced an even more difficult battle. He lay on the bed in the basement and closed his eyes, and soon he was dreaming. He was running in his dreams, trying to escape the department store management, but they were closing in on him. He ran faster, faster, then he was asleep in his bed in his old apartment in Winnipeg and he could hear his landlord talking to the police about finishing Smokey off. It was a restless night for Smokey, fleeing demons of the past. It was 6:00 A.M., and Smokey could hear the birds chirping in the trees. There was the sound of an active robin nearby. Smokey got out of bed and made his way upstairs. His parents had finished breakfast but had a spot for him. He had some toast and coffee, and then he went out to the back porch to watch the robin dig for worms. There was a gentle breeze and the constant hum of grasshoppers in the grass. Smokey thought, *I've escaped the big city and all its demons and devil children. I am safe here.* But deep in his heart he knew that escaping would not be so easy. There would still be postmen and big business in a small town. He didn't have to worry about it today. He would unpack his things and spend some time with his mother.

Smokey's mom came out into the back porch. She was wearing red triangle earrings! Smokey looked at her, trying to read the signs. Was she a Satanist too? Didn't she know that those earrings were the devil's instruments? He would have to be very careful what he said to her. Maybe she didn't realize what she had gotten herself into. The devil's symbols were everywhere!

Chapter XXIII

Four days had passed since Smokey stepped through the door of his parent's house, and time had stood almost still for him. Each hour, minute, and second seemed to take an eternity. The pain of an ended relationship and the shame of living off his parents made each moment last forever.

Finally, on the fifth day, Smokey went for a long walk and on his way back he dipped into the U.I. office just for the hell of it. Smokey perused the boards and then saw an ad for office manager for a junk dealer. Smokey contacted the office and said he had the necessary experience. They said the employer needed someone right away. Smokey said, "I'll be there this afternoon."

On his way home he convinced himself that this is what he needed right now, a job that required some skill and expertise. It would keep him busy. When Smokey got home his mother asked him what was up. Smokey said, "I'm going to get a job and start paying my way around here."

Chapter XXIV

Smokey held out his resume to a tall man with steel gray eyes and knew he was contracting work with the devil if he got the job. The man never smiled or shook his hand but his son seemed like a really nice guy. Smokey was pleased with the interview but they didn't hire him right away. It was the following day that they called him at home and said to start the next day.

The first day of his new job was hectic between posting sales records and answering the telephone, which never stopped ringing. He had to weigh in trucks as they came onto the scales. It was now autumn, and farmers were coming in by the dozens to sell scrap metal. Smokey worked hard and fast; it was tough getting a handle on everything. He was responsible for cheque payments, records, and payroll. It seemed that every day someone would come in and ask for an advance.

The first two weeks went by quickly and Smokey held his first pay cheque in his hands. It felt really good to be earning a buck. He could pay his parents for food and save the rest for school. Things were going well. That evening Smokey gave his forwarding address to the department store in Winnipeg, where he still had an outstanding account. It was a difficult decision because now the store management knew where he was again, but Smokey believed in honesty; he had to pay his bills. He also contacted the University of Winnipeg and asked them to forward his marks to him in Weyburn.

Each night Smokey would sit out on the back porch and look up at the stars. It seemed to him that his life was very small in comparison to the universe and yet he knew that life was important, a gift. He thought, *God's gift of life to us, we must make it count! I will be a constitutional lawyer, and I will fight for what is right!*

Chapter XXV

Smokey opened the envelope slowly. This is what he had been waiting for, his marks at University. Political Science, 1000 B+, Political Science, 2300 B+, Administration 2000, A+, Sociology 2150, B+. Smokey breathed a sigh of relief. He had a B+ average. He showed his marks to his mom. She gave him a big hug and said, "I knew you were a fighter." He had also received his account balance from the department store, which he paid in full and then cut up the credit card.

Chapter XXVI

It was nearing the end of September but it was still surprisingly a hot day. It had been a hectic day so far at work. Smokey was busy posting the sales journal for the previous days transactions when the boss came in and told him to stop work. Smokey stopped. His boss said, "There are three hundred dollars missing from the deposit. Did you take it?"

Smokey said, "No, sir"

The boss said, "Well, I think you better pack your things and go home."

Smokey left not knowing whether he was fired or not, but he had told the truth. He was innocent.

The next day the company had his final cheque prepared for him and someone had already taken his place. Smokey checked his separation slip to see what it said. Under the reason for termination of employment they had put, "Call us." Nothing was in writing, but they could bad mouth him all they wanted over the phone. The more he thought about it, the angrier he got. These were the type of things he would try to fight if he became a lawyer, but right now he had to face the facts. He was fighting against a big frog in a small pond. He couldn't win, and he knew he would never work in Weyburn again.

When Smokey told his parents what had happened they were as angry as he was. Then his mother said, "Maybe it's all for the better. We have some news to tell you. We are selling our house and moving to Ontario to be closer to your brother Ross. We think you should go to Regina and see about a place to live with Janet. She said there's room in the house she shares with an older gentleman from her church."

Smokey said, "Thanks for telling me, I think I need to go to my room."

Smokey sat in the basement listening to the chatter in his head. There was a thunderstorm coming up. He heard the distant rumble. He used to love thunderstorms but not anymore. The voices would come during the storm and torture him. He waited, then like a flash of lightening the voices screamed inside his head. "FUCK THE HOLY SPIRIT. FUCK THE HOLY SPIRIT." Smokey put his hands over his ears, not realizing the voices were from within. He trembled with fear. This was the unforgivable sin. Christ forgave all sins – but not blasphemy of the spirit. A man who spoke against the spirit was DAMNED FOR ALL ETERNITY. But I am not responsible for those voices, Smokey thought as he paced the bedroom floor and wrung his hands. *How can I be responsible?* Then he thought, I played with the ouija boards, *I read books on sorcery, I created those sculptures with the devil's hand. I am responsible. I AM DAMNED, DAMNED FOR ALL ETERNITY. Rejected by God forever!* He began to weep. The tears streamed down his face. *Not only does the woman I love reject me but I am rejected by my God. What is there to live for?* He wept for half the night, pacing the floor until he was exhausted.

Chapter XXVII

The sun shone through the basement window. It was morning and he had to go on living. But what was there to live for? He could become a constitutional lawyer and fight for the little guy, but he could find no true redemption. For it is not by works that thee are saved lest any man boast, so it stated in Romans. Smokey thought, *I am imperfect and my imperfection will mean my death!* Smokey felt great sorrow, which filled his being. Then he heard the phoenix singing a song of sorrow in his mind. A double form of suffering from this spirit.

Smokey lay in bed and stared at the ceiling for several hours. It was only personal necessity that forced him upstairs to the washroom around noon. His mother was busy making a lunch for everybody. She smiled at him and said, "Are you going to phone Janet today?" Smokey said, "Yes."

Janet said that there was room in the house for him and his birds and she would come down and pick him up. It was all settled.

That evening his parents presented him with a parting gift, the keys to the old Dodge Dart, plates, and the registration in his name. Smokey was overcome with emotion. He lowered his head and said, "Thank you." He phoned Janet back and told her that she didn't have to pick him up, but she said she wanted to come for a visit with everyone anyway. She would be there Friday to help him pack. There were three days till Friday.

Now that the move was going to happen, it couldn't happen soon enough for Smokey. He had everything packed after the first day with still two days to go till Janet came down.

The following day Smokey walked down to the center of town to a mall coffee shop where they made great egg salad sandwiches. He ordered his sandwich and sat down at a vacant table. His sandwich came and he began to eat.

A lady he had never seen before sat down at his table. She didn't smile or introduced herself. In fact, she curled her lips up and hissed a gentle "Fuck off." At first

Smokey didn't know what to think but then it dawned on him, she was one of those! In the late seventies all the people who were kept in the Weyburn Mental Institution were released into society. It was independent living; some survived on the outside and some did not. The causalities were high.

The woman sipped her coffee and said nothing, so Smokey finished his sandwich and left. He felt sorry for those who had mental problems. He could understand how it could happen, but he was thankful that he had a strong mind, a mind that could fight against evil entities and apparitions.

As he headed home, overwhelming sadness came over him. He couldn't explain it; it was just there inside him like a rock in his belly. He began to think about his death and the death of his father. He remembered the evening the minister came to say good night to him and his brother. He remembered how his father would sit by his bed and stroke the back of his head and sing him a German love song he learned while flying overseas flights. Smokey realized that night that nobody would ever stroke the back of his head again. It filled him with sorrow as he remembered that night. The sound of a morning dove vibrated through his chest as he exhaled into the dusty prairie air.

It was Friday morning bright and early. Smokey's mom said they had accepted an offer for the sale of the house late last night. Smokey said, "I'll have to come down and help you pack and clean the house."

Smokey's mom smiled and said, "It will all happen in a couple of weeks, but let's get you settled in to your new place first."

Janet showed up about ten o'clock, and Smokey's mother set the table for an early brunch. There were cheese and cold cuts, coffee and tea. They ate and chattered about their mom's move to Ontario, which was very exciting for everyone. Smokey's stepdad, John, said the move would be a new beginning for them and he sounded very enthusiastic.

After brunch they slowly packed up Smokey's car. They filled his car and Janet's too. Last in were Smokey's birds. They said their goodbyes, and Smokey got a big hug from his mother.

Smokey and Janet were off to Regina, promising to return in two weeks to help with their parents' move. Janet led the way. As they drove Smokey thought what he might do in Regina again. He most certainly wanted to finish his education, if at all possible, then apply for law school. He knew he had what it took to be a lawyer, and he knew that he would be good. But first things first. He needed at least an undergraduate degree and an MA to prove his academic abilities.

As the cars reached the outskirts of Regina, his sister pulled into a Robins Doughnuts. They sat over a cup of coffee. She said, "It will be good to have you with us." Smokey smiled and said, "I have no place else to go."

They reached the little house on Lorne Street and met with Walter. Walter was the owner of the house and seemed pleased to have a second boarder to pay a bit of rent. It was cheap rent, just $125 for the room with access to the kitchen and bathroom. An excellent deal. They unpacked Smokey's things in his new room and put the birds on a table. It was cramped, but it could be home if he relaxed and let things unfold.

Smokey wondered if Alexander Kazzer was following his moves, trying to find a way to get to him. He didn't believe for a minute that these corporations would let him go. They were there to control people, including their thoughts, but he must have faith in himself and his ability to sniff out evil before it happened.

The fall and early winter were a difficult time for Smokey as it was too late to go to school and he had to survive on about four hundred dollars a month from Unemployment Insurance. Each day he awoke to an empty agenda, nothing to do. He phoned his friend Bill and they met at the Utopia Café about two or three times a week. It was a hangout for the arts crowd and just about anybody was welcomed. Roger Eng, the master chef and experimental artist, might flip you a burger for three dollars or paint you a picture for the same amount. His work was stunning and original. He brought with him some of the old style Chinese painting along with a new contemporary impressionist style. You might get a painting of birds sitting on a fence or a picture of Bart Simpson. The thing was you never knew when the paintings were done. He stopped and started again. It was really up to you to decide when the pictures were complete. If you were a minimalist you bought early; if you like details you bought later. Everybody knew Roger.

Smokey spent many a morning with Bill over a cup of coffee at the Utopia Café. Bill was in transition as well, his disease having kept him from several types of employment. He still had his art but he couldn't make a living from it. They were two peas in a pod trying to understand the meaning of such a life and poverty, and four hundred dollars a month was definitely poverty. Bill talked about working for a preschool as an instructor and was hopeful of getting permanent work. Smokey said he was returning to school to get an education. Both had their plans and dreams. The days passed slowly at the Utopia Café!

Smokey needed to go back to Weyburn to see his parents off. They all washed the walls and cleaned behind the toilet and many other nooks and crannies. His parents were going to drive all the way to Owen Sound, where they had rented an apartment for the first month. It was difficult when the time came, but Smokey knew that everyone needed to say goodbye to Weyburn. They drove off and never looked back, and Smokey returned to Regina to his new little house shared with his sister. It wasn't always a blessing being with his sister though. She was planning a career in singing, and she really had only an average voice. She would spent hours practicing Billie Holiday, enough to drive everyone crazy. Smokey thought, *Get a grip on reality, girl, you haven't got the voice for it.* But the nightly singing continued. Walter didn't mind the singing though. He was half in love with Janet - that was obvious. Smokey wondered if that was why the rent was so cheap and felt a little bit guilty.

It was January before Smokey realized it, and he applied for a student loan to go to the University of Regina. He selected his classes and waited for the final word. Yes! He was accepted and could start classes immediately! He had to survive on a Canada Student Loan plus eight hundred dollars savings till he could find work in the summer, if he was lucky. Smokey sat in the counselor's office. They were going through his classes from the University of Winnipeg determining which classes he could use in his MA program in Regina. He lost about five classes in total, which was a lot; but still, it could have been worse since he had transferred CMA classes into the University of Winnipeg also. The counselor set him up with classes for the January to April semester. He would take a class in international trade, a class in political theory and economics. It would be a tough semester, but Smokey felt confident that he could handle it. He had a goal and a dream that needed realizing.

It was a bitterly cold day in January, nearly -30 Celsius. Smokey stood shivering at the bus stop in the north end of Regina. He had to catch the bus downtown then transfer to a university bus to the south end. The bus was late according to his watch, either that or it came early. Smokey usually timed the bus so he wouldn't have to wait in the freezing cold for long.

The bus arrived, and the driver was his cousin Allan, so they chatted for fifteen minutes as the bus made its way downtown. They agreed to have coffee soon. Smokey transferred to the University line and sat in the back of the bus. There appear to be a lot of foreign exchange students riding on the bus now, not like the 70s when it seemed like everyone had their own car.

Smokey got to school in time for his first class in political theory. They were studying Machiavelli, and the professor lectured at length about the discourse. The second class was in international trade, featuring Canada and United States trade negotiations, especially the Free Trade agreement. His final class for the day was economics, with which he knew he would have difficulty.

At the end of the day he sat in the coffee shop in the university reading Machiavelli, making notes about possible essay questions for mid-term. As he sat there reading, a tall, slender, beautiful Chinese woman sat down next to him. He smiled at her and she smiled back.

She said, "You are in my economics class."

Smokey replied, "I find the class difficult."

She said, "I can help you if you can help me with the English class." It was agreed that they would meet once a week to go over class notes, etc.

"By the way, my name is Sharon." "You can call me Smokey. Sharon, can I buy you a coffee?" Sharon replied, "No, thank you. I'll see you next week here after classes." "Bye." Smokey thought to himself, *This is great I have a tutor for economics. I need all the help I can get.*

The week passed and Smokey studied his class notes and read his textbook every night. It was Tuesday. Smokey met with Sharon after class.

Sharon said, "I have my first assignment, can you help me?"

"Let's take a look," replied Smokey.

The assignment was to analyze a poem called the "Black Rose." Sharon said, "I don't understand black rose. Is the rose evil or something like that?"

Smokey replied, "It has to do with romance and sorrow. Maybe a lover who was a cheat." They talked about the black rose for a long time trying to understand what the author might have meant.

Sharon finally said, "I think I know what the black rose is. It is my child conceived in rape". They worked on this angle for some time and finally came up with the words:

My child, the black rose,,
Whom I love and hate/
Conceived in rape,
He has his father's eyes.

Smokey said "That's perfect, Sharon. Good analysis."

She replied, "Thank you for your help." Smokey knew that she would do well. She had imagination and insight into poetry.

They turned to Smokey's economics, which wasn't nearly as much fun. They worked on problems for a couple of hours, then had a light dinner in the cafeteria. Smokey said, "I better be getting home, its getting late." Sharon smiled and said thank you again.

As he left, he truly felt that he had received the greatest help. He liked Sharon; she was honest and wanted to help if she could. She cared about school. She was here to learn like Smokey, and she had dreams of being a psychologist if all went well. Sharon was starting with a B.A. in psychology.

It was the first midterm, and Smokey had his essays to which to look forward. The first essay Smokey had to work on was on Machiavelli. As Smokey had been reading Machiavelli, he came to believe that he was much more than just a sophist, cruel and heartless. In fact, Smokey felt that Machiavelli had true heart. He described the role of the citizens and the senate as being accountable, far more accountable than the public servants and politicians of contemporary democracies. In some ways a Machiavellian society was superior to modern democracy. Smokey worked on the essay for several days, digging up quotations to support his work. He was going against the grain in this essay, but he felt if he supported his work, he would receive a fair grade. He turned in his essay "Machiavelli, The Philosopher with Heart," and he waited enthusiastically for his marks.

He met with Sharon the following Tuesday and she was excited. Bubbling over she described the comments and the A+ she had received for the assignment on the "Black Rose." She was so excited she gave him a hug.

Smokey had an economics paper due in five days. He hadn't started on it. He had spent so much time on the other two classes that he hadn't had time for economics. He still wasn't done his essay on international trade in which he was illustrating the negative side of Free Trade with the United States. This included the demise of the family farm and other small business. He had to leave that aside for now and work on economics while Sharon was with him to help.

The topic Smokey chose was the trickle-up economics of the Canadian Lottery System. He would illustrate how the system took from the poor, the hopeful, the desperate, and the addicted to feed sport programs for upper-middle class children. It was a tool of tyranny in the guise of hope. It replaced religion for those who stopped believing.

Sharon said, "This sounds very honest, but can you say such things without reprisals?"

Smokey thought again of Alexander Kazzer. Finally Smokey said, "I'm going to do it anyway." They set out the task of determining lotteries distribution in Canada.

Smokey turned in all his essays on time with both fear and excitement. He knew there was a chance that his work might fall into the wrong hands, but it was a chance he had to take. Alexander Kazzer hadn't killed him yet. However, after turning in all his essays he began to worry. What if they came after him? How could he defend himself? They controlled the police and other major institutions. He was like David without a slingshot facing Goliath. He thought about Janet and Walter; could he trust them? Did they know he may be the reincarnation of Adolph Hitler? Would they try to poison him like his last landlord had or try to gas him in his sleep?

Chapter XXVIII

Smokey felt the talons of the phoenix, the demon bird deep in his chest. It filled him with sorrow. He was at the university when it happened. He was sitting across from a young man when suddenly the demon bird attacked the young man. Smokey could see it in his mind's eye, the talons working into the man's head, the beat of the wings. The man fell to the floor and started convulsing. This wasn't in his mind's eye. The man was convulsing on the floor. People gathered around, and someone shouted, "Give him room."

"He has been attacked by the demon bird," Smokey shouted. A woman grabbed him and took him aside. "He's epileptic, you know. It's upsetting, but there is nothing we can do for him," she said.

Smokey seemed confused, but he snapped out of it. He told himself it was his imagination; the man had a medical condition. The demon bird could hurt no one in the physical form. But then he felt the talons pinch his chest, and he wasn't sure what was real.

Smokey left the university early that day and headed straight home. He knew that he was in some way responsible for what had happened to the young man. This demon bird had power that could cross the spirit realm into the physical realm. It was very dangerous, and he was responsible for it. But how could he control it? The demon had its own entity even if they were bonded together.

That evening Smokey went into his cupboard and brought out the picture of the phoenix or demon bird. He stared at it, trying to communicate with it. Suddenly he thought he saw its talons move. A shiver went through his spine. It truly was alive. As he sat there looking at it, a warm burning began to fill his chest—not a bad feeling but one of power and strength. Was the demon bird entering his flesh? He had always felt it externally before, its talons and feathers about him. He had never felt the heart of the bird, which he believed he was now experiencing.

As he glared at the bird its features changed into Barrie's face, the shaman who gave him the bird, and he heard a voice say, "Hello, my friend."

Smokey said, "Hello."

* * *

It was Judgment Day at the university; students were getting their midterms marks back. Smokey was filled with anticipation. At the end of his class in political theory, the professor handed back the papers. Smokey look at his paper—75 percent, the marker said, "A good effort." Smokey was a little disappointed; he had hoped for an A. He received an A, though, in international trade and a B+ in economics, so overall he was satisfied. There were no more essays to write except a second essay in political theory, which was due shortly. Smokey had a choice; he could write on John Locke or Thomas Hobbes. Smokey thought about it for a long time but finally decided on Thomas Hobbs and the Leviathan. He would draw comparisons between the Leviathan and the OPEC Oil Cartel. It was an interesting perspective and a challenge.

Smokey met with Sharon to help her with an analysis of John Donne for her English paper. Basically she didn't need much help. She was a deep and thoughtful thinker. It was spring and the end of the semester. All that was left was the final exams. Smokey had written his economics exam already and felt that he had passed, but just barely.

Smokey waited with two hundred other students at the doors of the auditorium. In ten minutes he would receive his essay questions for international trade. He was very nervous, but he had studied hard and was ready as he could be. The doors opened and the students went in. Smokey sat near the front of the auditorium. The professor said, "You may begin." Smokey flipped over the paper.

The first question said, "Explain the purpose of the I.M.F. and discuss its strengths and weaknesses." Smokey had little trouble with this. He thought about the third world countries selling cash crops to pay the interest on their debt. He knew the weaknesses for sure. The second question was, "Is the United States and Canada free trade policy fair?" Smokey knew he would do well on this question. Three hours went quickly, and Smokey was surprised when time was up.

The next day Smokey wrote his final in Political Theory. He could write on Plato's "Republic" or John Locke. Smokey chose Plato's "Republic." He discussed the myth of the metals in the "Republic," where it was stated that some men were born with hearts of bronze, silver, and gold. This would determine their station in life. Of course this is symbolism. Nobody has a metal heart, but could it be that ones' genetic makeup determined his position in life? True, a man born with one leg would never be a champion marathon runner. A man with one leg can win the heart of the people, e.g., Terry Fox. It was an interesting question for Smokey. How much was class structured, civilization, and how much genetics? He wrote for three hours, giving examples of every situation he could think of. At the end of the day Smokey was exhausted.

He and Sharon went for a cup of coffee. She was going home for the summer, but she left Smokey an address in Hong Kong that he could write her.

Smokey said, "Have a great summer."

"See you in Septemberm," she said.

Yes, it was spring, and that meant the end of student loan money and empty bank accounts. He had to get a job within two weeks or apply for welfare. He had roughly sixty dollars to his name. Smokey began his job search with the usual places: Saskatchewan Power, the post office, the provincial government. He applied to ads in the paper for accounting positions and general labor, but after two weeks of solid searching he had to apply for welfare. It was going to be a long summer.

Smokey sat in the Welfare Office and waited. He had brought all the information with him, but despite this fact, the processing would take three weeks. Smokey thought to himself, "I'll never make it. I have thirty dollars for three weeks. That's impossible!"

After the welfare office interview he went to the Super Store and bought twenty packages of dried noodle soup for twenty-two cents each, a dozen eggs, and some frozen vegetables. That just about finished his ten dollars for the first week. He went home and made himself two packages of dried noodles soup and an egg. The noodles filled him up; they seemed to expand in his stomach. Smokey thought, *I don't even have enough money for a cup of coffee.* Smokey wasn't looking forward to three weeks without coffee.

By the fifth day of noodle soup, Smokey had a fever and diarrhea. He thought maybe the noodle soups were poisoned. Yes, poison the poor. It made perfect sense to Smokey. Corporations would love to torture the poor. Smokey decided to go to the doctor.

The doctor examined him and said, "Here's a prescription."

Smokey said, "I have no money."

The doctor said "Aren't you on assistance? That's what you told me." Smokey said, "Not for another two weeks." The doctor said, "This can't wait for two weeks." He went to his cupboard and pulled out some samples of a drug. He said, "Take these. They will help. Come back in a week, I want to see you again."

Smokey made his way home. He was feeling depressed and like a helpless victim of society. He needed a job more than anything else, but nobody was interested in him. The jobs went to the young and the boys from the south end, the wealthy middle class who voted P.C. and held jobs with the city and provincial government. There were no jobs for the lower class except maybe at Mac's or 7-Eleven, if you were lucky.

The next day Smokey was feeling much better, so he took his canoe down to Wascana lake for a short paddle. He unloaded the canoe and set it on the dock. He retrieved his paddle and began a slow steady stroke out to the center of the lake. He crossed the lake and followed the perimeter of the lake. Some female joggers on the shore caught his eyes. *Yes, there are still some great blessings in the world,* Smokey thought.

The next two weeks past with an agonizing slowness. He had gone almost three weeks without a cup of coffee when Bill called and said he would buy him a cup at Utopia Café. Smokey had to walk there; there was no gas left in the car.

Bill had done some dynamite new pictures. One was of an owl reaching for his prey, a young rabbit.

Smokey said, "That will sell for sure."

Bill said, "Yes, I think so too." Bill's work just got better and better.

Both men were now bachelors and talked about the life of bachelorhood and what they really would like. Bill said "We just have to open ourselves up to the universe and be ready for a relationship if it happens."

Smokey couldn't honestly do that yet; he was still hurting. It hurt every single day. He had given his all in the relationship with Sherry, and there was nothing left to give right now. It would take time, but there was the physical withdrawal as well as the emotional. He still dreamed about her and would wake up soiled.

They finished their cup of coffee. It was pretty good that day, and they went for a walk in the park. They used Bill's car to get there.

Bill was doing some photography as they walked along. His photography, like his art, was original. He took pictures of certain knots in trees that looked like faces or animals. Smokey thought about his own sculptures. How had his art turned so ugly, so evil? Why couldn't he have talent like Bill without sacrificing his mortal soul? He needed to create too, it was in his blood.

The next day Smokey received his Welfare cheque of $125, payable to the landlord, and $140 for food, clothing and transportation. It worked out to $4.50 a day. It wasn't much, but it was better than nothing at all. If he continued to eat at home and go for coffee only once or twice a week, he would manage.

The call came the following evening; it was his mother in Owen Sound. "Hi, dear," she said. "We have some upsetting news. Grandpa has had a bad stroke, and he is in the hospital in Regina. I'm flying out there tomorrow to see him. I'll be staying with your aunt and uncle while I'm there. Hope we can meet and talk. Love you, bye." She sounded quite upset.

It must be very serious, Smokey thought as he hung up the phone. He had always felt that he and his Grandpa had a special connection. He remembered the thousand games of Aggravation, a game played with marbles on a board and a deck of cards. It was Grandpa's favorite game.

Smokey's mother arrived in Regina the next evening and gave him a call. They met for coffee at a Robin's Doughnuts. He had never seen his mother look so fragile. She was always the one to say, "Stiff upper lip and carry on." But not this time.

The following day they met at the hospital. His mother smiled at him as they walked up the steps. They made their way to Grandpa's room. He was lying perfectly still. His breathing was labored. His mother sat in a chair next to his grandfather, and Smokey pulled up a second chair. "How are you, Dad?" his mother asked.

There was no response, just labored breathing. Then he lifted his hand and moved it with hers. Smokey looked into his grandfather's eyes. The light of the spirit looked weak in him.

Then a voice spoke in Smokey's head. "*Die, you old cunt.*" Smokey put his hand over his mouth, not realizing the voice was internal. When he did realize, he also knew his grandpa had heard him anyway. Before you die you are granted telepathic powers if you haven't got them already.

Smokey spoke inside his head to his grandpa. "*Grandpa, I'm so sorry. I didn't mean that. Sometimes evil spirits control my brain. They make me say awful things. You were right; I should never have played with the ouija board or other things that I did. Now I'm possessed, Grandpa, and I can't break free of the demons. Soon they will control all of me. I'm sorry, Grandpa. I should have listened.*"

As Smokey gazed into his grandfather's eyes, they seemed to glisten, and then the life was gone from them. His mother began to weep quietly as she held her father's hand and closed his eyes. Smokey said in this mind, "*If there is a heaven, I know you'll be there. I just might not be there with you.*

He took his mother's hand, and they walked to the nurses' station. He gave her a hug. His mother said, "Go home. I'll handle the rest. I'm okay."

Smokey walked home slowly. He had a lot on his mind. Near the end Smokey had felt his grandfather's spirit throughout the room. It was as if his soul was expanding to encompass them. He also knew his grandfather still loved him and would forgive him. In fact, now he felt he could talk to his grandpa. Smokey began, "I think my whole relationship with Sherry was like an evil spell which I enacted from writing poems. I think she was from the dark side of the universe, at least part of her was. Grandpa, I think she was a lover from a past life in ancient times. I think that she may be a demi-god of sorts, a tiger or a golden dragon. She had such power over me. Grandpa, I feel like I've been raped by a god or demon. And now I've lost control of my thoughts and words. What will happen next? Grandpa, I think I had one great love in my life, and it was with a demon."

When he got home he checked his wallet. He decided to put ten dollars of gas in the car so he could take his canoe to the lake. He needed release, and the stroke of the paddle would give him that needed release.

Smokey unloaded the canoe and grabbed his paddle. It was a perfectly calm day, no ripples on the water's surface. As he paddled along, he no longer dreamed of being a national champion. He dreamed of being a constitional lawyer. He imagined himself in court defending some poor person's constitutional rights. As he paddled along the lake, his thoughts returned to his grandfather. "Grandfather, some day you are going to be proud of me. I won't always be a failure." A slight breeze seemed to come from nowhere and sent a ripple across the bow of his canoe. He thought, *I should write Sharon a letter, let her know the things that have happened.* He pulled his canoe into shore and headed home.

The funeral was held on a dark and cloudy day, but just as they lowered the casket into the ground a ray of sun came through the clouds. The service had been short, and Grandma had held up very well. Smokey saw uncles, aunts, and cousins he hadn't seen for years. The family was actually quite large. He had been the only one who couldn't get a job, who had been a bit of a failure. They were eager to find out what he was doing, so he just said, "I'm going to school right now. Don't know where it will lead, maybe law if things go well." That was all he said, and that was enough.

The following day he said goodbye to his mother. Things moved too fast; there was no time for proper grief.

Smokey said, "Grandpa was like the father I lost early in life."

His mother said, "He was good to you and your brother."

Smokey asked, "How's Owen Sound?"

She stated it was fine, but he could tell that she was lonely there. Retirement is never an easy thing, especially when you are still young at heart and willing to work. They said their goodbyes, and his mother headed off to the airport. Smokey sat in silence. He knew his mother needed support too, but how could he help when he was thousands of miles away and struggling desperately himself? He struggled with demon voices every day now. There were periods when he lost control of his mind.

—— Chapter XXIX ——

It was Sunday, the day of rest. Smokey sat in front of the television half listening to some programs. Then a program came on Christian Feed the Children Foundation. There were pictures of starving children with flies in their eyes and swollen empty bellies. Smokey began to giggle, then he laughed out loud.

His sister came in from the other room and asked what he was laughing at. "You're not laughing at these poor children are you?"

Smokey said, "I think I'm possessed.

She grabbed him by the shoulder and said, "In the name of the Lord Jesus Christ I command you out of this man, Satan."

"*Fuck your Jesus up the ass! Jesus is a cunt licker! Cunt Licker! Cunt Licker!*"

"I'm sorry I didn't mean that," Smokey said.

"You didn't say anything, Smokey. Just have faith God will heal you."

"*Cunt Licker!*"

Smokey said, "I think I'll go to my room for a while." He went to the bathroom instead. He closed the door and sat on the toilet. He thought to himself, *I thought I was the reincarnation of Adolph Hitler, but it may even be worse than that. I may be the devil's son. If God could have a son, why not the devil?" Maybe I don't have free will, maybe I'm bound to my real father, the devil. Did I ever really have a choice? Am I the devil's son?* Smokey said to himself, *I still have some choices. I can die with dignity like Christ.*

He opened the medicine chest and pulled out a bottle of sleeping pills. He poured them into his hand and then took a glass from the shelf and poured a glass of water. He swallowed the pills and took a long drink. It would be his last taste of water, he thought. He went to his room and lay down on his bed. He became aware of his heart beating in his chest and he grew tired. His heart beat slower and slower. Smokey's mind entered the void. He slept.

* * *

The sun shone with all its brightness through the curtains, which were partially open in Smokey's room. Smokey became aware of himself and an awful stench. What time was it? What day was it? Realizing that the stench was him, Smokey raised himself out of bed and stripped the sheets. He threw the sheets in the washer and then stepped into the shower. He was alive. He wasn't sure how he felt about that, but in a way he knew he had been foolish. Janet always checked the days off on the calendar. If she had done so this morning, it was Wednesday. He had slept almost three days.

Smokey decided he should see a doctor, get a physical after taking the pills. He went to a nearby clinic. There was a lineup, so Smokey sat in the waiting room with sick children screaming and parents yelling. His name was finally called, and he went into a room and waited. The doctor came in shortly and asked him what the trouble was.

Smokey said, "I want a physical. I did something that I regret."

"What's that?" the doctor asked.

"I took some pills."

"What kind were they? Why did you take them?"

Smokey thought for a moment. How could he explain in five minutes what he had been through? He started to talk about the ouija board and its evils, then about his sculptures, evil corporations, and finally his thoughts on being the reincarnation of Adolph Hitler or the son of Satan.

The doctor listened, put his hand up to his chin, and said, "I think you have schizophrenia, son. I'm not an expert, but we will get one for you." He went to his list of psychiatrists and pulled out a name of a good doctor. "Just a minute and I'll make a call," he said. He left.

Smokey knew almost nothing about schizophrenia or perhaps he might have recognized some of the symptoms. He wasn't sure he believed the doctor. They could be trying to trick him. Maybe there were even certain people from the dark side who were trying to help him with his struggle. Was he to rise to power somehow, as a political leader or something? He wasn't sure, but he knew that he had reached a crossroads in his existence. He must submit or continue alone with his struggle.

The doctor came back and handed him a card. "You have an appointment next Monday. Promise me you won't take anymore pills till then."

Smokey said, "Okay, doc. Thanks."

The doctor performed a physical on Smokey and gave him a clean bill of health physically.

Smokey made a decision after being at the doctor's office. He was returning to the Lord. No darker forces, only the light of Christ. He would beat those demons back. He would start over. That evening he went to the cupboard and took out the picture of the demon bird. He took it out of the frame and rolled it up. It was nearly dusk and the moon was just coming up three quarters full. Smokey took the picture into the backyard to the gravel patch. He took out a book of matches and lit a match. He unfolded the picture and lit it on fire. He watched the flames engulf the bird. "Burn in Hell," he said as the flames devoured this spirit bird.

He felt its talons tighten into his left shoulder. He heard its cry! The ground under his feet seemed to weaken all of a sudden. Before he realized it he was falling through the earth carried by the demon bird. It was dark all around him. There were a few torches lit just enough to see close up. Smokey stumbled along until he came to a great burning fire. There were corpses everywhere. Most of them had sores and pustules on their bodies. A shiver went through his spine. There were the dead, mostly North American Indians, the curse of smallpox so evident on their bodies.

Smokey noticed that he was wearing a long dark robe with a silver cross around his neck. He came across a small boy crying in the dirt. He reached out for the boy, but the boy spat on the cross and said, "Your God did this." Smokey said "No! No! This is not the will of God." But the child, with the wisdom of ages, said, "You do not know your own God."

The next thing he knew he was back in the yard on Lorne Street, the picture completely burned to ashes. He buried the ashes and went inside. Smokey said to himself, "I'm going to church this Sunday, I am!"

* * *

Smokey rose early Sunday morning, had a shower, and shaved. He put the iron on low and began to press his pants for church. Smokey thought to himself "I'll close the book on those demons in my head. With God's help I can do anything."

Smokey caught the bus and headed downtown to the Baptist church. It was a bright and beautiful day; it was going to be a warm one too. The bus stopped about three blocks from the church. Smokey cut through the park to get there. The church was full, but Smokey found a seat in the middle rows. The pastor raised his hands and said "Welcome to the house of the Lord."

They sang some old hymns, and everything seemed to be going okay when Smokey felt himself rise to his feet. "Sweet Jesus," he shouted, "suck my cock!

"Oh no! I didn't do this–I couldn't have."

There were two burly looking young men headed in his direction. Smokey headed down the aisle as fast as he could walk, but before he could reach the back of the church he was lifted by the elbows and catapulted through the doors. As he went through the doors he tripped and went tumbling down the cement steps to the street. He hit his head on the curb. Smokey sat up. Blood trickled down his forehead and into the right eye. He blinked and saw the world in crimson. He picked himself up and walked slowly down the street to an old coffee shop.

Bell was working the counter when he came in. She took one look at him and said, "Oh my God, what happened to you?"

Smokey sighed and said, "I went to church."

She took him into the bathroom and washed out his eye and made him a cold compress out of paper towels for his head.

Smokey said, "Thank you."

Bell smiled and said, "One apple fritter and one large dark roast coming up, no charge today." Bell brought him the food and drink and said to him "The apple fritter is the body and the dark roast is the blood. Just think about it, and you're a better man than half the people that go to those fancy churches."

Smokey ate his fritter in silence and starred out the window. He thought to himself, *I'm not just thinking things now. I'm also saying them. The devil really has a hold on me.*

What about this schizophrenia? Could it be true? Is there something wrong with me? Tomorrow is my appointment with the psychiatrist—what should I say to him or her? When Smokey got home he looked up schizophrenia in the dictionary. It was a delusional disorder. Smokey thought to himself, "I'm not delusional, there must be some mistake. The doctor is probably wrong."

Smokey sat in the reception room of the mental health clinic. It was ten to two. His appointment was at two o'clock. He could almost hear the clock on the wall ticking. *Tick, tick, tick. What am I doing here? Tick, tick, tick. There's really nothing wrong with me. Tick, tick, tick. I've just been under a lot of stress moving from Winnipeg to Weyburn and then Weyburn to Regina! School, then welfare and poverty. Tick, tick, tick. Unemployment, the unfairness of society, love and loss, relationship gone sour. The loss of God's love, eternal damnation. Tick, tick, tick. Demonic pictures and sculptures, the attack of satanic cults, the postman. Tick, tick, tick. Corporations and their misuse of power, government and power. Tick, tick, tick. There is nothing wrong with me.*

The receptionist called his name. He went to the door, which had an automatic lock on it, and waited to be buzzed in. A small man with glasses met him at the door. The man introduced himself and said he would be talking with him today. They went down a long hallway to an office.

"Please be seated" the psychiatrist said. Smokey sat with his hands clenched together. "Try to relax. It's really not so bad. I know that this is your first time, but things will be all right. We don't bite."

The psychiatrist began with some preliminary questions on family history and mental illness. After a while the psychiatrist started asking him funny questions about spaceships and things. The interview lasted for two hours. At the end of the meeting the psychiatrist wrote Smokey a prescription for Stelazine, an antipsychotic drug. "Please take these three times a day," the psychiatrist said, and that was it. Smokey began to wonder about the psychiatrist. Maybe he was employed by the department store or the government to see to their needs. Should I take these pills or not? What will they do to me?

Smokey had the prescription filled at a pharmacy in the Cornwall Center downtown. He decided to have dinner downtown as it was already late afternoon. There was a submarine shop in the mall which Smokey liked; he would eat there. He could watch them prepare it so nothing else got in his sandwich by mistake or on purpose. Smokey ate, then caught the bus home.

That night he decided to write Sharon a letter. He told her about his grandfather dying, and he told her about the trip to the mental health clinic. He was surprised at how much he had to say. He wrote, "It's a good thing you went home for the summer. There are no jobs here it seems, unless you have connections."

When he'd completed the letter he picked a maple leaf from the tree in the backyard and enclosed it the envelope with the letter.

The psychiatrist had suggested that Smokey go to the club sponsored by the Canadian Mental Health Association on Albert Street. The doctor said, "You can go there and get a hot meal and meet some people like yourself, maybe make some friends." Smokey thought he would do this tomorrow. If the weather were nice he would walk there for the exercise. He decided that evening that he would try the pills.

He slept late. It was almost noon when he crawled out of bed and he still felt tired. He took his morning pill. It turned out to be a lovely day, about 24° celsius with just a smattering of clouds here and there. Smokey walked out the door fully intending to walk to the club, but he found that by the time he had walked a few blocks he was too tried to go any further so he caught the bus.

He opened the club doors and stepped inside. There was an old man sitting in a chair chewing on a handful of cigarette butts and laughing hysterically. Another woman was singing softly to herself a stream of profanity. Then a young man came up to him and looked him in the eye and winked. "I'm the Son of God," he said.

Smokey smiled and said, "I'm the reincarnation of Adolph Hitler."

"I forgive you," the man said.

"Thanks," Smokey replied.

They talked for a while, and Smokey found out the man had been a pre-med student before he had become ill. Smokey told him how he had wanted to be a respiratory technologist but was not accepted into training. They had things in common.

There was a loud banging and cursing, a woman's voice. Smokey looked around and saw a woman who had to be five hundred pounds banging her fist on the table. The Son of God said, "That's Shirley Temple."

Smokey couldn't help himself, he began to laugh. They both laughed for several minutes; then Smokey's laughter turned to tears. Perhaps it was a momentary insight that there was little difference between a five hundred-pound woman who thought she was Shirley Temple and a man who thought he was the reincarnation of Adolph Hitler or the Son of Satan. There was no difference, and it wasn't funny. It was a tragedy.

Smokey left the club vowing not to return. He got home around 3:30 in the afternoon and decided to have a short nap. He slept till 5:00 P.M. Smokey made himself supper and took another pill. He watched television with Walter till 9:00 P.M., took another pill, and went to bed.

Again Smokey slept late, and it was nearly noon before he rose. He noticed another thing—he was always tired and hungry. It seemed to be the only two emotions he had left, tired and hungry.

He began to suspect the pills as the cause, and he was partially right. Schizophrenia can lead to a lack of motivation and tiredness, but so can the drugs that combat other symptoms, such as hallucinations and delusions. By the end of the summer Smokey was still ill but fifty pounds heavier. The drug had slowed his metabolism down and he still had the appetite of an athlete.

It was late August when he decided to do his income tax. He had been afraid that the federal government might want him dead, so he didn't file. Today he decided he would file. It was the law, and to his surprise and sheer delight he was going to get eight hundred dollars back. He could use that after a summer of welfare. He needed new shoes desperately as he had used duct tape to tape the toe of his shoes together. He deserved this break, and he wasn't going to tell welfare that he was getting the money. He could buy a good winter coat, use the rest for the fall semester at school, and of course he could plate his car one more year. The old Dodge Dart was still going without even a tune-up since he had received it.

* * *

It was the first day to sign up for autumn classes. It had been a long summer. Smokey knew that there were certain classes he had to take, like his language requirement and his math requirement. These were obstacles he had to face sooner or later. It might as well be now. Smokey signed up for French class and calculus. His third class was advanced political theory. It made for a really tough semester, but Smokey thought he could handle it.

He sat in the cafeteria and watched all the students go by. They were all so young. He had to be at least ten years older than anybody else. Smokey thought to himself, *I should have been doing this years ago when my mind was bright and fresh from high school.* Initially Smokey had gone to university after high school, but he had dropped out after a year and half. Luckily some of those old classes could still be used for credit.

It was only four o'clock, but Smokey was tired. It seemed that he was always tired, and he knew it was the drugs he was taking that caused it. He would have to plan his days carefully in order to get the maximum from each day. Smokey rode the bus home. He only drove his car in emergencies and weekends when the bus service was poor. He just couldn't afford the gas to run his car full time, and a bus pass was only forty dollars a month.

He arrived home about five o'clock and started to make supper. Pasta with a little bit of cheese was on the menu for this evening. Smokey had pasta two or three times a week. It was fattening, but it was also economical. A meal of pasta with sauce wasn't much more than a dollar, maybe a dollar fifty. The only problem was the lack of exercise necessary to burn all these calories. He thought to himself "I'll go for a long walk after supper and burn some calories off." After supper Smokey felt too tired to go for a long walk; besides, he was getting an eerie feeling about the evening. The dark forces were out tonight. He could see the demon bird in his mind's eye. It hadn't left him. It was still a part of him. There were other forces out there tonight, though, very dark forces with a lot of power. He could feel it in his fingertips, a tingling sensation that warned him of the dark spirits. Smokey went to his room and took down the crystal from the window where he had set it to attract positive energy. It could attract negative forces this evening. Even the birds were silent. It was a creepy feeling.

Smokey set his Bible on the table. He opened it to a passage about a dove among the crows that shall be treated as a crow. A shiver went through his spine. Was he the dove among the crows? He closed the Bible and said a short prayer that the evil forces would not control him tonight, but he could hear voices in the distant realms of his brain, voices that cursed God. He knew that he had become a receptacle for these demons. *Is schizophrenia just a name given to satanic possession? Do we deny the truth about this illness?*

Smokey had been doing some reading on schizophrenia. They said it was a chemical imbalance in the brain, but maybe it was a demon brain. Maybe the chemical imbalance was due to demon possession. The medical profession knew so very little. Hell, twenty years ago they were drilling holes in our heads as a last resort. The medical profession hadn't come that far in twenty years. The drugs don't stop the voices; they sedate you and confuse you about what reality is.

Smokey could hear the voices clearly now. They were demon voices cursing the name of God. He took his evening pill, put a pillow over his head, and crawled into bed. That night he could feel death's hand surrounding him. In his dreams he was struggling for life against the dark forces of the universe.

Smokey woke the next morning feeling very tired and groggy, but through the fog in his brain he immediately sensed something was wrong. He realized what it was after a few minutes. The sun was shinning through the window, but the birds were silent. He got dressed and went over to the cage. One of the birds was dead and the other one was sitting on its perch shaking.

Smokey got a bag from the kitchen and put the dead bird in it and then put it in the garbage can outside. He cleaned the birdcage out thoroughly and then put down fresh papers and filled the dish with seed. He said to the bird that remained, "It's just you and me now, bud."

Smokey thought about what had happened. Had the dark forces retaliated? Smokey had burned the demon bird. Did the dark forces kill his budgie as an act of revenge? A life for a life or an eye for an eye, as in the Old Testament? He had felt the darkness the previous night and the hand of death within his room. These things could not be explained in terms of logic.

Chapter XXX

Classes didn't start until next week but Smokey went to the university and picked out his textbooks. His student loan had gone through. Smokey thought, *I'm going to have to get a good paying job next summer to pay down some of my debt.* He purchased his textbooks and sat in the student lounge looking through them. The first few French classes looked easy, but he knew it would get tougher later on. Calculus looked like a nightmare, but he had little choice about that. As far as he knew he had to take it.

The third class, political theory, started with Rousseau. Smokey began reading the "Discourses" and the "Social Contract." There was more depth to Rousseau than the classical philosophers like Hobbes or Plato. The classical philosophers had believed in the physical inequality of man. Rousseau saw more than a physical inequality; he saw a moral equality as well. Then there was the whole notion of man having a changeable nature, a free will, which allowed for the social contract. It was societal institutions which created inequality, but man accepted this inequality. Smokey became confused and frustrated with Rousseau before the classes even started. Did he lack the critical mind to fully understand Rousseau? Could he not get beyond classical thought? He rode the bus home feeling like he had made a mistake in all his classes. But there was no choice; he had to take these classes.

Smokey sat in his calculus class and numbers swirled in his mind. The numbers changed into shapes, mostly triangles, then pyramid-type images appeared in his mind's eye. He was having trouble listening to the professor. Every time the professor spoke a voice in his head would shout out something else. He tried reading the text, but it was difficult to understand without lecture support. At the end of the class he realized he had learned absolutely nothing. A similar thing happened in his French class. The voice in his head confused him and he couldn't hear what the teacher was saying. By the time his third class began, Smokey was in a very confused state. He tried desperately to understand what the professor was saying, but it was no use. His own mind wouldn't let him think. (He thought to himself, *Rousseau is a lot like duality or arguing against duality. The fact that you argue against is an opposite and therefore remains a form of duality.*) There were so many ambiguities in Rousseau. How could he even hope to understand? Moreover, every time the professor explained something, the voices would cut in and leave him confused.

At the end of the first three weeks Smokey knew that he was in trouble. Calculus was simply beyond him at this point. He had failed his first French test, and Rousseau eluded him. But it was more than that—it was the voices in his head, all the time now an inner dialogue with the devil, if you will. Still, Smokey felt he couldn't give up. He struggled with his classes up till the last possible day for withdrawal without failure. On that day Smokey withdrew from all three classes and left the university feeling ashamed and beaten.

Because he withdrew so late, there was no refund from his classes. The student loan money would not see him through till spring. It was now December, and he had less then one thousand dollars to pay for next semester's classes, pay rent, and buy food till the end of April. He had to decide if he was going to go back to school in January and try again. If he didn't go back and pass all his classes he would never get another student loan, but he didn't have enough money left to pay a full semester of classes. What was he going to do?

He went to the Welfare office to ask for help, but since he had taken a student loan out he was unable to get assistance until after April the following year. The next five months Smokey would have to live on two hundred a month. After rent was paid he would have seventy-five dollars. He definitely was in trouble.

Smokey sat with Walter and watched afternoon soap operas. Walter had lost his job in September and was having trouble making the mortgage payments on UIC. Smokey's sister was working a minimum wage job and paying $250 a month in student loans repayment. Nobody had any money!

It was the twentieth of December when Smokey received a call from the welfare office. They wanted him to take a vocational rehabilitation and assessment program. He would work for an employer and they would assess his value while the government paid his salary. He would work fours hours a day, five days a week, and earn about four hundred dollars a month. Smokey thought this would work out. He could work in the morning and go to school in the afternoon and evening.

"For whom will I be working?" Smokey asked. When he got the answer, Smokey was pissed off. It would be the same department store chain that had hired him to stock shoes in Winnipeg. The same department store that had sprayed him with solvent and destroyed his brain would now determine his merits as an employee again. This was tough to swallow, but he needed the money desperately. He said, "Okay."

It was Christmas Day. There were no presents or tree, but they had all chipped in and bought a turkey. Walter was busy carving it down to the bone. Smokey's sister was making a salad. Smokey sat in the living room and relaxed. There was hope for the New Year. He would make enough money to pay rent and attend university too. Things didn't look so bad. He's had one bad semester; he could recover from that, no problem. They ate dinner and there was lots left over for turkey sandwiches the next day.

* * *

The holiday season was over and Smokey sat in the counselor's office at the university. He explained his failure the past semester and also pointed out his weaknesses in language and math. He asked, "Is there any alternative to Calculus?"

The counselor said, "Yes, there is! You can take logic as an alternative for your math requirement. As for your language, you should really try Cree. A lot of people have had success with learning a Native language."

Smokey decided to take the two classes, and he thought with work in the morning that would be plenty, especially with the drugs he was on. He signed up for Cree 100 and Logic 151 and bought the texts at the University bookstore. Classes would start next week.

Smokey walked through the doors of the department store determined to maintain his dignity, but it wouldn't be easy. They had him doing every shit job you could think of. They had no intention of training him in any particular area. He was just there to do the jobs that nobody else wanted to do or would do. Some days were better than others. He didn't mind the display work, but it bothered him that the man next to him doing the same job as him got eleven dollars an hour and Smokey got five dollars an hour. For the first few weeks Smokey really tried to impress people, but soon he realized nobody cared. He was just a loser, a mental patient the government paid to have around. The other workers viewed him with suspicion or ignored him. There were a couple of good guys there; the boiler inspectors were always fair to him. However, after a few weeks Smokey did the bare minimum to get by and that was all. He knew they would never hire him when the government program ran out. They would say he was unfit as an employee. He just survived each day the best he could and looked forward to school.

His two new classes started out easy. In logic the arguments were so simple. Roses are red; apples are red, therefore roses are apples. It was that simple in the beginning. Cree was a lot of fun; there was no English spoken. Smokey learned greetings in Cree the first day: *Tanisi, namoia nanatoe.* He was really enjoying these classes, and the voices that had plagued him the previous semester were much reduced—not completely gone but much improved. He could concentrate on the subjects at hand and not have to fight with the devil.

Nevertheless, Smokey wasn't normal, as one would classify it—though who is to say what normal really is? He still heard voices, and he still had feelings of intense paranoia. He still wondered about Alexander Kazzer and the department store management. He still wondered if the government was bugging his apartment. These feelings died hard. It took a lot of insight to realize that these thoughts were symptoms of the illness. Smokey wasn't convinced that it was all in his head.

The days passed slowly at work, but he had his classes to which to look forward. He felt if he could get a good summer job things would be okay. Spring came and with it the end of classes. He had done very well with a final grade of 86 percent in Cree and 72 percent in logic. Even though he had only managed two classes out of a minimum of six for the student loan requirements, he felt he had done well to recover. The fact that he had only completed two classes, however, meant he would never get another student loan. He had to find work. The four hours a day he worked at the department store paid his rent and food, but he was still unable to save any money.

With spring came new problems, one of which was Walter had defaulted on his mortgage payments and was now in a situation where he would lose the house. Walter said, "I'm sorry, Smokey, but I have to give you notice. I'll be having to turn over the keys to the bank in less than thirty days. Even if I got full time work now, it is too late to save the house." Smokey said he understood and he would start looking for housing right away.

That same day his sister gave him some other news. She was moving to Ontario to find better opportunities. In one day Smokey would lose not only his housing but also his only remaining family support. Smokey had gotten used to her singing. Just to be able to touch base with a family member was important. Suddenly Smokey felt overwhelmed. It was too much to handle—he couldn't do it! Smokey felt sick to his stomach. It had been too much, the last year or so. Leaving Winnipeg for Weyburn, then Weyburn for Regina, saying goodbye to family, poor paying jobs, welfare, and student loans. And being diagnosed with depression and schizophrenia was something to this day he barely had a grip on. He just couldn't cope with another move, and yet there was no choice in the matter. The bank would lock the doors at the end of the month, so he had to move.

It was soon evident that he could not find a place for one hundred twenty-five dollars a month. The very cheapest places were double that and there weren't very many nice places to live.

Toward the middle of the month he phoned his friend Bill, who was looking for a place as well. Then Bill said, "How do you feel about sharing a place? It would be cheaper and we could get a nice place."

Smokey said, "Sure, it sounds great to me." The next day Bill picked Smokey up after work and they went hunting for a place to live. Most of the two bedrooms were over five hundred dollars, but there were a few in the four hundred dollar range. They had little success the first day of looking, but they felt toward the end of the week would be better.

Smokey woke to the sound of shattering glass. He looked out the window and saw three kids running down the street. He slipped on his jacket and went out to see what had happened. The windows in his car were smashed out, except for the front windshield. Smokey got a cardboard box and some work gloves and began picking up the glass off the seats and floor of the car. He was calculating the cost in his mind, the price of four side windows and a rear window for this car. He had no insurance other than what came with the registration, which meant he had nothing. The cost of the replacement windows would be more than the value of the car.

Smokey did what any poor man would do. He walked to Canadian Tire and bought a roll of clear plastic and a roll of duct tape. He made windows out of the plastic and taped them on the car. He knew if the police stopped him he would be charged. The clear plastic distorted images and was unsafe.

The next thing Smokey did was phone Red and ask if he could store a canoe for him for a while. Red said, "Sure, no problem. Bring it over."

Smokey brought the canoe over that evening and they sat around and talked about old times. It felt good. Smokey had missed Red. Red said "Any time you want to use the canoe, just let me know. I'm off work at 3:00 P.M." Red noticed Smokey's car and asked, "Are you going to get some windows for it?"

Smokey said, "No, I can't afford it. It needs engine work anyway and the plates are due. I'll phone the auto wrecker at the end of the month."

After leaving Red, Smokey took a drive out into the country. It was a beautiful night. All the stars were out. Smokey thought, *I'm going to miss the freedom of transportation. I am giving up a lot this month; my family, my home, and my car. If I didn't have my four hours a day work I think I'd go insane. Even if there is no chance of permanent employment, it keeps me busy for at least fours hours a day.*

When Smokey finished work for the day, he rode the bus home. Janet's little Datsun was three-quarters packed when he got there. She said "I want to make it to Brandon tonight if I can."

Smokey said, "That's a long drive. Don't push it too hard."

He helped her with the remaining things; the last things to go in were her guitar and her dog, Hobo. She gave him a hug and said, "I know you're going to be all right. I've prayed about this. Things will work out for you and Bill. You'll find a nice place. Goodbye."

"Goodbye." Smokey said as the Datson let out a puff of blue exhaust and putted down the street.

Smokey understood her need to move on. There were no jobs in Regina other than minimum wage. You can't pay your student loan on five dollars a hour, not when you're twenty thousand dollars in debt like his sister was. Twenty thousand dollars for a philosophy degree. Was Smokey's aim of a political science degree any better? If he couldn't get into law school, what good would a political science degree be? There was journalism, but Smokey really wasn't interested in that. There were public service jobs, but how to get hired on? It was the same old problem. He must get his masters in political science and gain admittance to law school.

Smokey went back into the house and phoned Bill. Bill had three places for them to check out. They agreed to meet after supper about 7:00 P.M. Bill pulled up to the house at five minutes to seven. Smokey said, "Right on time."

The first place they looked at had lots of stairs and it was in the north end. The stairs would be difficult for Bill to manage. They decided to turn the place down. The second place was also in the north end but a way from the bus route. It was on the main floor, but neither of them liked the place. It was also too much money. The best place they checked out was in the Cathedral area near downtown and bus routes. It was a cozy little two bedroom on the main floor and the price was just $450. That would be $225 each plus hydro. Smokey thought he could handle that. He made $400, so it left him with $175 for food, clothing, transportation, and hydro. They both agreed that this was the right place. They got the place for the beginning of the month.

Smokey went to Welfare to see if he could get anything for hydro and the increase in rent since he became eligible for assistance again when classes ended in the spring. He received $125 from Welfare, plus the $400 he earned at the department store.

It was the end of the month and time to move. They got the keys to the new place on the twenty-seventh, which gave them time to move in slowly. Bill had arranged a party of people to help with the move. Smokey packed his own things in the car. He filled it full in less than an hour. The last thing he put in his car was his bird. He drove over to the new apartment and started unloading things into his room. When he was finished he brought the bird into the apartment.

The building manager met him at the door and said, "No pets allowed."

Smokey said, "It's only a bird."

"Birds make noise," said the building manager. "This is not allowed."

Smokey said "Well, give me a few days to find a home for him."

The building manager grudgingly said, "Okay."

Bill arrived with the gang a half hour later, and Smokey helped unload Bill's things. Bill had a couch and a television, which would be great. Together they pieced together a stereo. When the crew had finished moving everything in, Bill ordered pizza for everyone. They sat around eating and talking.

Smokey said, "Anyone want a budgie?"

They were silent.

Bill said, "I think my brother would like it. We'll take it over to him later."

When everyone had gone Bill said, "Okay, let's get rid of the bird." They took Bill's car and headed over to Bill's brother's place. Bill's brother met them at the front door.

"What's that you got there?" he asked.

"It's a present," Bill said.

"What kind of present?"

"It's a bird, a budgie."

"For me?" Bill's brother's eyes lit up. "Cool," he said. "Really cool. Thank you!"

Smokey said, "Higgledy, meet John. John, say hello to Higgledy."

They stayed for coffee and talked with John for a while. John had muscular dystrophy also. Of the four boys in the family, two developed the disease, both Bill and John. John was a bit of a backyard mechanic, but he no longer had the physical strength to do a lot of the work. At times his bitterness boiled over, but who could blame him? It was a horrible disease to have.

Who said God was just? I think not, Smokey thought to himself. *At least it's something I'll never understand, why God would create such diseases, diseases of the body or diseases of the mind.*

They arrived back at their new apartment late that evening. Smokey no longer had a bed so he curled up on the couch for the night. Tomorrow they would go looking for a bed after work.

* * *

Smokey had been to every used furniture shop in the city by the end of the day. Everything was too expensive.

Smokey sat with Bill at the Utopia Café. "I guess I'll just have to use the couch for a while."

Bill said, "Let's see if Jack comes in. He often has deals on furniture and things."

Jack came in about twenty minutes later. Bill said, "Jack, got any beds and dressers for sale?"

Jack said, "How much you want to spend?"

Smokey said, "A hundred bucks."

"I can get you something for that, I guess. When do you need it?"

Smokey said, "Yesterday."

"I'll drop it off here tomorrow," Jack said.

"Can you deliver it to our apartment?" Smokey asked.

"Okay. Give me the address," Jack said.

It was done. Smokey was getting a bed and dresser for a hundred dollars. Not bad! They had finished their coffee and were just about to leave when Roger brought out his latest painting, a picture of the Mona Lisa. It was really cool. Bill had to have it. Ten dollars later they brought back a Mona Lisa for the apartment living room.

That evening Smokey called the auto wrecker and had his car hauled to the dump. Smokey thought to himself, *If I were making a decent wage and working full-time things would be different. I could afford to fix the car, but it doesn't seem likely this year.*

Smokey continued to look for full-time employment through the summer, but by August he had given up hope. It looked like school was out of the question for the coming fall. Smokey thought to himself, *How much more do I have to take, living on five hundred dollars a month and half of it going to rent with no opportunity to educate and improve myself*? The more Smokey thought about it, the more depressed he became. There had to be a solution. If he couldn't work for the money and he couldn't get a student loan, how could he get the money to go to school? There was only one option left. He phoned his brother in Toronto that evening and asked to borrow the money for two university classes for the fall. His brother said, "Never mind repaying it. It's a gift."

Smokey said, "Thank you."

Knowing that he could go to school lifted Smokey's spirits a great deal. He could manage on five hundred dollars a month for a future of promise.

It was late Friday afternoon when Bill met him at the Utopia Café. Bill said, "How would you feel about a trip to the Bad Lands, the Big Muddy?" Smokey loved the Bad Lands. It was always a spiritual experience of sorts when he could go.

Smokey said, "I would love to go."

Bill said, "I invited Barrie to come along too."

Smokey felt a pang of dread. This was the man who had given Smokey the demon bird. Would he know that Smokey destroyed it? Should he confess? Should he stay home? What should he do? He almost feared the man's power. The man was truly a shaman. Just for a moment he felt again the talons of the demon bird tighten on his left shoulder, and in his mind's eye he saw black feathers about his head. A shiver went through Smokey's spine. Then Smokey snapped out of it and said to himself, "I'm going, that's all there is to it. I have nothing to fear!"

They went home and packed their things. Smokey hadn't used his tent for years, but it was still in good shape. Bill had a camp stove and an old coffee pot for the morning coffee. Barrie showed up ready to go about seven o'clock the next morning. They hit the highway by eight. Bill and Barrie talked about art and other things. Smokey sat in silence and looked at the landscape as it changed. He felt a burning in his chest, not a bad feeling, sort of warm and comforting. He also felt a tingling in his hands. This meant that he was close to power. He could feel Barrie's power.

They reached the valley of the Big Muddy by noon. They followed the road to a small campsite not far from Rock Glen. They set up their tents and unrolled their sleeping bags. It was hot—hotter than hot. It had to be close to 100 degrees in the shade, and there wasn't much shade. There were shrubs but no tall trees in this part of the world. It was grassland and tumbleweeds with sand and clay cliffs carved out by the winds. There was no wind today, however, it was completely still. The only sounds one heard were the locusts buzzing. Then they heard an eagle cry. They looked up, and there were three of them.

Bill said, "Three of us and three of them!"

"That's not insignificant," said Barrie.

They took off for the cliffs on the other side of the valley. With every breath Smokey took he could feel his spirit strengthen. This was God's country, not useable for farming but, oh, so beautiful, a refuge for eagles, hawks, deer, and other wildlife.

Smokey said, "This is where I want to be when I die. Scatter my ashes into the prairie wind and let me soar like an eagle."

Barrie said, "We will do that for you."

Bill said, "There's my brother sitting on that post." On the post sat a red-tailed hawk with its talons in a mouse or small rodent of some kind.

They walked further into the cliffs. Bill used a cane to help himself balance on the uneven earth. Each man then separated from the others and went off on his own journey. Smokey was wandering through the grasslands looking at the cacti in bloom. He saw a dark shape in the grass and went over to see what it was. It was a very large feather. Smokey took it with him. He knew it would be important.

They all met back at the cliffs an hour later. Barrie asked, "What did you find, Smokey?"

Smokey said, "A feather."

Barrie exclaimed, "That's an eagle feather! The one who holds it must speak the truth. Would you like to trade?"

"What have you got to trade?" Smokey asked.

Barrie brought out a small leather pouch.

Smokey said, "Sure I'll trade!" and gave Barrie the feather.

Barrie said, "Now I'll speak the truth." He undid the leather pouch and poured out six stones. Actually there were only five stones, but one was split in half. Barrie said, "These stones represent the journey of your mind. Look at them, pick them up, and feel them in your hand. The first stone is a very dark stone, split in half. This represents your present state of mind. You are often confused and torn on which way to go. Old beliefs systems will fail you in this struggle. You will grow, and as you grow your mind will become more clear and focused on life. Each stage in your mind's growth is to be cherished. Pick up the last stone and feel it!"

The last stone was a smooth, round, white rock. It felt small in his hand, but it represented clarity of mind and strength of character. He felt a warm glow in his chest as he felt the white stone.

Barrie said, "This progression of mind is your life, a journey not unlike my own. I can't help you with your struggle; it is yours alone to deal with. But I want you to know I love you like a brother."

Smokey found that as he held the stones in his hand he was weeping. The man loved him like a brother and Smokey had feared him. Smokey wanted to say, "I killed your child, the demon bird," but he couldn't. He was silent in his new found love and guilt.

They went back to their campsite, and Bill brought out the coffee pot. They sat in a circle around a fire pit. It was too dry to light a fire. A few stray sparks and the land would be in flames.

Smokey said, "This cowboy coffee is pretty rough stuff."

Bill said, "It's as good as Robin's Doughnut's coffee." They all laughed.

That evening the moon came out round and full. As they sat in the glow of the moon they listened to the coyotes howl.

Smokey crawled into his tent for the night. He had a lot about which to think. The most important thing he had to figure out was love, friendship, and self-preservation. He felt that killing the demon bird had been self-preservation on his part, yet it had been the murder of a child—Barrie's child about whom he cared. Barrie said that he loved him. Would someone who loved you hurt you? Perhaps if it was to help you grow. No, Barrie had never meant to hurt him; it was the gift of a helping spirit. How had the spirit turned so dark? Was it always a dark force? *I can't help feeling I have killed his child and it's a terrible feeling of guilt. You can blame it on cultural differences or misunderstandings; nevertheless, I am responsible,* Smokey thought.

That night Smokey dreamed of Sherry. Her hair was long and a flaming red. No, this wasn't Sherry, it was someone new. They were holding hands and lighting fires with their free hands. When Smokey woke the next morning he could smell the smoke in the air. It was distant, but there was definitely a prairie fire burning somewhere.

They broke camp and took the car up the valley to some new cliffs. As Bill parked the car at the side of the road a white-tailed dear sprang out from behind a clump of bushes. They all went their own ways for about an hour, then they returned.

Barrie was planting something in the ground, at least he was making a digging motion.

Smokey asked, "What are you doing?"

Barrie said, "I'm burying my old spirit and starting over with a new spirit. It's symbolic, like when a Christian is baptized in water, he dies and is brought back to life with the breath of the spirit. The breath of the Spirit is in this land. All we must do is open our hearts and shed our old selves." Barrie said, "You have something for me?"

Smokey said, "How did you know?"

Barrie just smiled.

Smokey brought out the rock he had found. It looked like a serpent's head. Smokey said, "It's Satan fossilized."

Barrie laughed and said, "I love it. I can feel the power it has!"

Bill had found a piece of wood that looked very interesting. It looked like a small whale trying to come through a wave. "With a little carving here and there, I think we will have something," Bill said.

It was a great weekend. They returned to the city with just a touch of sadness. They dropped Barrie at his apartment and said their goodbyes.

On the way back to the apartment, Bill said, "Do you want to stop somewhere for coffee?"

Smokey said, "Sure!"

They sat at the coffee shop and the subject matter returned to art. Bill said, "You're not creating sculptures anymore. Why not?"

Smokey said, "It has to do with my illness. I thought I was possessed and I was capturing spirits from hell."

Bill said, "There are forces that we can't explain when we create, but I think it's a gift. You have the gift too. I really like your sculptures. An artist, and I consider you a folk artist of sorts, needs to create. You will never be happy unless you are creating."

Smokey knew it was true. Even with school he had felt an emptiness without his sculptures. Even if he could hear his sculptures talking to one another, it was a gift. He would create again.

Chapter XXXI

Smokey said, "I'll pick up some clay this week."

Bill said, "Good man, you will be happier for it; also, there is an artist co-op you can join and show your work to the public."

Smokey said, "It seems almost a tragedy that I have to return to the department store tomorrow after the weekend we had."

"Yes," said Bill. "We have a special connection with that place. It's spiritual."

"At least I have school to look forward to in a couple of weeks."

"And I have my new job at the pre-school as an art instructor."

Smokey said, "Congratulations on the new job, it should be great."

The next day after work, Smokey bought forty pounds of red clay. It was heavy and hard to carry on the bus, but he made it home safely without any problems.

When he got to the apartment, Bill handed him a package that had come in the mail. Smokey opened it with enthusiasm. It contained the money order for the university classes and a book, *The Sun My Heart* by Thich Nhat Hanh, from his brother. It was a book on meditation.

Smokey brought out the sitting cushion that his brother had given him for Christmas years ago. He had never used it, but as he looked at it and held the book in his hand, he knew there was a lot of love being sent forth from his brother.

Smokey said, "I'll read the book and sit for ten or fifteen minutes a day. I'm looking for new paths; I'm not sure I'm ready, but I'll try."

To sit for fifteen minutes a day seemed like a small commitment, but Smokey found out that it was harder than he first thought. He learned from his brother in a telephone conversation that he could count his breath when he sat and that that would help him stay focused and in the moment.

* * *

Smokey sat at the table with a lump of clay. The artist co-op was having an opening in two weeks. Smokey needed to have a piece ready by then. He would have to work fast. He felt the clay in his hands; he moved his fingers this way, then that. Gradually a head formed out of the clay and from the head Smokey sculpted a body in robes. Then came the arms, which held a large cross. It was going to be a priest. Next he sculpted a large erect penis coming out of the priest's robes. He thought a moment, *What should I call this sculpture*? Then it came to him. It would be called, "Lord, Forgive That Flirtatious Altar Boy." Then he laughed. He set the sculpture on the window ledge to dry.

He wasn't done sculpting. It had been a long time and creativity was raging in his blood. He sat in silence for a moment waiting for the spirit to move him. Then he heard the call of a loon in his mind. He began to sculpt the body of a loon, then the head. At first it looked more like a duck, but gradually he got the shape right. As he did the feathers on the body of the loon, a face began to appear on its back. Soon there was a complete face embedded in the back of the loon. It looked great. "I will call this the spirit rider," said Smokey. He put the sculpture of the loon on the window ledge with the priest and put away the clay for the day.

Bill came home a little later and said, "I really like the loon."

Smokey said, "It's yours when I'm done showing it at the art co-op opening."

It was time to register for classes at university. Smokey rode the bus there, arriving at about 1:00 P.M. after finishing work for the day at the department store. Smokey already knew which classes he would take. He would finish his language requirement by taking another class in Cree, and he would take an advanced political science class. The class he chose in political science was called Prairie Populist Movements. He decided to walk home after paying for his classes and getting his texts. It was a lovely day in late August, and Smokey decided to stop by the lake to see if any canoes were on the lake or maybe a sailboat.

* * *

It was the middle of September, and Smokey had just finished his political science class for the day. It was interesting to find out the politics in the 1930s. He found out that there was a large KKK following in rural Saskatchewan. There were no black people so the Klan focused their hatred on the Catholic Irish.

As he wandered down the hall he bumped into Sharon. She smiled and asked, "How have you been?"

Smokey said, "Fine." "Will you come for dinner tonight?" she asked. "Sure, I'd love to."

"See you at seven this evening," she said. "Bye."

Smokey decided he would stay at campus until 7:00 P.M. Sharon had a campus room with a shared kitchen and bath.

Smokey knocked on Sharon's door at 7:00 P.M. She answered and let him in. "Dinner will be a few minutes," she said.

Smokey sat in the kitchen with her and they talked as Sharon prepared the meal. This was Sharon's last semester here in Canada. If she continued her studies, she would do so in Hong Kong. She said, "I love Canada, but Hong Kong is my home." Smokey helped her set the table. She smiled at him and said, "Thank you for sharing dinner with me." They sat down to their meal. Smokey felt a darkness come over his mind. It sent a shiver through his spine. Then it happened.

"*Fucking slant-eyed chink*!"

"Oh my God, I didn't say that! I couldn't have said that. Dear God, no!"

Smokey looked down at his plate. He didn't want to look up but he knew he had to. He saw her brush a tear from her cheek. Smokey said, "I'm very sorry."

There was silence, a deathly silence. Then she spoke in a whisper. She said, "Please go."

Smokey got up and made his way to the door. He looked back, but she was gazing out the window.

Smokey started walking home. As he walked he became more and more angry. Finally he stopped and shouted into the wind, "Thank you, Jesus! Thank you, God!" with all the bitter sarcasm he could muster. "What kind of God are you to let this happen? I didn't want to say that. How does this shit come out of my mouth? I know I'm not possessed anymore. I have a disease. But you are the creator and you made the disease. What kind of God are you? Are you some kind of Nazi? What happened to the loving, caring God, the God who died for us? What happened to the compassion of God? How could you let this happen? She was my best friend in the university. Why? Why? Why?" There was only the wind in his ears. God was silent.

When Smokey got home he flopped on his bed and stared up at the ceiling. He opened up his book, *The Sun my Heart*, and began to read. His mind was very agitated, but as the book said, if you sit, you will settle, so Smokey pulled out his cushion and sat. He thought about what had happened and he was filled with a deep sorrow. He began to count his breath. Soon he couldn't hear the numbers in his mind. He was gone. When he came to he felt the pain in his legs. He felt his cheeks wet with tears. He sat for another ten minutes and counted his breath, trying to stay in the moment.

Smokey got up and went to the drug store. He found a blank card with some beautiful prairie flowers on it. In the card he wrote, "Please forgive my ignorance!" He signed it and mailed it to Sharon. He had done what he could to repair the damage, but he knew it would take time.

It was opening night at the artist co-op. Smokey had finished his two pieces in time, and he was excited about showing them. There was a lot of folk-type art there. It was good stuff, and it was a fun evening. Smokey met a lot of young artists, some of whom were very talented. Bill's work was the best, however.

At the end of the evening Bill and Smokey went for pizza. Bill said, "You seem a bit down. What's up?"

Smokey said, "It's my illness. It's getting worse. I thought it was really bad when I stood up in church and shouted obscenities, but things are even worse now."

Bill asked, "How can they be worse?"

"I can't say, but trust me, they are," Smokey said.

Bill said, "It is time to see your doctor."

Smokey nodded. "I'll see him tomorrow."

* * *

Smokey sat in the waiting room of the mental health clinic. This time he didn't question why he was there. He knew he needed help.

They called his name and Smokey went in. The secretary said, "You will have a new psychiatrist today. Don't worry, she is nice."

Smokey went in and the psychiatrist introduced herself and told him to have a seat. "I have just been reviewing your file. You are doing pretty well," she said.

Smokey said, "I'm not doing well, doctor. I'm saying things out loud."

"What kinds of things are you saying?" she asked.

"Does it really matter?" Smokey asked.

She said, "Yes, it does."

Smokey said, "First of all I stood up in church and asked Jesus to suck my cock. Then I called my best friend a slant-eyed chink. I didn't want to say these things. They just came out of my mouth like shit from a goose."

She smiled and said, "I know it's painful, but this is the nature of the disease. It's a chemical imbalance in your brain. We'll try a heavier dosage of medication, but it will make you tired."

Smokey said, "I'm tired all the time now anyway and I'm always hungry, even when I haven't done anything. Before medications I was 180 pounds. Now I'm 240 pounds tired and fat!"

She said, "There are limits to what we can do for you. We don't have a magic wand, but let us try this and see what happens."

Smokey said, "Okay."

Smokey sat in the university cafeteria, half hoping to see Sharon, half dreading it. It didn't happen, so he brought out the draft essay on which he was working. He had decided to do an essay on a contemporary movement in the prairies. He would compare the Grant Devine government with its views on privatization, anti-abortion, and family planning centers with the New Christian Right in the United States. It was a delicate study, but there were definite parallels between the two governments, and it was a populist movement. He worked on his essay for about two hours, and then he took a coffee break.

It was lonely at school sometimes, thousands of students but no real friends. The one friend he had in Sharon he probably lost forever. It was his fault, and yet it wasn't. The words had come out of his mouth, therefore he was responsible, yet he had never wanted or intended to say such a horrible thing. It was the malfunction of his brain which had caused it. Smokey thought to himself, *Will I lose all my friends? What if I make some rude remark about Bill's disability? Will I lose him as a friend too? This disease is a social time-bomb–you never know when it's going to explode into a socially unacceptable statement or behavior. Thank you, God...bastard!*"

How do you reconcile a loving heavenly father with a God who dishes out mental and physical disabilities? Why must some suffer so much more than others? The more he thought about it, the more he began to realize that his childhood concept of God was flawed. He couldn't find the answers to his questions–if there were any answers to be found in Christian fundamentalism. He began to question all that he had been taught.

He began to think about the possibility of past lives and about karma. Karmic influences could explain why he was given this disease. Though karma is far too complex to understand completely, one can begin to understand the world as an organ of balance, and we must balance ourselves. There may be consequences from past life experience which result in some mental impairment or physical disability. It was a topic he could discuss with Bill some time, Smokey thought.

* * *

Smokey walked along the shores of Wascana Lake on a chilly November afternoon. He knew that he was making progress at school, and he had Bill's friendship, plus his art and sculptures to work on. Yet his life felt incomplete. It lacked female companionship and intimacy. He wasn't sure how to resolve the problem. He had no idea how to go about getting a date. Even in high school he had been a misfit. He walked around the lake twice thinking about how nice it would be to have female companionship or a lover once again. When he got home he opened the classified section of the newspaper he had bought and checked out the companions wanted section. There was nothing in there that caught his eye. He sighed and sat the newspaper down. He thought he should create his own want ad, sort of a personal résumé of sorts, just in case an ad turned up that he liked. It would give him something to think about, how to describe himself in a positive, desirable light. He thought about the things that were important to him, then sat down with paper and pen to compose.

What's important to me? What do I like? Smokey started to write. "I'm an intelligent man in my thirties, a late bloomer still working on an education. I hope to be a lawyer. I love the smoky blues of T-Bone Walker and the soul-searching of Leonard Cohen. Music is very important to me. I love a good movie or a book by Robertson Davies. My passion is canoeing." Smokey thought, *I can work on this and develop a letter with real polish.*

The next day an ad appeared in the paper. "Hi. I recently moved to the city. I'm a slim, good-looking woman in her mid-thirties. I'm looking for an educated, intelligent man who is fit and enjoys a variety of things from music to hockey."

Smokey thought, *I'm going to give it a try and write her a letter.* He wrote the letter and let Bill review it. Bill said, "It's very good. I know she'll like it." Smokey sent the letter the next day.

It was a week later when she called him. Her name was Heather and she loved Leonard Cohen and canoeing. She said, "Send me a photo of yourself."

Smokey said, "Okay." He mailed her a photo and waited.

He waited until December, but then he realized that he would never hear from her again. He was fat and ugly in his present physical condition and nobody would want him. Tired and feeling rejected, he sat down to a lump of clay. He decided he would sculpt a self-portrait. He let his fingers move through the clay, thinking about who he was not just physically but also spiritually. He thought about the changes in his life over the past five years, from a very physically active man to an overweight student struggling for an education. Then there was the spiritual education, which had just begun. After half an hour he gave up on his sculpture and simply said, "I have yet to take form. I am very old, yet I am a child."

That evening Smokey took out his cushion and sat. He started counting his breath. Thoughts would come and go, but he tried not to judge them, just to observe them like his little book, *The Sun My Heart,* said. Time passed, and before he realized it, he had sat for a whole hour. When he was finished he felt rejuvenated, totally refreshed. At this moment Smokey realized that he had indeed found something valuable in the practice of meditation. He gained a sense of peace and a keen sense of awareness. It didn't matter that he couldn't reconcile his concepts of God. He could count his breath.

The next day Smokey phoned his brother, and they talked about Zen meditation for half an hour. His brother promised to send him another book that would be helpful in his practice.

Smokey said, "I still believe in God, but I think I see the truth in karma. I know that I have lived before. This isn't my first time."

His brother said, "It's enough to know karma exists. Don't spend your life trying to understand it; it's just too complex."

Smokey felt a real warmth after talking with his brother, a sense of kindred spirits.

It was Christmas day. Bill carved the turkey that they had chipped in for and bought. Barrie came over for dinner as well. It was a small feast; not only the turkey, but potatoes, carrots, green beans, and squash were all nicely prepared.

After dinner Smokey opened the envelope from his parents. It contained a money order for two more university classes. "Dear second son, we want you to continue in your studies. Merry Christmas." This was a very generous gift, for his parents were by no means wealthy.

Bill said, "You really do have loving parents. You can tell they care about you a lot."

Smokey said, "Indeed, I'm blessed with good friends and family."

Smokey had made each of his two friends a sculpture for Christmas. One was of an Egyptian woman for Bill and the other was a Buddha for Barrie. They were both pleased with the gifts. As evening came on they watched a video called *Lady Hawk,* which everyone enjoyed.

New Years came and went, and it was time to sign up for classes again at university. Smokey would take a class in social statistics and another political science class about regionalism in a federal state. The following day, after signing up for classes, Welfare phoned him and asked him to come in for an interview. When he got to the office, he was worried sick about what could be the problem, but it was nothing serious. His work grant had ended and the department store had deemed him as unfit for employment.

The worker said, "I know you tried really hard there. It's not fair, but we have to go by what they say. You are no longer considered employable. It's not much, but there is a small increase in your living allowance as a result. We will pay your rent plus $195 for food, $40 for a bus pass, and $40 for disability needs. You no longer have to look for work."

Chapter XXXII

Smokey had mixed feelings about this news. He was expecting it but it still made him angry. That department store had used him for a whole year before stating he was unfit for employment. If that were the case, they should have been able to determine his value in a month or two. He had to face it, he had been royally used!

Smokey went and had a talk with the vocational rehabilitation worker. The worker said, "It's a racket there. Nobody ever gets hired on. They just use the employees until the government grant is finished. Don't take it personally. Your replacement won't get hired on either. I'm sorry. We should have done better for you, but placements are hard to get for the mentally ill." Smokey could tell that the worker felt bad, so he let it go.

The worker, whose name was Larry, said, "Come to my office at the club. Sometimes I have odd jobs that need to be done. Don't think it's over. If we find you a part-time job and it works out, your status may change."

* * *

Smokey sat at the table in the university cafeteria. He was reading his text on regionalism in a federal state and drinking coffee when he looked up. There was Sharon standing before him. She said, "I've come to say goodbye. I go home to Hong Kong at the end of the week. I got a B.A. in psychology with honours."

Smokey said, "Congratulations!"

She held out her hand. He took it and shook it gently. He was dripping with guilt and shame. There was so much he wanted to say but he couldn't find the words.

Then she smiled and kissed him on the cheek. "Don't look back," she said. "Look ahead." She turned and walked away.

At that moment Smokey realized that he had been forgiven, or at least it was behind them and there was a tomorrow. Even when you have been forgiven there is a shame that lingers for a moment, and Smokey felt this with intensity. But it was behind him now; he could move on. He could hold his head up once again. Sharon understood compassion.

The winter semester passed quickly. Smokey studied hard and was well prepared for his exams. His exam on regionalism was surprisingly difficult, but then it was an advanced class.

After his exams Bill and Smokey went for pizza to celebrate. Smokey said, "Keep your ears open for cheap bike. I need some form of transportation."

Bill said, "Barrie wants to sell his mountain bike. It would be perfect for you." They drove over to Barrie's and asked about the bike. Barrie said, "For you, fifty dollars."

Smokey said, "It's a deal," and he paid Barrie right on the spot. Smokey rode his new bike home, feeling free as a bird in the wind.

It had only been a week since school was out and Smokey was going crazy with nothing to do. He would ride his bike around Wascana Lake for exercise, but this only filled an hour or two of every day.

Just when he thought he couldn't take another empty day, his uncle phoned him. "Listen, I need an extra man to build grain bins and install windows in homes. Are you interested?"

Smokey said, "I sure am."

"We start tomorrow," his uncle said.

It was tough getting used to the manual labour after a winter of sitting at a desk as a student, but Smokey wasn't going to give up and his uncle was a patient man. Smokey thought, *This is my chance to make a few bucks for classes next fall.*

After two weeks Smokey received his first cheque from work. He now had a dilemma on his hands. If he was honest he would tell Welfare he was working, but if he did that, all his earnings would go into paying rent and food. There wouldn't be enough for university classes in the fall. He knew it was dishonest, but he asked his uncle to cash his cheque for him. Smokey took the money home and put it in a sock in his drawer.

Smokey worked part-time all summer, right up until school started in September. He saved almost two thousand dollars, enough for a full year of classes at university. In September, Smokey registered for classes. Another winter passed, and Smokey did well at school. He had completed the B.A. requirements in political science and was starting his master's program.

* * *

It was the summer of 1993 and Smokey was out of work. His uncle had retired, so there were no grain bins to build or windows to install. Smokey was on welfare again with no job prospects in sight.

Smokey met the postman at the door. His heart gave a little flutter remembering past experiences. He retrieved his mail from the box and went back to the apartment. There was a telephone bill, a letter for Bill, and a statement from the bank for him. Smokey opened the bank statement. It had a letter enclosed. It showed student loan arrears for eight hundred dollars. They were giving him five days to pay the arrears or the loan would be sent to the Secretary of State of Canada and the government would come for the money. The monthly amount was $100. Smokey's personal income for a month was just $275. He couldn't give them $100 every month.

Smokey realized that day that he would never be able to complete his master's program or finance law school if he could get in. Like his dream of being national champion in canoeing, he fell short. He would have to graduate with just a B.A. in political science. Smokey felt like he couldn't handle another failure. If he wasn't going to be a constitutional lawyer, what was he going to be? A second dream was dying.

That night he talked over his situation with Bill. Bill had some good advice. He said, "Go to your doctor and get a letter stating your disability and send it to the Secretary of State of Canada with a letter requesting forgiveness for your student loan."

Although it was good advice Smokey felt terrible about it. It meant that he would further be recognized as useless, someone incapable of employment or paying his debts. It took Smokey a week to actually make up his mind that this was what he must do.

Smokey read the dismal prognosis his doctor gave him in the letter to the federal government. He asked himself, *Am I really that hopeless?* He thought back to Plato and the myth of the metals. *Perhaps I have a bronze heart, one whose existence remains at the bottom of the heap no matter how hard he struggles*, Smokey thought. He began to see clearly how society was structured. There was no way up. If you were born at the bottom that is where you stayed, with only a few exceptions. His brother had crawled to the middle classes, but he was a very bright man and there was the two of them working together, him and his wife, Kathryn. They kept their debt low by taking turns working while going to school. Nevertheless, Smokey was having trouble letting the dream die. He kept hoping for some form of miracle.

Smokey spent the spring and summer at the club although he had vowed never to go back. He found himself drawn to it for the company. He soon became good friends with the vocational rehabilitation worker, Larry, and he would have coffee with him every morning. Larry gave him odd jobs to do and some contract work through Canada Post. He was able to earn an extra $160 each month just doing odd jobs contracted through the Canadian mental health organization.

* * *

It was early August when Smokey received a telephone call from Red. "We need a paddler for our dragon boat team. Are you interested?"

Smokey said, "I haven't done hardly any exercise this year. I'm fifty pounds overweight."

Red said, "It doesn't matter. You have the experience. These races aren't three hours long. They are less than five minutes."

Smokey said, "Okay."

This was the first year for the dragon boat festival in Regina. It was established to promote Asian culture in the West. There were only four boats and sixty-three teams signed up for the competition, including a team from Alberta. The boats held a team of eighteen paddlers, a rudder operator, and a drummer. The drummer set the stroke rate for the paddlers to follow. There was one week of practice before the races began. Sixty-three teams had three half-hour practice sessions throughout the week.

After the first practice Smokey said, "Boy, are we bad!" Everyone laughed. By the third practice, however, they could get their stroke rate up to eighty-five beats of the drum per minute, and they could hold it at that rate with reasonable rhythm. They were ready to be the prairie dragon boat champions.

To start the ceremonies off, an elderly Chinese dignitary told the story of Qu Yuan. More than two thousand years ago, in the Chinese kingdom of Chu, a poet-statesman called Qu Yuan lived. This kingdom was corrupt. The emperor was convinced by others that it was Qu Yuan who was corrupt. He was banished from the kingdom. As a final protest against the government, Qu Yuan threw himself into the Milo River. Local fishermen dashed to their boats to rescue him. They did not reach him in time. Each year on the fifth day of the fifth moon, dragon boat races take place to re-enact the fishermen's attempt to save Qu Yuan. Now this history is shared with Canadian cities.

At the end of his story there was a loud round of applause from all the teams and the crowd on the shoreline. The first four teams lined up at the start line. The gun sounded and they were off. There was the splash of paddles and the *thump-thump-thump* of the dragon boat drums. The crown roared with enthusiasm as two of the boats nearly collided.

Smokey paced back and forth on the shoreline. They had half an hour to wait before their first race. Red was busy handing out new team t-shirts prior to the first race.

Smokey's team was called the Swill City Stokers, and it was a team made up of beginners as well as seasoned marathon paddlers. With twenty-five minutes to go until their first race, Bill came by with his camera. They all stood in a group with their paddles in hand. Bill snapped the shot and took a couple more just to be sure. "Good luck," Bill said. Then he headed for the finish line across the lake so he could catch the winning boat as it crossed the line.

The ten-minute warning sounded, and everyone made their way down to the docks with life jackets on and paddles in hand. They began to find their places in the canoe. Smokey sat at the very back on the right side. With less than five minutes to start-time, they paddled out to the starting line. They waited there for the other three boats. One minute to start time, Smokey's heart pounded in his chest. He flexed his arm and back muscles. The official raised the gun into the air over his head. *Bang*! There was a frenzy of paddles splashing and drums beating.

Smokey's team pulled out in front. They were now pulling their paddles through the water eighty-five times a minute. The crowd began to chant, "Stroke, stroke, stroke!" The drummer yelled out encouragement to the paddlers as they began to gasp for air. They were halfway across the lake. Just a couple of minutes more and they would be there. Smokey concentrated on the beat of the drum and watched the paddler in front of him. They had good rhythm and were closing in on the finish line. They were way out in front of the other boats. They crossed the finish line and their time was recorded. Even if you won your race, if your time was too slow you would not advance to the next round.

After several hours' wait, the Swill City Strokers were told they would advance to the semifinals. Once again Smokey found himself paddling his heart out for three and a half minutes. They won the semifinal heat and would enter the finals against an Alberta team and two others. This was a matter of pride. They had to beat the Alberta team. The two teams were just seconds apart. It was going to be a hell of a race.

There is very little that the teams can use as strategy with such a short race, but Red had a plan. They would start off slow at sixty-five strokes a minute and then increase their stroke rate gradually. This would cut down on the splashing and ensure good rhythm from the start.

The four finalists lined up their boats at the start line and waited. The gun sounded and they were off. The Swill City Strokers dug their paddles in deep and pulled at a steady stroke rate of sixty-five strokes a minute. As they pulled out of the hole, the drummer increased the stroke rate. Soon they were stroking eighty-five times a minute. The Alberta team was right beside them, not more than a foot apart in terms of position. They sped down the lake side by side. They were halfway across the lake now. Smokey felt the muscles in his arm burn, but he kept in rhythm with the others.

The Stokers had pulled out in front by a couple of feet, but the Alberta team started their sprint to the finish line. Then it seemed like the Alberta team was burnt out and the Strokers pulled half a boat-length in front. Smokey gasped for air as he paddled his guts out. They crossed the finish line! It was close, but the Swill City Strokers won by four seconds. They were the prairie dragon boat champions!

As the boat reached the shoreline people gathered around, making it difficult to get out of the boat. They shook hands with the officials and talked to the media. Red was the spokesperson for the team. Smokey was really excited about being a dragon boat champion. He could see himself on the podium with the group. Then fear struck his heart! What if he said something rude or offensive while he was up on stage in front of all those people. He knew that it was a possibility given his mental illness and past experiences. What should he do? Should he stay away from the award ceremonies, or should he go and trust himself?

This dilemma was a new reality for Smokey. He always had to weigh the odds between being with people and enjoying their company and the security of solitude. Solitude meant safety but also loneliness, whereas socializing could be great but it brought about certain risk, such as the risk of humiliation, or worse, confrontation. After what had happened with Sharon, Smokey had avoided people from the Chinese community. He was embarrassed and ashamed. He knew that avoiding people was not the answer, but he couldn't risk another experience like before. Now he would be on stage in front of hundreds of Asians from the community. Could he control these outbursts of garbage? Was it worth the risk?

Smokey sat down at the edge of the lake. The sun was setting, a large red ball with pink clouds around it. Smokey knew he had to make a decision about the coming evening. Could he trust himself? He skipped a rock across the lake. He counted the skips—one, two, three, four, five, six. Six was not an unlucky number like four, but three sixes was the number of the beast. Red came up beside him. "Need a ride to the award ceremonies?" Red asked. The decision had to be made, now or never.

Smokey said, "Yes."

"Let's go!" Red said.

The Swill City Strokers sat at two tables near the front stage at the center of the arts where the ceremonies were being held. After a few minutes' introduction, the third-place team was announced, and they went up on stage to the sounds of hoots and hollers. Then it was the second-place team, the Alberta team's turn to take the stage. Finally the announcer called the Swill City Strokers to the stage to a thunderous round of applause along with a few catcalls as well. Each Stroker received a medallion, handmade by the Chinese ladies' auxiliary. They were very unique with colours of red, gold, and silver.

When the medallion was placed on Smokey's head all his anxiety faded into nothing. He was being honoured, and it felt wonderful. Smokey wore his medallion every day for a week after the celebrations.

That evening when he got home and settled on his cushion for an evening sitting he thought to himself, *Yes, there are still some good days, and I am thankful for them.*

Smokey sat with Larry in the club office and shared a pot of coffee. As Smokey sipped his coffee he thought about the coming months. He said, "I've saved $480 from the part-time work you have given me this summer. I'm wondering what I should do with the money. I really need new clothes, and it would be nice to go to a show once in a while. The problem is, what do I do with myself all day if I don't go to school? I have enough money for one university class. It seems futile, however, to continue to go to school without hope of ever achieving my master's degree. At the rate of one class per semester, I'll be fifty before I graduate."

"I think you need to go for the intellectual stimulation," Larry said. "I don't think you're ready yet to give up studies."

Smokey thought for a few moments, then he said, "I think you're right. I have no illusions anymore about achieving a master's degree, but I can go for the sheer stimulation of the class. I'll sign up next week."

"A couple of things you may be interested in this fall are trash clean-up after pro football games and yard clean-up when the leaves fall. If you're interested you can take charge of a work crew for both these items."

Smokey said, "Yes, I'm interested." So although Smokey didn't have a lot of things to keep himself busy, with one university class for intellectual stimulation plus part-time work, he had enough to maintain sanity.

Chapter XXXIII

It was the last week in August. The sun was blisteringly hot. Smokey sat by Wascana Lake and thought about his spirit. *It is true I have an illness, but I also believe in the power of the spirit, he thought. I know I have certain powers and gifts of the occult. I don't understand everything, but I know I have powers that influence the weather like a rainmaker in ancient times.* "My breath is wind, hot and dry," he said as he exhaled a breath of air from his lungs.

Smokey felt the wind accelerate and the clouds begin to form. He could feel the change in the weather begin to happen. There was going to be a storm! He could feel his chest constrict and the electrical currents like lightning pulsed through his body. He began to beat the ground with a stick in rhythm to the electrical impulses in his body. The wind blew briskly against his chest, and clouds moved swiftly to block out the sun. The clouds darkened. With sudden awareness and foresight, Smokey realized what he had done. He had summoned up the wind and rains in excess. There was going to be a tornado somewhere close by! The rain began to fall, and there was a crack of lightning that lit the darkened sky.

Smokey sat under a large elm tree and contemplated his actions. *If lightning strikes anything in the city I am responsible. If a tornado touches down in an urban center I am also responsible.* A wave of guilt came over him. *How could I have allowed this to happen?* Smokey thought to himself. *I must learn to control my emotions when I'm angry or frustrated with society. I must learn to vent it in constructive ways. How do I control this darkness that swells inside me?*

Smokey made his way home through the pouring rain. When he got home he jumped into a hot shower, then made himself a pot of coffee. As he drank his hot coffee he thought about the contemporary rainmaker. He brought out his block of clay and set it on the kitchen table. He began to sculpt a figure of the contemporary rainmaker. It was to be a sculpture of self. *What do I look like? What exists but is unseen? Do I have wings? I think I have both wings and hands. I hear the beat of the drum. I'm beating a drum. I feel the rhythm.* He let his hands flow through the clay, shaping and reshaping until finally it was finished. It was half human, half beast, with wings of darkness and hands of light. It was both angel and demon whose hands beat a drum. The drum echoed into the voids of space. He could hear it in his mind. "I am the rainmaker," he said, and gently placed the sculpture on the window ledge.

He prepared himself for evening sitting meditation. He tried to see himself clearly in the moment, both man and beast. He tried to go beyond this duality but found himself unable to find release. He counted his breath, and with every number he asked for clarity of purpose in his life. He sat for nearly an hour, and then he retired for the evening.

The sun was just beginning to poke through the curtains in Smokey's bedroom. He could hear some birds chirping outside in a nearby tree. There was coffee on the brew. It permeated his nostrils. Bill must be home. Smokey turned on the clock radio. The first thing Smokey heard was the news.

"Three people are dead after a tornado struck a small town just south of Regina," the news anchor said.

That was all Smokey needed to hear. He was stricken with guilt. "How could I have done such a thing? Damn it anyway!" he said. He knew no one would understand his suffering of guilt, not even Bill. He must suffer this alone and beg God's forgiveness.

"Smokey, are you up?" Bill called.

"Sort of, I guess," Smokey said.

"Come have some coffee. We need to talk."

Smokey pulled on a few clothes and headed to the kitchen. Bill was sitting there with the coffee pot in his hand. "You probably noticed I haven't been around much lately," Bill said. Smokey nodded. "I have a lady friend now and things are going well," Bill said.

Smokey smiled and said, "Lucky dog."

"Anyway, I want to give notice at the apartment and move in with her next month if possible."

Smokey nodded again. That meant he would have to move again to a cheaper place and he would be on his own too. He didn't relish the thought of living alone, but perhaps it would give him more space to be in his own environment. Smokey said, "Well, let's get it done and give notice today."

Smokey poured himself a cup of coffee and said, "So tell me about your new lady friend."

"Well, she is into the arts and is very interested in new forms of spirituality. She loves my work, and she is hot," Bill said.

"It sounds like a good match," Smokey said. "My congratulations on finding someone with similar interests."

Smokey had a lot to think about as he walked to the university to sign up for his one class. He had to decide what to do about his special powers as a weather spirit. Was he really responsible for three peoples' deaths? Was he a murderer? He thought about this for some time as he walked along. *If it's true, I need to find a way to control things. Secondly, I need to decide what class to take at university. Since I have only one class I want it to hold my interest.* Finally, he made a mental note to himself to check out apartment prices and start a search.

Smokey walked up the steps to the university and entered the faculty of arts where classes were posted. He got a calendar from the main desk and looked through the class selection in political science. He found the class for which he was looking. It was in international law. Smokey thought to himself, "I may not be able to finance law school, but this class, if I do well, will prove my ability." He signed up for the class and headed to the cafeteria.

He sat amidst students chattering about their new classes. There was a real excitement in the air. Even Smokey felt a bit of the enthusiasm rub off on him. As he sat there the aroma of the lunch special, beef stew, curled up his nose. He loved beef stew, but lately he had feelings of guilt about eating beef. These animals had a degree of intelligence; they had feelings and emotions, even if it was what man called instinct. They were living, breathing things. He decided to forego the beef stew for now.

This semester would be different than in the past. He had no lofty goals. He would be going to class just for intellectual stimulation and to prove to himself that he had abilities. He also knew that this would be his final semester. He wouldn't let his hopes drag on indefinitely. He knew there had to be an end.

Smokey started to walk home from the university. He was really tired, but he knew that he needed the exercise. He wondered what the pills he took really did for him. He had been compliant, but he felt that for the most part he was normal. He was just more developed spiritually than others. He was given larger demons to fight. People just didn't understand the battles he had to fight. It made perfect sense to him that he was chosen to be a weather spirit.

As he walked along he also thought about his move coming up. It would be hard to find a place as nice as the one Bill and he had been living in. He felt a moment of sadness for what he was losing and for the good times he and Bill had shared together in that cozy little apartment. Bills' company had truly been a Godsend when Smokey couldn't face solitude. Smokey thought, *I think I'm ready for solitude. I can decorate my own place and make it entirely mine.* He walked the rest of the way home counting his breath and trying to stay relaxed and in the moment.

It was the first week of September, and classes at the university had started. Smokey listened to the professor talk about how to prepare a proper defense for the international community's ears. He found the class exciting. He only wished he could make a career out of it somehow. At the end of the class the professor said, "Think about a position or defense you would like to present to the class." Smokey thought about this for some time after the class but he couldn't think of a position on the international stage that he could defend as yet.

When Smokey arrived home from university there was a phone message from Larry. Larry had indicated that he felt that by next week there would be enough leaves on the ground to start up some work crews. Smokey called Larry back and said he would drop in the next day in order to establish a work crew and look at the contracts. After talking with Larry he opened the paper to the classified section and started looking for one-bedroom and single apartments. Most apartment owners wanted working tenants.

It was difficult to get an apartment even if Welfare would pay the amount of rent asked. It was society showing its prejudice again. Welfare would pay up to $325 a month for a disabled person's accommodation. Most landlords placed rent above that amount, even if the place was a dump! Smokey didn't find anything in the paper that looked good.

The next day after class Smokey went to the club to see Larry about the leaf-raking contract. Larry said, "These three guys are my best men. They will work for an hour or two without any problems. You can take them with you next week."

Smokey asked, "Do you want me to call them?"

"No, I'll tell them to be here at 9:00 Monday morning," Larry said. "This won't interfere with your school work too much, will it?"

Smokey said, "It's okay, I can miss a few classes."

Smokey spent the first four days of the following week raking leaves. He would pick up the work crew in the Canadian Mental Health half-ton and drive out to the site—usually a home in the south end of the city. The boys were eager to work at the beginning of each day, but usually after three or four hours of raking and bagging leaves they called it a day. The week passed quickly, and by Friday everyone was looking for weekend cash. Larry handed out the cash in tens and twenties and the men were off to buy smokes.

That evening at home Smokey brought out a pen and paper and began a poem about the week. He wrote:

> Winds through barren branches
> Fallen leaf my soul
> No redemption
> Just decomposition
> Rake up the dead
> Five dollars an hour.

He was trying to make his poems more Zen-like, but it took practice to see things in the moment.

Bill was out with his lady friend, and that left Smokey alone on the weekend. For the first time Smokey got a taste of solitude. It was something that he had avoided whenever he could. It was a double-edged sword. If he remained in company he ran the risk of offending people, however, staying home alone meant an inner struggle with his mind. Tonight he was alone with his mind, and the seconds seemed like hours. Each tick of the clock in the living room was like a lifetime passing. Smokey felt a deep sadness. As he sat there, darkness fell. He did not turn on a light. He just sat on the couch in silence without music or television. He felt his heart beat slowly in his chest.

An hour passed in darkness, then two. He felt himself falling, falling through space. He envisioned himself in a deep dark well. He lifted his arms trying desperately to touch the surface of the wall and feel the brick and mortar. There was nothing that would gauge the parameters of his body or his mind. He lifted his knees to his chest and encircled them with his arms. "I am alone," he said, "life is above me. Yes, above me there is laughter, there is happiness." He felt cold, a coldness that started at his fingers and penetrated to his chest. Time passed and he could no longer feel his fingers. He was simply a cold mass on the floor of a well, deep in space. He no longer heard the laughter of society. He felt only the emptiness of his own solitude.

Smokey sat on the couch in the dark until the first light of dawn came through the curtains. He got up and went to the kitchen to make a cup of coffee. With the taste of dark-roast coffee on his lips, he felt a bit better. It was a new day, and the plan was to find an apartment for the next month.

Smokey trudged down the street to the drugstore to buy a paper. He took the paper to the nearest coffee shop and had his second cup of coffee for the day while perusing the paper for apartments for rent. He circled three places that were reasonably priced and in decent areas of the city. Even in a small city like Regina there were undesirable areas. The smell of the fresh-perked coffee was enticing. He almost had a third cup, but he found some self-control at the last moment.

His search first took him to a small apartment block in the west end in the Rosemont district, not far from where he grew up. The landlady, a short rotund gal with whiskers on her chin, said, "No pets, $375 a month, laundry extra." Smokey looked at the place, but it was $75.00 more than his budget would handle. He thanked her and crossed the place off his list. It was a nice place, and he had known the price from the paper. He just thought he could take it if he got stuck.

Smokey hopped on the bus and headed east to downtown, then up Victoria street to his next stop. This place was just $320 a month. He could afford it, and if it was nice he would take it. The landlord, an elderly man with a Polish accent, looked him up and down. Smokey introduced himself, and they went up to the suite which was on the third floor. The place was freshly painted with new carpet and an air conditioner. Smokey couldn't believe it. It was like a miracle. He paid the landlord a hundred dollars as a deposit on the suite. The old man said, "You can move in tomorrow if you like. I won't charge you any more for the rest of the month. I just want good people." Smokey couldn't believe his ears. The landlord gave him the keys and said, "Don't be late with the rent at the end of the month."

Smokey felt a huge weight lift from his shoulders. He had a place to live and he could move in any time. He decided he would walk home and get some exercise. When Smokey arrived home Bill was there with his new woman. They made the introductions and chatted for a short time.

Smokey said, "I found a place today and I can move in anytime."

"That's great," Bill said. "We will help you move and you can help us move!"

Sunday Smokey was alone again, but this time he had things to do and think about. He began by taking his pictures off the walls and packing them in cardboard for the move. As he worked he also thought about his class presentation at university, which was due in the near future. He had decided to defend Canada's three hundred mile limit of ocean. This could be supported because there was a need for fisheries regulation due to depletion of stocks. He spent the day preparing a defense to be presented to the international community class. He considered all possible arguments. The day passed quickly, and Smokey realized he was almost ready for a truck to load his things.

That evening Smokey and Bill sat down to a game of chess. It had been a long time since they had played. Smokey had forgotten just how good Bill was at the game. He had a steel-trap mind, and he was ingenious at setting little traps for Smokey. Smokey lost his queen in less than fifteen minutes. The game was over in an hour, Bill the victor.

After the game they sat around and talked. Eventually the subject of Smokey's illness came up. Smokey said, "I've been thinking a lot about my mind, and schizophrenia really doesn't entirely fit. I know I have a lot of the symptoms, but I think it's more than that. I believe that something happened to me when I stayed with my landlords in Winnipeg. I believe somehow, some way, I was brainwashed, at least partly, as a white supremacy goon. Ever since I lived at that house I've had these thoughts that don't jibe with how I feel. And sometimes I say these things out loud and hurt people."

Bill was silent for quite a while before he spoke. He said, "It's what's in your heart that counts. I think something happened to you also, but I don't know what or how.. You are still a good person down deep."

Smokey said, "I wish I had never gone to Winnipeg. I feel half destroyed, like I lost the only battle that counts, and I must live the rest of my life in disgrace."

That evening Smokey lay in bed with the covers up to his chin, yet he felt a shiver run through his spine. What if they were brainwashing him in his sleep with the use of satellites? Maybe it was the government that had brainwashed him. Was he safe here? Had they tracked him down from Winnipeg? He stared at the ceiling trying to think of how he could protect himself against such forces. Could he program his mind to resist brainwashing? He thought to himself, *I have friends of various nationalities and backgrounds, and they have been good friends. I won't give them up to some darker force within my mind till I die.* Smokey pulled the covers over his head and drifted off.

That night they came for him, pure white ghost-like creatures with swords, chanting racial slurs. He had no weapons to defend himself. They called him brother. Smokey woke up screaming, "I'm not your brother! I'm not!"

It was early morning and the sun was just coming through the kitchen curtains. He put the coffee pot on and sat there in silence thinking about the night. He remembered seeing these creatures before when he had lived in Winnipeg. They were some sort of demon supremacists that could penetrate your mind through your dreams or when you astral-traveled. They were very powerful and could destroy a human mind with one swipe of their sword, killing the human spirit and replacing it with a death rattle of racial slurs.

He knew they were real. He remembered now! He had been struck in the chest with a sword. He remembered he was dying, and he could feel the dark force fill his body. He didn't die. He woke up in bed sweating with chest pains. He was about to call a doctor when the pain subsided. He looked down; there was a scar across his chest. He sat there in silence. In the morning he had forgotten everything, but now he remembered! "I have been touched by the dark forces," he whispered to himself. He drank his coffee.

Smokey thought to himself *I have both sides in me now, sort of like Luke Skywalker's father was supposed to have. I have been marked by the devil. It is so obvious that God loves diversity and the devil does not.* Smokey felt a deep sadness fill his soul. He poured himself a second cup of coffee. He sat in silence. A dull pain radiated from his chest down his arms to his fingertips.

It was time to catch the bus for school. Smokey didn't want to face the world. He had a feeling that today would be a hard day to face. Slowly he packed his papers in his knapsack and put on his fall jacket. He opened the door and stepped into the world. As he walked toward the bus stop a woman was raking the last of the leaves from the ground in her yard. She looked up at him eyes filled with hate. "Bigot," she snarled. Smokey did not respond and he kept walking. He thought to himself, *Others know what happened to me. They can read my mind.*

It was the same when he got to university. Students looked at him and muttered, "Bigot," under their breath. Everywhere he went he heard "Bigot, bigot, bigot!"

Smokey thought, *They don't understand. I'm trapped with this brainwashed mind. They don't understand how every racial slur I make causes me suffering. But it's all in my head . How do they know? They must be able to read minds.* After calling his professor a nigger in his head, he decided he had enough for the day and caught the bus home. He was too ashamed to look at anyone. He knew what they were thinking anyway. His nerves were shot. He headed for the bathroom, and he dropped to his knees and smelled Santi-Flush as he emptied his stomach into the bowl. He knelt there shaking. It had all been too much for him, the judgment of society, the solitude, fighting demons with nothing but his honor and integrity. Where was his dignity now?

Smokey stood up and looked into the mirror. "How do they know," he asked himself. "Is there a mark on my chest or forehead? How can they possibly know what I think unless I'm communicating by telepathy?" He had had enough for the day. He went to his room and closed the curtains. He sat on his bed in the dark and found himself trembling. He crawled into bed and slept.

Smokey slept the rest of that day and all night, waking late the next morning. He had time to get to class, but he couldn't do it. He couldn't face the outside world today. He just couldn't do it! He thought about the previous day and also his dreams. "How much of yesterday was real?" he asked himself. He was truly afraid to find out. He put the coffee pot on, and soon there was the aroma of fresh perked coffee in the air. Smokey sat at the kitchen table and sipped his coffee. It was a darker blend mixed with French roast, a strong cup. He thought, *I can't face whatever reality exists outside my apartment. I must plan a day indoors.*

There was no problem with things to do. All the apartment walls needed to be washed before they moved, plus the place needed a really thorough cleaning. Smokey finished his coffee and went to his stereo. He found an old Van Morrison tape and put it on. Then he went to the closet and pulled out a bucket to begin the day's work. There was something calming, almost soothing about the manual labour. He worked steadily, completing the living room and hallways by noon. At noon he took a break and made himself a sandwich, old cheese and dill pickles. It was his favourite.

The day passed quickly, and soon it was dark outside. Smokey put away the cleaning materials for the day and put on his jacket. He was going for an evening walk. He stepped out into the glow of the street lamp and walked cautiously down the street. He noticed a large moon in the sky. He thought, *Maybe the moon made me crazy the last few days. Maybe none of it is real.* But he knew better than to fool himself. It was real, it was all real!

After his walk Smokey tried to do an evening meditation. He sat on his cushion and tried to free his mind of concepts. He thought, *Can you ever really be free of duality? Good and evil are such important concepts here on earth. Even on earth the light blends with the darkness, there are many shades of light.* He thought about what had happened to his mind. His mind was both dark and light. He was able to see his ignorance; he just wasn't able to prevent it. But being able to see your ignorance was a gift.

The last few days had been really stressful. He had to come to grips with people's opinions about him, and he had to face his own ignorance. Smokey continued to sit trying to give up thought and just count his breath. Thoughts would still enter his mind but he tried to just let them pass without judgment. It wasn't easy!

The next day Smokey still wasn't ready to face the world, so he stayed home. He listened to music and prepared for his university class. That evening Bill brought the truck he borrowed from his dad for moving. Bill said, "You might as well load up what you can throughout the day tomorrow. We will move tomorrow night."

The move went smoothly, and Smokey found himself alone in his new apartment. He spent most of the evening hanging pictures and arranging furniture, but there came the feeling of solitude at the end of the day. He hung the picture of the four loons guarding a nest in the living room. It looked great, deep and mystical. He found a special spot for his meditation cushion. That night Smokey went to bed early, determined to return to university the next day.

The next day Smokey caught the bus to the university. He kept his head down and didn't look at people. If people made comments about him he would just have to ignore them. The university was busy with student elections for the coming year. For those just starting university it was exciting, but for Smokey it didn't matter anymore. This was his last semester.

The semester went by quickly, and soon Smokey was working on his final paper on international dignity. He did a lot of research on dignity, but he often found that human rights were equated with human dignity. They really weren't the same thing. Smokey used an example of a Canadian Welfare recipient. The Welfare recipient may have basic rights, but does he or she have dignity?

It was January. Smokey had survived a solitary Christmas. He had applied for graduation and received confirmation in the mail that he had completed the requirements for a B.A. in political science. He could expect his diploma shortly. With classes over, Smokey had an enormous amount of time on his hands. He received some casual labour from the club and Larry, but it didn't fill the days.

Chapter XXXIV

Each day Smokey rose late in the morning; sometimes it was even afternoon. He put on long underwear and his sweater then jeans and a parka. Finally he wrapped his scarf around his mouth and put on his fur hat. He stepped out into minus thirty weather. The snow was crisp and broke under his feet. Even through the scarf the air was cool.

He made his way to a new coffee shop called Roca Jacks. They were roasting beans and the air was thick with the smell of fresh coffee. Smokey ordered a high test, which was Columbian coffee mixed with espresso. He sat in the window and watched the people trundle by in their parkas. He sat at the window for almost an hour trying to pass the time. One thing was certain when you have the whole day to yourself. You tend to observe the little things, like who is sitting next to you in the coffee shop and what they are wearing.

Smokey noticed a woman in the far corner of the shop. She was wearing a bright yellow dress. He thought this a bit odd. Wasn't a colour like yellow for spring? Maybe she was just hopeful this January. He finished his coffee, wrapped himself up, and headed out the door towards the library. That is where a lot of the unemployed and retired hung out in the winter months. As long as you didn't smell too bad and were reasonably quiet, you were welcome to stay there the whole day.

Smokey checked out the Canadian Authors section first. He selected a Robertson Davies book called *Bred in the Bone*, and he was soon lost in the story. He read for perhaps three hours straight, then left the library, checking out the book and heading to the club to see Larry.

Larry, the big Irishman, had his gigantic hands around a cup of coffee when Smokey walked through the door.

"You're just in time for a cup." Larry bellowed.

Smokey poured himself a cup and sat down across from Larry. "Any work coming up?" Smokey asked.

Larry smiled. "Sorry," he said. "Things almost come to a stop in January. If we get a blizzard I'll send you out on a snow shoveling crew. That is about all I can do for you. If you want, there are some art classes being taught today. It is something to keep you busy."

Smokey said, "Why not?"

Larry and Smokey drank a whole pot of coffee and talked about employment and then politics. They were both frightened of the surge to the right again. Saskatchewan had just finished eight years of the Grant Devine conservatives and then returned to the New Democratic Party when it looked like the right was gaining strength again.

Smokey said, "The day Grant Devine took power I moved to Manitoba, and then Garry Filmon took over there and there was no place else to run. All the prairie provinces were conservative! Under the NDP I sometimes find work, but it seems I'm always unemployed when the conservatives are in power." It wasn't always true. It just seemed like it.

Larry nodded and said, "Conservatism is a narrow view of the world, and it benefits the wealthy and tortures the poor." They both agreed that the Grant Devine government had caused endless havoc, greatly benefiting the rich at the expense of the poor.

At three o'clock the art class began. Larry went along just for the fun of it. The art teacher was a little man with a short beard. He talked about using colour to express emotions. Most people did pictures of winter such as sleighs and horses and people skiing. Smokey decided he would do a self-portrait. It took him almost an hour to complete the detail around the eyes and mouth, but when he was done he could almost see himself in the picture. He left the painting to dry, put on his winter attire, and left for home.

Smokey hadn't eaten all day, and he was starving by the time he got home. There wasn't much in the apartment though. He had a bowl of chunky soup and a peanut butter sandwich. Such things were luxuries, and his general food supply was running low. If he went to the club every day he would get a free sandwich and a bowl of soup. He decided he would go to the club three days a week, visit with Larry, and get something to eat.

Smokey passed the winter months at the club, doing art and joining a writing class in the evenings.

It was a bright and sunny day in February when Smokey received a package in the mail. It was his diploma from university. Basically all it said was that he had completed a bachelor of arts, but Smokey felt a tinge of pride. He said, "If I had the money I could have done a lot more." He set the diploma on his dresser and headed out the door to the coffee shop.

Each day was a copy of the previous day. He went to Roca Jacks for his first cup of coffee for the day. Then it was off to the club to either chat with Larry or do some art work. In the evenings he would pull out his clay and sculpt.

* * *

It was the first day of spring. Smokey went for a long walk around the lake before going to the club to meet with Larry. When he got to the club he noticed all the art work was gone. The art instructor said, "We are having a public showing of the art along with poetry from the writing class."

Smokey never thought his work would be on display. His name would be on his work. That meant that people would know him as a mental patient. He didn't like it, didn't like it at all. They should have asked his permission to display his work. Smokey fumed about this for half an hour, then he relaxed and accepted his fate. He selected one of his poems to be read during the event. After that he decided he would talk with Larry about his feelings. He found Larry in his office sipping a cup of coffee.

"Come in and close the door," Larry said. Smokey sat down. "What's on your mind?" he asked.

Smokey said, "They should have asked our permission to display the work."

Larry grinned and said, "You are right! Do you want your stuff taken down?"

Smokey said he had reconciled himself to being on display as a mental patient.

Larry said, "It's a tough call. The exposure is good, especially with funding agencies, but sometimes individuals get hurt."

Smokey said, "I have been trying to hide my mental illness. I didn't want to admit it to myself and certainly not to others and the general public."

Larry put his coffee cup down and said, "There are benefits to exposure and there are drawbacks. Did you know you qualify under affirmative action as a disabled person with the government?"

Smokey said he didn't know that but doubted it would make any difference.

Larry said, "You are probably right, but you shouldn't give up hope."

That evening Smokey received a call from the mental health clinic. The psychiatrist wanted to see him immediately. Smokey wondered what was going on. Had someone complained about his behavior? He couldn't imagine why the psychiatrist would want to see him. He worried about it half the night. The next morning he made an appointment to see the psychiatrist that afternoon.

Smokey sat in the mental health clinic waiting for his appointment. The same old clock on the wall ticked off the seconds then the minutes. Smokey thought of everything he had been through in the past few years. A hopeless feeling fell upon him like a sheet of ice rain, numbing his brain. What was next? Was he saying things out loud again? Why was he here?

The door opened and his psychiatrist greeted him with a smile. She asked him how he had been feeling and noticed that he had gained a few more pounds over the winter months. "I'll get right to the point," she said. "You have been selected for a new drug because you are a higher-functioning schizophrenic. It is possible that with this new drug you will be more motivated. Perhaps you might even find something part-time in the work force. Most importantly, though, it has better results in terms of reducing hallucinations, including auditory hallucinations. This drug should benefit you a lot. Would you like to give it a try? The choice is yours."

Smokey didn't hesitate. He said he would like to try the drug.

"The first thing we must do is take you off the old drug. This will take about two weeks. Then we will start the new drug and see if it works for you. Okay, we will start tomorrow. You will need a special letter to get the drug at the pharmacy at no cost. You can pick that up at the front desk later in the week. Reduce your current drug by half tonight and tomorrow. Then come in and see us again."

Smokey followed all the instructions and soon was off the old drug and started on the new one. He didn't notice much difference except for the fact that he couldn't sleep as much. This meant he had more time to fill throughout the day.

After a couple of weeks, Smokey seemed to have a clearer mind. He realized that thinking that he was the reincarnation of Adolph Hitler or the son of Satan, or even a weather spirit, were all delusions. He felt his rational mind take control of these delusions and all the emotional baggage that came with it. He could see that he had indeed been ill, but not all the delusions disappeared. Certain thoughts proved difficult to overcome. He still believed that some people could read his mind and could communicate telepathically. This symptom, if it really was a symptom, remained in Smokey's consciousness.

It was the day of the mental health celebration. The poetry readings were first. Smokey listened to his poem being read. He was surprised how it moved people. He was pleased. During the evening there was a silent auction of the club members' artwork. Smokey had two pictures displayed. At the end of the evening he was informed that his two pictures sold for fifty dollars each. Smokey didn't know whether to be happy or sad. Why would the public want his silly old picture? Was it a trendy thing to have a picture drawn by a mental patient, or was the work really good? Smokey couldn't decide which it was. Maybe it was a bit of both. One thing for sure was, he could use the one hundred dollars. He desperately needed some new jeans and shoes. Welfare under the NDP was a little more compassionate than under the Conservatives, but it was still tough making it to the end of each month. If you didn't buy a bus pass and walked everywhere you could save forty dollars, but there was no allowance for things like dental care. Smokey needed to see a dentist! He had to choose with his one hundred dollars what was more important: decent clothes or a couple of fillings. If only he could get some part-time work, cash, under the table. At the end of the day, however, Smokey was more than pleased to have $100.00.

That evening, as he sat in meditation, he thought about how much he did have and how much he had been given. He had been given the chance to compete nationally and internationally in canoeing. He had been given the privilege of attending university for five years. He had family, loved ones, and friends. Indeed, he felt he was blessed. Most importantly, he had been given the best possible drugs to combat an illness that he still knew little about and barely had a grip on now.

After a few moments of gratitude, Smokey began to count his breath. With each exhalation, he counted in his mind till he reached ten, then he started over. He sat and counted for thirty minutes. Thoughts would come and go, but he just let them pass through his mind, trying hard not to judge.

The next day Smokey spent at the club with Larry. There wasn't a lot left to talk about. They had covered every topic under the sun except religion, and Larry said "I don't talk about religion. There's enough bullshitters out there now already."

Smokey smiled and said "Yeah, I suppose you're right."

They drank a pot of coffee and chattered about yesterday's news. The day passed and Smokey headed home. Just as he opened the door to his apartment, the phone rang. Smokey answered it.

"Hello?"

"This is your big brother."

"Hi."

"What are you doing in July?"

"Nothing."

"How would you like to spend ten days with a bunch of Buddhists in the Algonquin forests of Ontario?"

"I don't think I can meditate all day."

"You will be building a cabin."

"That sounds like fun."

"Then you'll come?"

"Sure!"

"I'll send you an airline ticket in the mail. We can discuss the details later."

"Bye."

"Goodbye."

Building a cabin in the woods with a bunch of Zen Buddhists. It sounded really interesting, and Smokey felt that he was up to the challenge. That night he had a dream in which he and his brother were standing on top of a mountain overlooking a winding river. When he woke up the next morning he could see the river clearly in his mind.

He was just about to walk out the door when the phone rang. It was Bill.

"Long time no see," Smokey said.

"How about we meet at Roca Jacks in half an hour?" Bill said.

"Okay, sounds good."

By the time Smokey walked to the coffee shop, Bill was already seated at a table near the window at the front of the shop. Smokey ordered his coffee and took it over to the table. He sat down across from Bill. Bill looked weary; in fact, he looked down right fatigued.

Smokey said, "Good to see you."

Bill smiled thinly. "My relationship is over," he said.

Smokey didn't know what to say. He just nodded understanding.

Bill said, "I have to move at the end of the week. Can you help?"

Smokey nodded again. "No problem," he said.

Bill said, "So you've heard my earth-shaking news. What's new with you?"

Smokey told Bill about going to Ontario to build a cabin in the woods with a group of Zen Buddhists. "That sounds exciting," Bill said. "I wish you all the energy you'll need to haul those logs." Bill didn't have much else to say. He was very dejected. They sat in almost total silence and sipped their coffee. Every few minutes Smokey would see that Bill was gazing out the window. They finished their coffee and Smokey was getting his clothes on when Bill said, "Let's have a second cup." They both got refills and sat back down.

Smokey understood that there didn't have to be a lot of conversation. It was enough just to sit together for company. Smokey realized just how much he had missed Bill's company the past few months. It was good to get Bill back, even though Smokey had wished him well in the relationship. He was now glad for the company. Bill said he would pick Smokey up Friday afternoon and they could start work packing things.

On Friday afternoon, Bill picked Smokey up at his apartment. "Would you like a cup of coffee first?" Bill asked.

Smokey said, "Sure."

They found a parking spot and entered Roca Jacks. There was only one table left, so Smokey grabbed it while Bill ordered the coffee. They sat at the table sipping their coffee.

"I really appreciate this," Bill said.

"I'm not doing anything otherwise," Smokey said. "I like to help."

After coffee, they headed directly to Bill's apartment. His ex-partner was out, so it was not too uncomfortable, but they still had to separate his things from hers and the things they had shared. As the afternoon progressed, Smokey could see the strain on Bill's face. The rest of the moving crew arrived about six o'clock, and they began to load up the heavy things onto a truck they had borrowed. It took the full evening to move Bill. Being the artist he was, Bill tended to collect a lot of materials. At the end of the evening, standing amid his things at his new apartment on Broadway Avenue, Bill thanked everyone for their generous help.

Smokey asked if Bill needed help setting things up, but Bill said he needed to be alone. Smokey said he understood and he would walk home. It wasn't that far. Smokey started his walk home. As he walked along he thought about his relationship with Sherry again. He understood how Bill would be feeling right about now. He remembered clearly the day Sherry left him. "Love hurts," he said to himself. "Love hurts!"

Smokey received his airline ticket by Purolator courier two weeks before his trip to Ontario was scheduled. It was a long two weeks. He was eager to see his brother and meet these Zen Buddhists who wanted to build a cabin in the woods. Finally the day came. Smokey phoned Bill for a ride to the airport. They arrived about an hour before the boarding time. Smokey checked his baggage at the Air Canada counter and proceeded to the boarding area, saying goodbye to Bill on the way.

After checking through security, he sat and waited for the boarding call. It was about a thirty minute wait in which time Smokey went to the bathroom three times. He hated to use the washroom on the plane. It was big enough for a child, but not for a full grown adult. You had to squeeze in, like getting into a cupboard. It was much better avoided if possible. The boarding call came, and Smokey entered the plane. He searched for his seat, hoping beyond hope that there would be an empty seat beside him. It was not to be. There was a very huge man sitting in the seat next to his. The man sort of spilled over into Smokey's seat. Smokey squeezed in the best he could and buckled up for take off.

Chapter XXXV

There is always such a rush one gets from the take off. It was the closest he would come to transcending time. While they were in the air, they were between time zones. Smokey sat back and relaxed as the nose of the plane began to level off. The man next to him was probably in his mid-fifties, OF stocky build, with large blue eyes. The man undid his buckle and then proceeded to untie his shoes and slip them off. He began to rub his feet together.

Smokey had to suppress a gag reflex. The odor from the man's feet smelt like a combination of burnt toast and feta cheese, though a little more rancid! People around began to mumble, but the man persisted on rubbing his feet together. After about half an hour, the stewardess asked people what they would like for dinner. It was not surprising that a lot of people declined dinner. When all you can smell is old socks, who wants dinner? Other than the atrocious smell, there were no other problems on the flight. The 737 touched down in Toronto right on time. Smokey made his way to the exit, then to the baggage retrieval area. His brother was there with a big smile. "Good to see you," his brother said.

Smokey retrieved his baggage, and they headed to the parkade where Ross had parked his car. It was a 1980 Saab. It looked classy, but Ross said it was a piece of junk. There was a light rain falling that evening, and the windows of the Saab steamed up with condensation as they drove home. Smokey told Ross about the man on the flight with his stinky feet. Ross just laughed and said, "It could have been worse. He could have been the guru of silent farts." When they got home, Ross took one of Smokey's bags and headed around to the front door. Kathryn, his wife, was sitting in the living room reading a novel by Rohinton Mistry. She smiled up at Smokey and Ross and said, "You both would like this book." She gave Smokey a hug and said welcome. They talked for perhaps half an hour. Then Smokey was ready for bed. Ross showed him to the spare room and said good night.

Smokey heard the alarm clock go off in his brother's room. The sun was just beginning to poke itself through some eastern cloud. The light hit the bed in full force. Smokey rubbed his eyes and sat up. Ross was at the door. "Rise and shine," he said. "We have a big day in front of us."

Smokey had a quick shower and shaved off his stubble. Ross had made toast and coffee. Smokey sat at the kitchen table desperately trying to wake up. The coffee helped, and soon Ross was talking about the plans for the day.

They set to work loading the Saab with tent, sleeping bags, groceries, and other camping gear. They said good bye to Kathryn, who wasn't the camping type, and headed through the early morning traffic. The first stop on the way was Second Cup for a large takeout coffee and a muffin each. Then it was on to Bethany, a small community just about an hour out of Toronto. This was where Tim lived.

Ross talked about Tim's background and how he had come to Zen. "Tim had a rigid Catholic upbringing," Ross said, "but he found his way to Zen through the martial arts, years later. You will like these men," Ross said, "I know you will."

When they got to Bethany, Tim was sitting on the front porch waiting. Tim had no hair to speak of; he was muscular, with clear brown eyes. They made their introductions and began transferring the camping gear from the Saab to Tim's van. After the van was loaded, they drove a short distance to a small café in the middle of nowhere, leaving the Saab behind. There were lots of cars there. They went in for a breakfast-brunch.

Tim and Ross ordered omelets so Smokey did the same. He realized that being with Buddhists for ten days meant no sausages for breakfast. Of course, there would be no one thanking Jesus for the food either. The waitress brought the omelets about twenty minutes later. They were huge! All three men had healthy appetites. They devoured the food in record time. There was time for one cup of coffee each, and then it was back to the highway.

Smokey sat in the back of the van while Ross and Tim sat up front. Ross and Tim talked about the Zen center and the work that needed to be done there. Smokey listened to two committed men talk about Zen sitting. He longed to go to a zendo and sit with others. Perhaps some day he would, he thought.

The world changed as they drove, from highways and industrial developments to country and the Cambrian shield. Soon there was just road, forest, and sky. It was beautiful! The sun beat down on the pavement, creating little heat waves that were visible from the van as they drove. Smokey gazed out at the tree line and thought about hauling those logs through the bush.

"Look, there's an eagle," Smokey said and pointed to a larger bird at the tree line.

Tim laughed. "That's not an eagle, it's a turkey vulture. But we do have eagles at the cabin site."

Smokey couldn't believe he had made such an obvious mistake. He watched the bird flying through the air. It had majesty to its glide, even if it was just a turkey vulture.

Just as they turned into Madawaska, two young deer stepped out onto the roadway. Tim slowed the van down to a crawl. The deer didn't care until the van was right up close. Ross got a shot off with his camera. "Got them," he said.

They stopped at the gas bar in Madawaska. It was an eclectic little shop, anything from bread to fishing lures. Smokey noticed the bear head on the wall. *How could you miss it?* he thought. Doug, the shop owner, smiled and said, "I got that feller up where you boys are building that cabin." he let out a laugh that sounded more like a weasel.

It was only a couple of miles along a dirt and gravel road to where their property began, but it was all uphill. Eventually they reached the end of the road. There was a camper set up there and a ton of logs piled just to the north of it. Ross said, "Come on, I'll show you the cabin site." They followed a thin trail through the bush until they came to a clearing where the floor of the cabin was. The cabin site overlooked a cliff, and below it was a river. Smokey had seen that river before in his dreams. It was the mighty Madawaska River. He stood there and took in the beauty of the site. "So what do you think?" Ross asked.

Smokey was speechless. Finally he said, "It's stuff that people dream of."

They went back to the van and found Tim already unpacking things. Smokey asked "When are the others coming?"

Tim said, "They will be here tomorrow afternoon."

Ross said, "If you are going to set up camp, Tim, we will start hauling logs. Come on, little brother, we have work to do."

Smokey picked up the end of a log and Ross grabbed the other end. It was unbelievably heavy. They ambled along the trail to the campsite and placed the first log down. This was going to be really hard work. As they wore the path down and the ground leveled, the job got a little easier, but by that time Smokey was so tired it seemed harder. They hauled logs for six hours that day. Tim was in such good shape he could handle a log by himself.

That evening they made a small fire near the camper and sat out under the stars. Tim made a pot of cowboy coffee, which was just grounds in water brought to a boil. Smokey sipped his coffee and listened to the two men talk about Zen. Tim brought out his flashlight and read from a book called *Zen Awakening*. It was a wonderful evening, but Smokey could feel his muscles ache. He knew it was time to turn in. It would be a big day tomorrow. He crawled into his sleeping bag and soon was fast asleep.

The next thing Smokey knew, he was being shaken. A voice said "Roll over, you're snoring." Smokey rolled onto his side and went back to sleep. He slept soundly for the rest of the night.

The sun hit the camper through the trees before six o'clock in the morning. Tim was already up and scrambling eggs for everyone. Ross was next up. He sort of growled and said, "The only one who got any sleep is still in bed!"

Tim laughed, "Yeah, we are going to have to do something about the man's snoring. I've never heard a man saw logs like that. He sounds like a bear." Tim added some salsa to the eggs.

The aroma penetrated Smokey's nostrils. Smokey wasn't really ready to get up yet, but the smell of the eggs and perked coffee was too much to resist. He crawled out of bed and said good morning to the two men. When the eggs were done, each man grabbed a plate and sat around the fire pit.

Breakfast was hurried, then it was back to hauling logs. The idea was to move all the logs to the cabin site before the others arrived. Perhaps they could trick the others, when they arrived at the camper, into believing the logs hadn't arrived. By noon, all the logs were at the cabin site and the others hadn't arrived. They took a short break. The others arrived at around 1:00 P.M. and the trick with the logs was a success. Brad looked almost lost when he was told there weren't any logs delivered. Smokey received introductions. There was Brad, a large, gentle soul; David, a man with a Cheshire grin; and Brad's wife, Emma, who volunteered to be the cook for ten days.

Brad had short black hair with a few wisps of grey and he was clean-shaven. All the men were clean-shaven except for Smokey and his moustache. David was a wiry fellow with a Zen haircut, like the Buddha. Unlike the Buddha though, he had an angular face and a square jaw. Emma had dark hair and looked like she may have been of Dutch descent. Emma's laugh was sharp as a razor's edge and went well with her style of humour. Each member of the Zen group brought character and a clear mind.

The group unloaded their gear, and everyone sat around the fire pit. "What are we going to do without logs?" Brad exclaimed. David knew something was up. Tim was just too relaxed.

Finally Ross said, "The logs are at the site. We've been hauling logs for hours!"

Brad said "I thought I saw truck tire tracks. I should have suspected something."

They spent the afternoon preparing the cabin floor for the first wall of logs. Each log had been planed with a tongue and a grove, and they were meant to fit together like building blocks. After the floor was prepared, they laid down the first logs for the exterior walls. It looked like everything was ready for the next day.

At about six, dinner was ready. Emma had made a vegetarian chili and there were fresh buns and butter.

"Well," Ross said after dinner, "It's time to set up a tent for those who snore."

Tim laughed. "Put him out in the bush," he said.

"Come on little brother, help me set up a tent for you," Ross said.

They set up a small pup tent on the dirt road twenty yards from the camper. Smokey was happy. He liked the privacy. As evening drew nigh and the stars came out, once again they lit a small fire and sat around for awhile. Sometimes there was silence. No one had anything to say. There was just a sense of fulfillment being out in the woods camping.

Tim and Ross were the first to depart from the fire and head to the camper. Smokey left for his tent. He crawled in and closed the tent fly. "Ouch," something was in his ear. Then something bit his face. Then he was being bitten all over. "Ouch, ouch! Damn, damn." He thought if he got into his sleeping bag they couldn't get him, but he was wrong. These creatures, no-see-ums or sand flies, were small enough that they could get right inside his bag, and man, could they bite. They were all teeth. After half an hour of being bitten, he gave up and went to the camper. "Give me the keys to the van. I'll sleep there." Tim gave him the keys and Smokey took his sleeping bag and curled up in the van for the night.

The next morning at breakfast, Smokey took his share of ribbing. Ross said, "The great outdoorsman was chased out of his tent by a few flies."

Smokey said, "More like a thousand flies with teeth. They were like bulldogs with wings."

Everyone got a chuckle out of Smokey's plight the previous night. Emma made a porridge that had raisins in it. It stuck to the ribs just fine. There was toast and coffee also. By 7:00 A.M. the men were up at the cabin site. It was Smokey's job to bring logs to the floor as they needed them. It became apparent that the logs did not fit together like building blocks. Each log had to be custom-fitted in place and spiked down. This took a lot of time, so the hours that everyone worked were long and strenuous. Even though the men had bug suits, the black flies would find their way to bare skin somehow. The bug suits were also extremely hot, and one would risk getting bit just to cool off.

After three days of building cabin walls, they decided they needed a break. Emma needed a break from cooking and cleaning too. That evening they drove into Bancroft, a small northern settlement thirty miles from Madawaska. There was a pizza-pasta restaurant that Tim recommended. They ordered two extra large pizzas with mushrooms, hot peppers, and green olives. When the waitress brought the pizza, Smokey's mouth began to water and his stomach gurgled in anticipation. It was the best pizza Smokey had ever had. The five of them consumed the two pizzas. There wasn't even a crumb to be found on anyone's plate.

On the way back to camp, the group talked about the next day's plans for the cabin. The walls were almost finished. One more day and the walls would be complete. Then would come the roof trusses and planking. A seemingly impossible task was being completed step by step.

The next day everyone was tired. Progress was slow but steady. It was hard work standing on a step ladder, sledge hammer in hand, pounding spikes into the logs. Around noon, Tim headed off to the chemical toilet in the woods, also known as the honey pot. Nobody paid him any mind until they heard a mighty roar and heard Tim come crashing through the bush. By the time Tim was in sight, mama bear was in close pursuit. Everyone started yelling and screaming and banging things. It was too much for mother bear. She stood on her haunches for a minute, then turned around and headed back into the bush. "Was that your girlfriend?" David asked. Everyone started to laugh. The danger had passed.

It was the first day of building the roof. The walls were all up. Smokey helped Brad bang the trusses together and measure the distance for each truss. They had done a good job so far; the walls were all square. Smokey stood on a ladder at the center of the cabin and centered each truss. The work was slow but not nearly as difficult as the walls had been.

By three o'clock that afternoon, the trusses were in place and it was time to start the roof planking. Smokey handed up the planks while Ross and Tim nailed them in place. Most of the time Smokey was just an extra hand, but he didn't mind. He could watch and learn some carpentry skills. As the sun was about to set, Tim hammered the last roof plank in place. "It's time for a swim," he said.

"Sounds like a great plan" David said.

The men changed and headed down the steep slope to the Madawaska River. In several spots, the Madawaska bursts forth into dangerous rapids, but at the cabin it was slow and meandering. Smokey was the last one down the slope. By the time he got there, the others were already in the water. He heard the screams as they entered the water with a splash. Even in the summer the Madawaska River was cold. Smokey put one foot into the water, "Brrrrrrr." Then, without warning, his brother sent a spray of cold water right onto his chest. He let out a scream then jumped into the river. It was refreshing after a long day of cabin building.

Smokey thought, *This has been the best vacation I've ever had since Bill and I went to Newfoundland on motorcycles back in 1979.* He thought about how relaxed he had been the past week. There were few thought disturbances and voices in his head except for normal conscious dialogue! For the first time, Smokey asked a serious question about schizophrenia.

Was schizophrenia advanced or exacerbated by urban living? If he lived in a cabin in the woods, would he be okay? Would the voices fade like they had this past week?

As he paddled around in the Madawaska River, Smokey thought about each one of these men, how special they were. They were bright, clear headed, and sensitive to each other. They seemed to understand that life is suffering but it is also very beautiful. Smokey reflected on fireside conversations about suffering and joy, ignorance and enlightenment, and the nature of the Buddha. It all started to make sense for him. In his mind, he thanked each man for sharing their understanding. The cold water was beginning to numb his brain. He made his way to the shoreline. Everyone was calling it quits for the day.

It was the last evening that everyone would be together. Tim started a small fire in the fire pit. Brad said, "Well, we did it. We have a cabin now. With some finishing work it will look great." There was lots left to do, but everyone was pleased with what had been accomplished.

Emma came out from the camper. "I'm not doing any more dishes," she said. The boys could see the exhaustion on her face.

Tim said, "I'll wash." The others grabbed drying towels.

Smokey grabbed a towel. There was something about doing dishes he liked. It was a simple task but required concentration. More than that though, it was the fellowship, the collective effort that counted. It reminded him of days at the cottage when he was young.

When the dishes were done, the men hung their towels on a makeshift clothes line and sat down to the blazing fire. The stars were beginning to poke through an early dusk sky. Each man gazed into the fire. It was their last night together. Smokey had only known Emma and the men for ten days, but he felt that they were family. Not only had they shown him carpentry skills, but they had given him back his dignity as a human being. They had asked him questions about his mind and listened without judgment. He knew he would remember these past ten days for the rest of his life.

Soon there were just embers glowing in the fire pit. There was a feeling of exhaustion in the air, but the forest gave back energy too. The others retired for the evening. Smokey stayed out and watched the embers cool. Tomorrow he would return to Toronto for a day, then it was off to see his parents in Owen Sound. Smokey made his way to the van for bed. He crawled into his sleeping bag. He said a short prayer to the universe. He said, "Thank you!"

About 5:30 the next morning, a crow started circling. It was an early morning wakeup call, but everyone was eager to start packing up. Smokey had most of his things packed in fifteen minutes, so he helped Tim load up the van. There was very little conversation. People were concentrating on the tasks at hand. By 8:00 A.M. the van and truck were loaded and they headed back to Tim's place in Bethany. They drove slowly through the forest, but when they reached the major highway, Tim put the pedal to the metal. They arrived in Bethany by noon.

Ross and Smokey collected their things and loaded up the old Saab. Then it was time to say goodbye. Smokey shook hands with the three men and Emma gave him a hug. She said, "We will think of you every time we use the new cabin." Smokey slowly crawled into the front seat of the Saab. Ross put the old jalopy into gear, and they headed out to the highway, back to Toronto.

Ross said "We've got to get you cleaned up before you see your mother." Smokey just smiled and nodded.

As they drove along, Ross started talking about Toronto, about employment opportunities and a better health care system. Finally Ross asked the question, "Would you like to live in Toronto?"

Smokey didn't answer. He just thought about it for a few minutes. It was true he had outgrown Regina. There were no opportunities for employment in Regina. The only advantage of Regina was that housing was cheap compared to other major cities. Ross, reading his thoughts said, "I can put your name in for subsidized housing, and we will try and get you a good doctor and mental health clinic to go to."

It would take some serious planning, but it was possible. Smokey said "I'll think about it."

They spent the rest of the day unpacking the car and getting a start on laundry. That evening Smokey crawled into a hot tub and soaked his aching bones. Tomorrow they would head to Owen Sound to visit their parents. Smokey slept late, but there was still plenty of time to get to Owen Sound. He shaved off ten days of whiskers and washed. Ross had finished the laundry. Kathryn said, "Well, it's goodbye again!" Smokey laughed.

Chapter XXXVI

The Saab cruised down the highway. Smokey snoozed in the passenger's seat. It had started to rain, and the rhythmic sound of the windshield wipers put him off to sleep. Ross woke him up on the outskirts of Owen Sound. When they reached the house, his mother was standing at the door, watering some geraniums that were growing in pots on the porch. She smiled and waved. Ross and Smokey got out of the car.

"My two sons!" she exclaimed.

"Hi, Mom!" Smokey said.

"I'll put tea on," his mother said, "or would you like coffee?"

Ross said, "I'll have coffee later, but I need a nap right now. I must head back in an hour or so."

While Ross rested, Smokey and his mother caught up on all the news. His mother smiled when she saw all the bug bites on his arms. Smokey said, "I even have a scab on the back of my head where the black flies sunk their teeth into me!"

He hadn't seen his mother since his grandfather's funeral. He knew he hadn't been well then. "I'm doing better mom," he said. "The new medication I'm on seems to ground me at least partly in reality."

His mother smiled and said "I'm so glad you've found something that works for you."

Smokey said "Well, it works some of the time anyway."

She took him out to her garden in the backyard. They sat and watched the birds at the birdfeeder. Smokey could see how his mother took joy in the little things. Feeding the birds and watering the flowers was like her Zen meditation. Smokey was reminded of a discussion the Zen men had on mindfulness, being present and in the moment. He thought his mother was mindful watering her flowers and feeding her birds.

Ross came out and joined them on the back porch. He said, "How about that coffee now?"

Smokey's mother smiled and said, "Coming right up."

They had coffee on the back porch, even though it was still drizzling on and off. Ross and his mother talked for a short while, then he said it was time for him to go. Smokey watched the Saab disappear around the corner. Then he went in to be with his mom.

At around 6:00 P.M., Smokey's step-dad came home from work. He looked exhausted. Smokey shook his hand and they retired to the living room. Smokey's mom was busy cooking supper. It would be baked salmon with new potatoes and green beans, Smokey's favourite! Smokey's step-dad, John, was now working as a commissioner. He enjoyed the work but got pissed off at how the others in his profession sloughed off.

The dinner was served promptly at seven. Smokey took an extra scoop of the new potatoes. The salmon melted in his mouth. He savoured the taste. It was perfect with just a tad of lemon. Smokey couldn't remember when a meal tasted so good. It was delightful!

After dinner and dishes were done, his mother brought out a deck of cards. They played a fun little game called ninety-nine. Smokey's step-dad was the winner. He seemed to get all the right cards. By nine that evening, everyone was ready for bed. Smokey crawled into bed and turned out the lamp. He gazed up at the ceiling in the dark. Once again, he said a short prayer. He said, "Thank you!"

He had almost forgotten tomorrow was July 21, his birthday. Smokey thought to himself, *Thirty-eight years old and still no career or meaningful employment.* Once again Smokey felt his failures and wondered if his luck would ever change. He thought that a move to Toronto might mean better employment opportunities. He began to think seriously about a move. He fell asleep, weighing the pros and cons of a move to Toronto.

The sunlight beamed through the curtains in Smokey's room. He had slept late. He could hear his mother singing downstairs. He made his way to the bathroom and hopped into the shower. He soaked in the shower for a good ten minutes before crawling out of the shower and looking for a razor. When he finished preparing to look his birthday best, he went downstairs to greet his mom.

"Happy Birthday, dear," she said.

"Thank you," he said.

"Would you like some eggs?" she asked.

"Sure."

After breakfast and dishes, they went out to the garden and watched the birds for an hour. A cardinal came right up close to them and sang his song.

Smokey said, "It must be nice to be a cardinal, but I'm afraid I have a sparrow's soul."

His mother smiled and said, "Sparrows are the ones with character. They stay for the winter, surviving on crumbs offered by humans."

Smokey said, "I think our relatives are cardinals. They always fly to Mexico or Hawaii in January, whereas I stay in Canada and eat moldy potatoes from the food bank."

His mother smiled and said, "You're too young to be bitter. It doesn't suit you either."

Smokey grinned. "Let's go down to the harbour front," he said.

"Yes! We can watch the Tobermory being loaded," she said. The Tobermory was a large grain ship that docked in Georgian Bay every year. It usually sailed in early August for ports unknown.

They walked side by side down the hill to the harbour. There were lots of smaller ships in the harbour that day. They watched them being loaded and unloaded. It was almost perfectly calm. There was just a slight ripple on the lake surface.

"A nice day for sailing," Smokey said.

"You might be becalmed," his mother said.

After watching the ships for a while, they walked over to a small doughnut shop. They ordered coffees and shared an apple fritter.

His mother said, "I hope chicken breasts are okay for a birthday supper."

Smokey smiled, and said, "Perfect."

They walked back to the house. Smokey's mom was huffing and puffing by the time they got to the top of the hill. When they reached the house, they were both winded.

They decided that a half-hour nap before starting supper would be good. Smokey retired to his room and slept soundly for over an hour. When he got up, his mother already had the chicken in the oven. John, Smokey's step-dad, would be home from work shortly. It seemed as if they had done very little, but the day had passed quickly.

That evening after supper, Smokey's mother brought out some gifts. "The first one is from us," she said. Smokey unwrapped the paper in flashes of green and blue wrapping. It even had a bow on it. Inside was a new wristwatch. Smokey said, "How did you know I needed a watch?" His mother smiled and his step-dad grinned. "Thank you," Smokey said.

The next gift was from all the folks up at the cabin. It was large and soft. Smokey tore through the paper. There was a large green sweat shirt. Smokey held it up. There was a bear's head on it, and printed around it was "Madawaska." Smokey said "It's cool, really cool. I'm a lucky guy to have such friends and family."

The rest of the week Smokey spent either in the back garden with his mother or else he went down to the harbour to watch the ships coming and going. The week went by too quickly. They had their last meal together when Ross came to pick up Smokey that same day. Smokey wore his new sweatshirt and watch.

They stood on the front steps. Smokey gave his mom a big hug and then shook his step-dad's hand. "Thanks for looking after me," he said. It was a hard goodbye to make. He felt he could stay there for months and be happy.

Ross grabbed Smokey's luggage and put it in the car. "Let's go, little brother," he said. They climbed into the old Saab and pulled away. Smokey could see his mother wave as they drove away.

Ross asked, "Was it a good visit?" Smokey said, "Yes."

"I feel like mom is isolated there," Ross said.

"Yes, but she gets out now and again. She teaches English as a second language once a week," Smokey said.

They drove home to Ross's place in almost complete silence. Smokey's vacation was over. Tomorrow he would get on the big bird and fly back to Regina. Smokey thought about what it would be like to live close to his brother and also his parents. He needed more than just his friends in Regina. He needed family too.

When they got to the house, Ross said, as if reading Smokey's mind, "I'll put your name in for subsidized housing. It will take a while to get it anyway."

Kathryn was just pulling a large vegetarian lasagna out of the oven when they came in the door. It smelled like heaven, deep and rich with aroma. Within minutes they were sitting down for their last dinner together.

Ross said, "Smokey's planning, or thinking of, moving out east."

"It's a big move but there's more opportunities out here," Kathryn said. "That's what everyone has been telling me," Smokey said.

The flight left at 7:00 A.M. the next morning, so everyone retired early that night. Smokey lay in bed thinking to himself about big city life. It would be different. There would be more stress, and stress may affect his illness. But what was left for him in Regina? There was no opportunity for employment, no opportunity to educate himself further, and there was no family support. He decided that night that he would do all he could to make a move out east.

They were up at 4:45 the next morning in order to get to the airport in time. Kathryn said goodbye at home, and then the two men headed to the airport. It was drizzling out. The Saab's windshield blades beat rhythm to the music in the car. They were listening to an old Bruce Cockburn tape.

They reached terminal one and Ross grabbed the luggage out of the trunk of the car. He set them down on the sidewalk. Smokey gave him a big hug then picked up his bags and walked into the airport.

Smokey checked his suitcase and went through the security check. He found his gate for departure, sat down, and waited for the boarding call. It was only a short wait, but it seemed like an eternity to Smokey. He wanted to be gone now, back to his little apartment in Regina.

There was lots of room on this flight. The seat next to him was empty. There was also a good-looking woman sitting across the aisle from him. He caught her eye. She smiled. She had long dark eyelashes and they were real. Her complexion was dark. She had deep brown eyes. She reminded him of his first girlfriend years ago.

The plane sped down the runway then lifted into the air. "I love take offs, don't you?" she said.

"Yes" Smokey said, "it's the best part of flying."

"Do you do a lot of flying?" she asked.

"Not anymore, but when I was a child we flew everywhere. My father was a pilot for Air Canada, Trans Canada Airline back then."

"I don't fly much anymore either," she said. There was a brief silence, and then something in her changed and became almost rigid. She pulled out a Bible and said, "Have you heard the word of God?"

Smokey's heart sank. "Yes," he said, "I've heard the word."

"Are you a believer?" she asked. There was silence. He could tell her the truth and risk attack or he could lie. He said, "I am the way, the truth and the light."

"God bless you brother!" she said.

Smokey felt like shit. These types of people always make you feel like shit. They have all the answers and they know they're right. Smokey couldn't hide his disappointment. She noticed. He took out a pocket novel and began reading.

The rest of the flight was uneventful. They served a cheese omelet for breakfast that Smokey devoured in a few bites. Before long the plane was over Winnipeg and would be starting its descent a few minutes later. Smokey gazed out the window watching the farmland. From the sky the crops looked good, but close inspection may reveal otherwise.

The plane touched down in Regina, and Smokey gathered his personal belongings. He followed a long trail of passengers out of the plane to the luggage retrieval section of the airport. Bill was standing there waiting for him. Smokey smiled and waved. Bill nodded with a smile.

"Good to see you," Smokey said.

"You too," Bill said.

Smokey grabbed his bags from the rotating machine and they headed for Bill's car. "So how was the trip out east?" Bill asked.

Smokey grinned and said, "It was the best holiday since you and I rode our motorcycles to Newfoundland."

"That was along time ago, back when I still had strength in my arms and legs," Bill said. "Let's stop at Roca Jacks and you can fill me in on the details."

"Sounds good to me," Smokey replied.

They reached the coffee shop and got out of the car. It wasn't busy yet, and there were two empty chairs and a table in the window. They took their coffees to the table and sat down. Bruce Cockburn was playing in the background. Smokey remembered that Ross was a real Bruce Cockburn fan. Smokey began to relate the events of the last twenty days with enthusiasm. Bill was always a good listener.

At the end of it all Bill said, "It sounds like you have some decisions to make."

Smokey smiled and said, "Yes, I'm thinking of moving east. I'll be closer to my family, there are job opportunities, and there are opportunities to learn about Zen."

They finished their coffee and Bill dropped Smokey off at home. Suddenly the empty room frightened him. There was no one to talk to anymore. He had returned to his solitude and found it extremely difficult, but after a while he remembered his mother and how she focused on the little things. He tried to do the same. First he slowly unpacked his things and got a load of laundry ready to go. Then he vacuumed the apartment and swept the kitchen floor. He tried to do each job with mindfulness, concentrating on the task at hand. Smokey managed to fill the rest of the day doing little things around the apartment.

That evening Smokey walked back to Roca Jacks for an evening coffee. Barrie was sitting there sipping a decaf.

Smokey said, "Hi."

Barrie asked, "Would you like to come over to my place and listen to some music?" "Sure."

They left Roca Jacks and headed to Barrie's apartment. Smokey hadn't really seen much of Barrie since their trip to the Badlands with Bill. He remembered the wisdom of the man, especially as it related to Smokey's future. Smokey thought about his mind and the five stones that symbolized his process of consciousness.

Inside Barrie's apartment were hundreds of stones. Some were painted with designs and symbols. Smokey sat down in an arm chair. Barrie was quiet. He was sharing his inner sanctum. He lit a candle and turned out the light. Barrie put on some music and sat down to watch the candle burn. The music was haunting. "It's called shaman flute," Barrie said.

"I like it," said Smokey.

Together they sat and listened to the shaman flute and watched the candle burn. They did not speak.

Smokey left Barrie's about midnight and walked home. On the way home he felt like a spirit was following him. He thought it was a bear spirit, but he couldn't be sure. It was just watching him. It didn't attack. He thought to himself, *Perhaps it is one of Barrie's sprit animals, an ally.*

When Smokey got home, he did a short Zen sitting on his cushion then went straight to bed. That night he dreamed he was in a cave. There was a bear dancer dancing around a fire. Smokey gazed at the shadows on the wall. There was a story being told in the shadows as well as the dancer's story. Smokey thought to himself, *That's how life is, two stories, one told by the rational mind, the other story told by the spirit.* He drifted off into space and time.

The next morning Smokey woke early. He probably hadn't adjusted to the time change between the provinces. It would be eleven o'clock in Ontario but only nine o'clock here in Saskatchewan. He had a quick shower then headed out the door to Roca Jacks for his first cup of coffee for the day. When he arrived, Barrie was already finishing his cup of coffee.

"You can have my table," Barrie said.

Smokey ordered his usual high-test, which was Columbian and espresso. He sat at the table and sipped his coffee. He decided he would go to the club and see if Larry had time to chat. He listened to Van Morrison playing in the background. A good cup of coffee and good music, life wasn't so bad.

Smokey thought about his dream the night before. *Yes,* Smokey thought to himself, *there are two stories of my life. First, there is the rational, the story of a struggling schizophrenic. The second story is one of the emotional spirit.* Smokey thought, *I have emotional memories that effect my rational thought and vice versa. It is a mix which forms total consciousness.* Smokey was beginning to realize that to understand himself he had to accept both versions of himself, even when they conflicted. He was both.

Smokey walked along Eleventh Avenue to the club at Albert Street. He reached the old brick building and went inside. Larry was in his office doing paperwork. He said, "Give me ten minutes and then we can have a coffee." Smokey said, "Sounds good to me." For about ten or fifteen minutes, Smokey sat in the lounge with the rest of the folks. There wasn't much to do at the club except play bingo and smoke. Sometimes there were art and music classes, but the results were generally primitive. There was nothing for the critical mind except writing classes in the evening. Smokey enjoyed the writing classes, but he wasn't very productive. Smokey sat and waited.

Larry came out a few minutes later and said, "Let's go to the coffee shop on Albert street. I need to get out of here." They headed out the door and across the street to a funky little coffee shop. Some contemporary music was playing, stuff Smokey didn't recognize. They sat in large lounge chairs around a wire spool table.

"How was your trip?" Larry asked.

Smokey talked about his adventures building the cabin in the woods.

"It sounds like you had a really good time," Larry said.

"Yes, I really did. I'd like to move out there if I can," Smokey said.

"Well that would be a big step, but I understand how you must feel. The fact that all your family is out east must make a big difference. I'm sure you feel it especially at holiday times like Christmas," Larry said.

"I have my friends here though," Smokey said, "It would be a tough thing to leave my friends behind."

Larry said, "Let's make a list of pros and cons and just see what you're giving up and what you might gain."

They did this together, and much to Smokey's surprise, he was giving up a lot to gain even more if he moved. It would be tough giving up friends, but there was the telephone and internet e-mail to stay in touch with friends.

"When are you planning this move?" Larry asked.

"Hopefully next spring," Smokey said.

"If you're going to be with us for the winter, then I have a plan for you," he said.

"Let's hear it," Smokey said.

Larry unveiled a government program geared toward employment for the disabled.

"I've been down this road before," Smokey said.

Larry talked about a program where Smokey would work for the Canadian Mental Health Association, one day a week, in the accounting department. Larry said, "I have already talked to Alex the accountant there, and the difference is we control the employer recommendation at the end of the program. We aren't dependent on a corporate entity with a different agenda who may assess your value unfairly. It's a way to regain some status as an employee."

Smokey smiled and said, "I'll do it."

Larry said, "The program starts in September and runs until April the following year. You will earn the maximum earnings in social assistance without penalty. You can earn some money before your move out east. Yes, this may all tie in together nicely," Larry said.

"Thanks for setting this up," Smokey said.

"You need something now that you're done school. I think you will like Alex too. We will talk more about your move as the time comes. It can be an easier transition with the right help," Larry said.

Chapter XXXVII

Smokey thanked Larry again and left the coffee shop feeling really hopeful about the coming winter. He had some employment in a meaningful capacity. He walked back to Roca Jacks and found Bill sitting at a table reading a book.

"Is this a time when you would rather not be disturbed?" Smokey asked.

"No, I'm happy for the company," Bill said.

Smokey joined Bill for a coffee. Smokey said "I have work in an accounting department one day a week, starting in September."

"That's good news" Bill said.

"I'll earn an extra $160 per month, which I really need," Smokey said.

Bill pulled out a wooden cribbage board from his coat. "Best two out of three," Bill said.

Smokey said, "Okay." Smokey won the first game, but Bill came back and won two straight.

Bill said, "I'll give you a ride home." Bill dropped Smokey off at his apartment and drove off.

The next month passed slowly. Between his friends, Bill, Barrie, and of course Larry, he had sufficient interaction to prevent solitude from becoming unbearable. During the month of August Smokey also did a little bit of recreational canoeing. He was trying desperately to lose a few pounds. He was embarrassed by his weight and physical condition. In a matter of only a few years, he had gone from being a trim athlete to being sixty pounds overweight. He knew the medications he took didn't help his weight problem, but they were necessary.

The first week of September, Smokey met with Alex, the accountant from the Canadian Mental Health Association. Smokey liked him instantly. The man had a sense of humour which was quite rare. They agreed that Smokey would work every Friday from 8:00 A.M. to 5:00 P.M.. Alex said, "This Friday you will be doing the bank reconciliation. Then you will have payroll and GST to calculate."

Smokey said, "See you Friday!"

Thursday night, Smokey set his alarm for 6:45 and crawled into bed. He couldn't sleep. He tossed and turned most of the night. He was just excited about his new job and the responsibilities that came with it. It had been a long time since he had done a bank reconciliation. Could he still do it? The alarm went off, and Smokey crawled into the shower. He dressed in his new pair of pants supplied by social services. They weren't size 34" any more. They were a 42" waist, but he shaved and put on his new shirt and he felt that he really didn't look too bad.

There was time for a fifteen minute coffee at Roca Jacks if he hurried. He hustled down the street. When he got to Roca Jacks, he noticed that Alex was having a coffee take-out.

Smokey said, "Hello."

"Good morning. Would you like a ride to work since you're here?"

Smokey said, "Thanks, but I think I'll sit for a few minutes then walk over."

"Okay, see you there," Alex said.

Smokey sat at a table near the roaster. He could smell the fresh beans. He drank his coffee slowly, enjoying each mouthful. It had just a slight bitter taste to it which Smokey liked. After he finished his coffee, he walked briskly the six blocks to CMHA. It was a cool morning, but the forecast was for heat. Luckily the offices at CMHA were all air conditioned.

When he reached the CMHA building, Alex took him to the coffee room.

"As I promised," Alex said, "there are two months of bank reconciliations to complete. I'd like you to get started on that this morning."

Smokey said "okay."

Smokey spent the full morning on the bank reconciliations. At noon his bank balance was three cents out. Alex said, "Just leave it, it's okay, I'll find it later." So Smokey left the bank unbalanced and went for dinner. There was a submarine shop close by and Smokey headed there. He ordered a tuna sub with all the trimmings. He was hungry, but he had to make his sub last. He was determined to lose weight.

The afternoon was hard work. It was time to do payroll. Although the payroll was computerized, Smokey had to check every entry. To everyone's satisfaction, Smokey had the payroll completed by 4:30 P.M. Alex got Smokey to do some work on Goods and Service Taxation for the remainder of the day. At 5:00 P.M., Alex came over to see Smokey.

"You're an honest man now," he said. "You've done a solid day's work, and I thank you."

"Next Friday?" Smokey inquired.

"Absolutely," Alex said.

Smokey smiled.

The walk home was warm. It was probably close to 26 degrees, but it was dry heat, very low humidity. The day's work had tired him out. He hadn't used his mind calculating numbers for a long time. He made himself some scrambled eggs for dinner then went right to bed. Smokey slept solidly through the night and did not rise until almost 11:00 A.M.

* * *

It was the middle of autumn. The leaves were changing colour and falling in silence to the cold ground. Soon the lake would be frozen and the snow would fall once again. Smokey made a little extra money raking people's leaves. It was like being surrounded by the dead, Smokey thought. It was beautiful.

Smokey worked one day a week, every week until Christmas. He did odd jobs also, trying to earn money for his move out east. He recognized how much he had in Regina, but he knew that the big city of Toronto was waiting for him.

Smokey spent Christmas with Bill and Barrie. They had Christmas dinner together on Boxing Day. Bill cooked a turkey complete with stuffing and vegetables. Everyone chipped in and helped with preparations. Despite the good friendships, Smokey felt a loneliness. He missed his family. They had sent him gifts and they talked on the phone, but it wasn't the same as being all together. Smokey was glad when the festive season was over and he could go back to his Friday job and any casual labour that came up.

Smokey woke one Friday morning in February to the sounds of screaming voices in his head. "*Nigger, nigger, cunt licker,*" the voices screamed over and over in his head.

Smokey thought, *Have I forgotten to take my medication*? His rational mind told him he was mentally ill and that the illness goes in cycles. There are good periods and bad.

But Smokey also thought about those ghost white creatures that chanted racial slurs in his dreams or when he astral-traveled. *Could it be that those creatures were controlling my mind? Have they penetrated my mind*? Smokey wondered.

He flopped on his bed with frustration and pulled a pillow over his head. It didn't help. The voices persisted. He phoned in sick. He couldn't go to work under these conditions. And perhaps some people could read his mind. He didn't want others to hear his voices. *What would they think*? Smokey thought.

The voices in his head persisted for several days. He became more and more disoriented. His own thoughts were mixed with the voices. It became very confusing, but it was the feeling that came with it that was the most damaging. He felt responsible for what the voices said. With this came a feeling of worthlessness. Was he truly becoming some form of Nazi? Smokey wondered. A shiver went through his spine. *What if I really am the reincarnation of some Nazi spirit? Or what if there is a portal to my mind that demons can enter*? Smokey thought.

It was February 14, Valentine's Day. Smokey's mind was finally silent. The quiet felt really weird, like he was in a sensory deprivation tank. He had become so used to the screaming that the quiet enhanced his sense of solitude. *Maybe it's better to have a screaming voice than nothing at all,* he thought. He knew that he would never be in love like he was with Sherry. *You're only granted one great love in a lifetime,* he thought. Still, a partner would break up this solitude. He got dressed and headed to Roca Jacks for coffee. It seemed that everywhere he went there were couples together. It angered him. He felt cheated by life. He was tired of being alone.

Smokey sat and drank his coffee in his new found silence. About half way through his coffee, Bill tapped him on his shoulder.

"Can I join you?"

Smokey said, "Absolutely."

Bill said, "I wrote a poem for today."

Smokey thought it would be something mushy, but he said, "Let's hear it."

Bill said, "It's called 'Fuck Off February.'" Bill's poem was a scathing criticism of society and how single people are treated. At the end of the poem, Smokey just smiled. He wasn't alone! Bill brought out the cribbage board. They played five games.

The winter months passed quickly. Smokey had saved nine hundred dollars from his work, which he kept in a sock in his dresser. The reason he didn't bank it was social service would take any funds in excess of five hundred dollars. They periodically checked his account for money.

It was the end of March when Smokey received a call from his brother Ross.

"It's time to put our plan into action. I've got subsidized housing for you starting May first," Ross said. "There are things that you will have to do. Check with social services and find out what they will pay for. We also need the mental health clinic to transfer your file," Ross said. "I'll send you a list of things to do at your end."

After the call, Smokey plopped down on the floor. His head was swimming with details and plans he had to implement. It was going to happen. He had housing in Toronto. This was a small miracle. People wait for years, sometimes, for proper housing.

A few days later, a letter and a to-do list came from Ross. Smokey followed the list step by step. It was well thought out. One of his jobs was to contact social services and advise then of his intentions. Smokey decided he would do that right away.

Smokey sat in the social services center that was combined with the mental health clinic and waited to see Shirley, his worker. A man with a fuzzy black beard and beady eyes was pacing the floor, back and forth. Every few minutes he would shout out an obscenity. Smokey smiled. *I've been there*, he thought.

His name was called and he went through the doors to Shirley's office. She smiled at him and asked how the part-time work was going. Smokey said it was going great.

"What can we do for you?" she asked.

"I'm moving to Toronto," Smokey said. "My family is there."

"I understand," Shirley said. "We will have things to do. When will all this happen?"

Smokey said, "I will be moving at the end of April."

Shirley was a pro. She had handled nearly everything in her day. To her credit, she never lost her compassion for humanity. She helped Smokey with all the details. As it turned out, social services would pay for a one-way bus ticket to Toronto for Smokey, plus it would ship his personal things by freight carrier. The truth was, since social services is provincially administered, they are more than happy to see a social assistance recipient move to another province. They will pay to help you move with the understanding that you do not return for at least five years.

The next step was to get letters from his psychiatrist stating his condition. They decided after a brief discussion that he should remain as disabled in terms of status. He was listed as a paranoid schizophrenic suffering from depression. The psychiatrist drafted the letter and let Smokey read it. The final letter would be ready next week, the psychiatrist said.

The next thing Smokey did was get employment references from Alex and Larry. He received a glowing report from Alex, which made him feel good. Larry's reference was both for employment and personal character. It was also very good.

The next step finalized everything and made it seem real. He gave his notice at the apartment block. After giving notice, he established final days for telephone and power, with the respective companies. Having done this he sat down on a kitchen chair and let his heart stop pounding in his chest. The fact that he was moving seemed to produced adrenalin with every step that he took.

The last few weeks passed very quickly. Bill would meet Smokey at Roca Jacks two or three times a week and they would play cribbage. Smokey worked at CMHA in the accounting department right up to the last week.

At last the movers came and picked up his belongings to be shipped to Toronto. Smokey cleaned the apartment and turned in the keys at the landlord's office. Bill picked Smokey up at the apartment's front doors and they went to Bill's place. Smokey left his suitcase in the car. The bus left for Toronto on Sunday night. It would be a two-and-a-half day trip.

They had about four hours to wait for the bus. Bill brought out the cards. They played a game called pig rummy. Smokey lost nearly every hand. His mind was elsewhere. About an hour before departure of the Toronto bus, Bill drove Smokey to the station. Smokey bought his ticket and then sat in the waiting room. Bill said, "This is a big step for you. Just remember you have friends here."

Smokey felt weak. He didn't know if he was making the right decision. Would he find work in Toronto? If not, what would he do in Canada's biggest city? He would be close to his family, but he was saying goodbye to these really good friends.

The bus let out a hiss of air brakes as it came into the station. People had ten minutes to board the bus. Smokey put his suitcase down in front of the loading zone. Smokey and Bill shook hands. He stepped into the bus and found a window seat. Bill waved and went back to his car. The bus pulled out.

Chapter XXXVIII

Smokey caught glimpses of his last prairie sunset even though he was headed east. He could see clouds with pink underbellies to the south. It wasn't long before he could see the moon. It seemed like the moon was following the bus down the highway. Smokey asked himself, "Have I done the right thing? All I really want is a little cottage by a lake with my canoe, but I'm moving to the biggest city in Canada!" If there had been room, Smokey would have paced the floor with anxiety.

Slowly Smokey began to calm down. In fact, it wasn't long before exhaustion overtook him and he fell fast asleep. Smokey woke just as the bus rumbled into the Winnipeg station. Instantly Smokey was filled with paranoia. All the old memories of Winnipeg came flooding back into his consciousness. Even though there was an hour to wait, Smokey didn't leave the bus. He was not going into that terminal, no matter what happened. The memory of being soaking wet from rain and living in the bus terminal was too vivid. He found himself shaking uncontrollably as he sat in his seat. The bus driver came back and asked if he was okay. "As soon as I leave here I'll be okay," Smokey said.

It was the longest hour of Smokey's life, but eventually the bus pulled out. The sun was just coming up in the east. The bus wound its way through the Cambrian Shield. There was a forty-five minute stop just outside Kenora, Ontario. Smokey took the opportunity to stretch his legs. It was a long way to Thunder Bay, the next major stop.

Smokey's mind went numb while he sat in the bus. Time just seemed to tick on. He didn't feel like reading, and sometimes he couldn't even look out the window of the bus. It was like he was in a trance. He did think about his brother, Ross, though, and how good it would be to see him and Kathryn. The bus was in Thunder Bay before he even realized it. It was dark out, but Smokey could see city lights up ahead. He had been riding the bus now for two days. The bus driver said, "We will arrive in Sudbury shortly." There was time for sandwiches and coffee in Sudbury, plus a badly needed bathroom break. Smokey's back was beginning to ache from all the sitting. He tried to do some stretches.

After leaving Sudbury, Smokey could no longer sleep. He felt his excitement build with each passing mile of highway. They would arrive in Toronto about ten o'clock in the morning. Smokey sat on pins and needles. He watched the landscape change from evergreen forest to farmland. The highway ran parallel to railway tracks. They caught up with a train headed south to the big city. Smokey tried to count the railway cars as they sped along.

Smokey watched as they went through underpass after underpass. There were commercial buildings and company advertising all around then. It seemed like an endless field of corporate America as they entered Toronto. There were smaller cities, but Smokey lost track of their names as they came to the edge of the big city.

Soon they were in the hustle and bustle of city traffic. It seemed like they hit every red light in the city. The bus rumbled along making two or three stops in the city. Finally the bus pulled into the downtown station in Toronto at Bay and Dundas Streets. It was actually one block north of Dundas, but those were the streets Smokey recognized.

Smokey looked out the window of the bus. He spotted his brother's graying hair in the crowd, and then he saw Kathryn. They both had come to greet him. Smokey took a deep breath and stood up. He followed the line of passengers out the bus doors to the landing. His brother and Kathryn gave him a big hug each, then they waited for his suitcase to be unloaded.

"How was the trip?" his brother asked.

"Long," Smokey said with a smile.

"Well, you have the rest of the week to recover, plus the weekend. Then we must get things done," Ross said.

Ross took them to a little restaurant on Yonge Street where they ate heartily. Then they drove home. Smokey was given the spare room, and the futon was made up as a bed. He lay down and slept most of the day. Ross called him for supper. "Tomorrow you should get used to the subway system. I'll give you some tokens," Ross said.

Smokey knew he had to learn the subway system, but he wasn't sure he was ready yet. The subway frightened him. There was the fear of power failures and being trapped in the tunnel, plus the crowds of people and possibly getting lost! Then there was the fears of an accident on the subway. The trains moved at such a terrific pace. If he could travel the subway alone tomorrow it would be a big step.

Kathryn had been busy that afternoon. She had been to the market and picked up some fresh salmon for supper. They were breaking with routine and cooking a big meal in the middle of the week. The salmon was done just right, and with just a touch of lemon, it was divine. During supper Ross gave Smokey suggestions for things he could do tomorrow.

Smokey was ready for bed by nine o'clock. The futon was fairly comfortable, and he slept soundly. By the time Smokey got up the next morning, Ross and Kathryn were both gone to work. They left him a key to the house and some subway tokens. Smokey had a quick shower, and then he headed out the door to find a coffee shop. His brother's house was only five blocks south of Danforth Avenue, a major artery in the city. Smokey walked up to the Danforth and found a Second Cup coffee shop on the corner. He ordered a dark roast coffee and sat on a stool facing the street. He watched the people go by. It was much faster than Regina. The big difference was coffee shops were for coffee. They weren't a place to meet people, like Roca Jack's in Regina.

Smokey sat at the coffee shop for almost two hours gathering strength of mind and spirit for his next adventure, the subway. Finally he could delay no longer, and he walked over to the Chester subway station. Smokey let his token fall into the little glass container, and with a deep breath he walked through the turnstile. He walked slowly down the steps to the subway line heading west.

He caught sight of the beaming light of the subway train and heard the high pitched horn as it approached the subway station landing. Several people got off at the Chester station, but the train was still full. Smokey could feel the knots in his stomach clench. He stepped onto the train. There was no place to sit. He had to stand in the aisle. It seemed like everyone was staring at him. Was he talking to himself? Why were they staring? Did he look like a country bumpkin? He rode the train to Yonge Street station, and then he got off.

Smokey walked down Yonge Street to Sam the Record Man's store. It was right where Ross had said it was. He couldn't believe the selection of music in the store. They had everything. Smoke found the tape he was looking for, a Leonard Cohen tape, and made the purchase.

It was time to catch the subway home. The ride home was even more crowded. He had to stand three inches away from someone else. He could feel the man's breath and smell it too! But other than the overcrowded cars, there were no problems. He didn't get lost or trapped in the tunnel. He realized most of his fears were unfounded.

The following Monday, Ross drove Smokey to the social services center in their area. The rules were different here. They needed more than one doctor's opinion on Smokey's mental health condition. Also, there was a question as to whether his situation was a federal or provincial responsibility. The bottom line, however, was that he was disabled and needed support. After filling out endless forms, Smokey would receive a personal allowance of about two-hundred dollars a month until he gained his own housing.

The next step was to attend an interview with the housing agency and view the apartment he would be given. The housing agency had an office right on the Danforth, so Smokey walked there. He sat in a waiting room filled with books and computers. Smokey noticed *The Deptford Trilogy* by Robertson Davies sitting on a shelf.

A tall slender woman with graying hair and deep brown eyes came in and sat at the desk. She introduced herself as Marg and asked him his full name. They filled out a form together. This organization also needed a doctor's statement of Smokey's mental history.

At the end of the interview Marg said, "We can show you the suite tomorrow if that's suitable."

Smokey said, "Yes, that would be great."

That evening Smokey filled Ross and Kathryn in on what had transpired. They celebrated with a pizza for dinner. The place where the apartment was situated was only a couple of miles away. Smokey decided he would get up early and walk there.

The alarm clock when off at 10:00 A.M.. Smokey had an hour to get to the housing agency. He skipped having a morning shower and quickly shaved off his whiskers. He walked south on Carlaw to Queen Street, then he went west on Queen to Lewis Street. He was at the right place. Smokey was surprised. It was a fairly new building.

Smokey met an intake worker named Nathan at the building. They talked for a few minutes until the building supervisor arrived with the keys. They went in together. The hallways were clean and bright. They opened apartment 1C and went inside. The floor was a dull grey-white and needed cleaning, but the walls were a nice pastel green and in good shape. The kitchen was clean with white cupboards. What sold Smokey on the unit were the large windows facing west.

Nathan asked "Do you think you could live here?"

Smokey said, "Absolutely. It's perfect."

Nathan handed him the keys and said, "It's yours. Just pay the monthly rent at the office this afternoon."

Smokey didn't delay. He went straight to the housing agency's office and paid the monthly balance due. The units were subsidized, and since he was only getting two hundred dollars from social services, the housing payment was minimal.

The following day Smokey had his first appointment with Spectrum, the mental health clinic his brother had contacted on his behalf. Smokey sat in a small waiting room with nice furniture. There were pictures on the walls and black leather sofas and chairs to sit in. He felt comfortable while he waited.

About fifteen minutes later, a tall man with curly black hair called Smokey's name. "Hi, my name's Edward. I'll be seeing you today," the man said. They went into a small office and Edward closed the door. "Did you bring your referrals?" Edward asked. Smokey took out his two letters from Saskatchewan and gave them to Edward.

While Edward read the letters, Smokey looked around the room. There were interesting masks made out of leather on the walls, and what interested Smokey most was a small meditation cushion in the corner of the room. Edward put the letters down and said, "Welcome to Spectrum. I'll be your worker."

They spent the next forty-five minutes getting to know one another. Smokey found out during that time that Edward was a Zen Buddhist and deeply devout. Smokey revealed his own inclinations towards meditation. He knew they were a perfect match. Smokey left Spectrum feeling like he had met a new friend.

When Smokey got home, there was a message for him. His furniture would be delivered to his suite tomorrow. There already was a hide-a-bed in the suite, so Smokey said to Ross, "It's time I made myself a home. Will you drive me over to the apartment?" Ross smiled and said he would be glad to. Smokey borrowed some sheets and a blanket for bedding, and he spent the first night in the apartment.

The hide-a-bed was uncomfortable. Smokey tossed and turned most of the night. He woke during the night with the feeling that someone was trying to choke him to death. It was such a strong feeling, he knew it had to be real. There were dark spirits in the apartment.

The next morning he met his neighbour below him. The man was an aging giant. He was probably three-hundred pounds and in his early fifties. Smokey learned from his neighbour Doug that the man who had lived in his apartment before him had died in the apartment during his sleep. Smokey was convinced that the man's spirit was still in the building. He walked back to his brother's place and waited to tell him what had happened.

Ross had to work late, so it was nearly 7:00 P.M. when Smokey told him his story. Ross went into the bedroom and brought out a rod of sweetgrass and a Buddhist drum. He said, "Let's go." They went back to the apartment together. Ross lit the sweetgrass and they chanted a Buddhist prayer for trapped spirits. They ended the ceremony with a recitation of the four vows. Smokey felt much better. He was ready to spend another night alone. Smokey said goodbye to Ross at the door.

Since Smokey hadn't been at his apartment all day, his furniture wasn't delivered until the following day, much to the anger of the movers. He spent the day unpacking his thing and hanging up pictures. He hung Bill's picture of the four loons over his bed. That made the place home. The dark spirit that had choked him in his sleep did not return.

Smokey spent the next few days making his apartment home. He went out and bought some plants. He still had about eight hundred dollar savings, so he bought himself a colour TV.

The next challenge was to get a telephone line from Ma Bell. Bell needed the name of his Welfare worker. Smokey thought that this was intrusive. He finally got a telephone line, but they definitely were not pleased to serve him. In a way, Smokey could see why Bell was reluctant to serve him. Welfare recipients receive so little they can't afford a phone, but if you want to be employment-ready, you definitely need a phone. How else can employers contact you?

Sunday Smokey was invited to Ross and Kathryn's for dinner. He was told by Ross to bring all his old resumes and to be thinking about presenting himself for employment in the near future. When Smokey arrived for dinner, Ross had the *Toronto Star* out on the table, open to the career section. He had several positions circled. The one job that looked the best was a position of coordinator for a small business. It stated that consumer survivors would be given preference.

Smokey asked, "What's a consumer survivor?"

Kathryn said, "It's someone who has been through the mental health system."

"Good," Smokey said, "I qualify."

Ross helped Smokey draft a letter of application to the agency advertising the position. Then it was dinner time. Ross said, "I'll have a resume printed for you at work with the covering letter. You can pick them up on Tuesday. Then if you're happy with it, you can send it off."

On Tuesday Smokey received a courier package. He opened the package and found a detailed resume geared toward the position of coordinator. There was also the covering letter, which Smokey signed. He mailed his resume and letter that afternoon.

Two weeks later, Smokey was the business coordinator for a consumer survivor cleaning company. He had really aced the interview, but already he was wondering if he could live up to expectations.

The first two weeks Smokey spent planning with the board of directors. There was a great deal of excitement in the air. Smokey still couldn't believe he had landed a job that paid forty thousand dollars per year. Smokey had strong accounting skills and good administrative skills. He brought the accounting records up to date.

After five weeks on the job, it became apparent Smokey needed help, possibly a mentor to assist him in his duties. He was determined not to give up. He didn't ride the subway all the way to Etobicoke every day to work for nothing. He came home every night exhausted.

It was crunch time and Smokey had to produce. There were many problems. The cleaning company wasn't even a legal entity. It wasn't a proprietorship and it wasn't a limited company, therefore it had to be a partnership. Unfortunately, none of the consumer survivors wanted to be partners because of the legal responsibility. As a result, Smokey couldn't register the company, file with Revenue Canada, or acquire workers' compensation. These problems, however, could all be overcome. The real problem was sales. After nearly seven weeks on the job, Smokey hadn't landed a single contract. It wasn't from lack of effort either. He had tried several cold calls and talked to people who said they were interested. According to a marketing survey done, there should have been lots of potential customers. But when Smokey called, some people were actually openly hostile!

After ten weeks on the job, the cleaning company was still not a legal entity and had no contracts. Smokey knew he must resign, but it hurt real bad. He had waited for a job like this all his life, it seemed. Now he had failed when the pressure was on. If he gave up this job, how could he live with himself? He couldn't bullshit anymore. He couldn't do the job. Smokey submitted his resignation and took the subway home for the last time.

As he rode the train, it seemed like people were laughing at him. Did they know he had resigned? When Smokey got home he phoned his brother and told him the news. His brother wasn't surprised. Both Ross and Kathryn had been coaching him on the job for several weeks. They were prepared for Smokey's decision. Ross said, "Go find yourself a nice coffee shop and relax. We'll see you Sunday for dinner."

Smokey did find a little coffee shop just a few blocks from his apartment. It was called The Eye of the Storm. Just as he sat down, a rather large fellow said to him, "You're in my building. My name is Peter."

"You can call me Smokey," he said. "Would you like to join me for a coffee?"

"I'll have tea," Peter said. "I bet you're born under the sign of Cancer. I can tell by your facial features."

They talked about astrology for the next hour. Peter knew all the zodiac signs and their traits, both physical and personal traits he could determine for people. Smokey couldn't believe Peter had guessed right. There are twelve zodiac signs. What is the probability of guessing the right one? They decided they would meet again for coffee another time. Peter gave Smokey his telephone number.

Chapter XXXIV

Despite finding a new friend, Smokey found the days long with little to do. He found himself getting quite excited about Sunday dinner with Ross and Kathryn.

On Sunday Ross presented Smokey with a new plan. He could help out at the Zen Centre on Fridays with yardwork and painting. "It will put some structure in your day," Ross said. Smokey agreed this was a good idea. He wanted to get closer to the Zen Centre and its people. The memory of building the cabin with Zen Buddhists was still fresh in his mind. He wanted that fellowship.

Throughout the remainder of summer and autumn, Smokey worked Fridays at the Zen Centre. He painted the trim of the building a rich blue-grey, including around the windows. Smokey also did weeding around the shrubs and flowers. He would spend four or five hours there on Friday, and his brother would pick him up after and take him home.

Things were starting to take shape for Smokey in Toronto. He had a friend in Peter, and he had volunteer work at the Zen Centre. If he could just find a similar job that didn't have a lot of stress, he would be satisfied.

It was a Tuesday afternoon when Smokey received a call from Ross. "Would you like to join us for an evening sitting at the Zen Center? Tim and David will be there," Ross said.

Smokey wasn't sure he was ready for an hour and a half of sitting, but he said, "Okay."

They arrived at the Zen Centre at 6:40. Sitting meditation started at seven. There was a sense of concentration in the air even before the zendo opened. Smokey changed into a robe and nodded to David on the stairs. He smiled back. Smokey entered the zendo. There was a sort of shelf waist high all around the perimeter of the room with mats and cushions carefully laid down on it. In the center of the room was the most beautiful Buddha figure Smokey had ever seen.

Smokey couldn't help but feel a sense of reverence for the atmosphere that was created.

Smokey sat on one of the cushions not far from David and Ross. At ten to seven a gong sounded as a warning to prepare for sitting. Smokey stretched his legs for the last time. At seven o'clock the zendo was full of people. This crystal clear sound of a small bell was sounded three times. Sitting had begun.

Smokey began to count his breath as he had been instructed to do. He was nervous with all the people there. Then it happened. A voice screamed, "*The Buddha is an ass-licking cocksucker.*" Smokey knew it was his voice. He waited to be removed from the zendo. He waited, and he waited. Nobody came to remove him. Had he really said this out loud?

He felt really bad. Everything that he held sacred was defiled by his own mind. Why does this happen? Then Smokey began to tell himself a story in his mind. He said, *Once a long time ago when God was in my mind, he spoke to me and said, "Do not eat of that fruit. It contains the knowledge of good and evil. Then I felt my mind was empty and God was gone! So I ate the fruit. Here I sit millions of years later struggling with duality, longing to be set free!* The bell sounded and the first round of sitting was over. There was a five-minute walking meditation. Then the second round of sitting began.

Smokey still didn't understand why he must defile what was sacred to him. He felt really awful inside. The very fact that he felt so bad was an indication to him that he knew good from evil. Then he remembered his brother sharing a koan with him. In this koan the Buddha is referred to as shit on a stick. What could this possibly mean? Smokey thought if he understood this koan his suffering would be reduced. Still, he had no answer. The bell sounded to end the second round of sitting.

During the third and final round of sitting, Smokey's mind had exhausted itself. The monkey chatter stopped. He counted his breath with renewed vigor. Then the final bell rang and they recited four vows. "All beings without number I vow to liberate; endless blind passions, I vow to uproot; dharma gates beyond measure, I vow to penetrate; the great way of Buddha, I vow to attain." The sitting was over. Each individual bowed three times to the Buddha and left the zendo. Ross and a few of the boys took Smokey out for tea after the sitting.

"How was the sitting?" Tim asked Smokey.

"It was a real struggle," Smokey said.

"Well," Tim said, "if it wasn't a struggle there would be little point in doing it."

Smokey smiled and said, "I guess you're right, but no one has a mind like mine."

They sipped their tea. The men were clearly supportive.

"See you next week," Tim said with a smile as everyone left for home.

On the way home, Ross talked with Smokey. He said, "Nobody can read your mind. We all have our struggles. Even if we could read your mind, what would we gain? In true Buddhism, there is no judgement."

Smokey said, "I can rationalize it, but my emotions haven't caught up. I still feel horrible guilt about all the things that go through my mind."

Ross dropped Smokey off at his apartment and said "Good night." That evening Smokey sat on his cushion alone and tried to make sense of his mind. "How can you have no judgement?" Smokey asked himself. "Isn't that just an illusion?" Yet we know that judgement and attachment is the root of all suffering. Smokey sat and pondered these questions until early in the morning.

* * *

It was late November. Most of the leaves had fallen and been gathered. There hadn't been a sunny day for over a week. Smokey could feel depression setting in. The fact that work had ended at the Zen Centre made things even more difficult. His only source of interaction and communication was with his friend Peter. Peter had not been well lately. As a result, Smokey was alone nearly all the time.

Smokey woke about 2:00 P.M. from a restless sleep. He didn't shower or shave. He hadn't showered or shaved for five days. He just felt like crawling into a hole till spring came. Despite his feelings, he decided to go to the store and buy a paper. Maybe there was a job for him in the paper.

Smokey left his apartment and started walking down the street. He noticed a man from the neighbourhood. He smiled and said, "Good afternoon."

The man's eyes flashed. He curled his lips in a sneer and spat, "Welfare shit!" The man then quickly walked by.

Smokey almost staggered with the impact of those words. It hit him really hard. He turned around and slowly walked back to his apartment. He went to the washroom and sat on the toilet. He thought, *I'm not the canoeing champion of Canada. I'm not a constitutional lawyer. I'm not a business coordinator. I don't even have a regular job*! He sat there absorbing his failures one at a time. They overwhelmed him. He remembered the days of his own home and having someone to share it. He thought about the past. Was the best part of life over?

Smokey looked into the mirror and saw the few grey hairs at his temple. "Am I destined to a life of Welfare?" he asked. He noticed the package of razors on the counter. He pulled one out of the package and stared at it. Then it was as if his mind went numb. He drove the blade into his left arm. He pulled down. A crimson flow trickled down his arm, off the elbow, onto the floor. Smokey just watched passively now. The pain was intense, but at the same time it was good. It was right. It was just.

Soon there was a substantial pool of blood on the floor. Smokey came to his senses and wrapped his arm in a towel. Then he bent down and put his index finger into the bloody pool onto the floor. He looked at his finger carefully. Then he wrote "W" on the bathroom wall with his blood. Next he wrote an "E." Soon it was complete. Signed in blood on the bathroom wall was "welfare shit." Smokey put his hands in Gassho, or prayer, and said out loud, "I bow to my new identity."

Smokey left the bathroom and lay down on his bed. He knew he had to go to the hospital, but he felt so tired. He didn't think he had the energy to ride the subway, yet he knew he must. He dragged himself to his feet and headed out the door.

When he arrived at the hospital he was greeted by a nurse who checked out his arm. "How did this happen?" she asked.

Smokey lied. "I was cutting carpet and the knife slipped." They applied some freezing compound to his skin then the doctor stitched him up.

On his way home, Smokey thought about what had happened. He had lost control just for a split second. He wasn't himself—or maybe he was his true self. "I can't let this happen again" he said. He needed to talk to someone about what happened. It was difficult. He wanted people to listen, to hear his cry, yet his silence said more.

When he got home he made an appointment to see Edward at Spectrum. He had to wait two days to see him, and by that time he thought he had a healthier perspective on the situation.

Edward invited him into his office and closed the door. Edward noticed Smokey's arm. "What happened?" he asked. At first Smokey couldn't find the words. He remained silent. Gradually however, Smokey spoke about the events that had troubled him so deeply. Edward listened.

When Smokey was done talking, there was silence again. Then Edward said, "It's all about attachment. You're attached to the concept of work versus welfare."

Smokey thought about this for a moment. He realized it was true. He was attached to the identity of welfare shit and all the despair it brought. But what he said was, "How can I not be attached?"

Edward said, "You can sit."

It was tough medicine, but Smokey understood. If he really believed in the Buddha way, he had to live the life. He went home feeling much better and prepared himself for a round of sitting.

Time passed slowly until Christmas. Smokey would spend time doing the little things mindfully, like watering his plants or doing his dishes. It was a period of letting go. He had to let go of old dreams and accept his present life, knowing that this new life had value too. Every night Smokey would sit on his cushion for thirty-five minutes. It charged him up and it helped through the days.

* * *

It was Christmas Eve. Ross, Kathryn, and Smokey traveled to Owen Sound to have Christmas with their parents. It was a nice evening. They decorated the tree and made eggnog in the blender. It was a time to be together. It was a time that Smokey had waited for for a long time, yet Smokey felt bad that he couldn't give gifts. All he could afford was a few cards. but they came from the heart.

It seemed time went much too quickly during family get-togethers and very slowly at other times. For Smokey it was the social element. He spent so much time in solitude that being with family was a real treat. Smokey savoured every moment. There was the usual family teasing. Smokey received a pig's nose that he was supposed to wear as a gift from his mother. This little gift had a sting to it, but Smokey laughed it off. Perhaps he was the pig of the family. He was the one in rumpled pants and needing a hair cut. It was all meant in fun anyway. Nevertheless, there is the inevitable problem of looking good on welfare. There is barely enough money for food, let alone good clothes and a nice haircut. And what about shaving requirements and deodorant? Smokey did his best, but often he looked poor and unkempt.

It was time to say goodbye to his parents. Smokey gave his mother a big hug and shook his step-dad's hand. Ross and Kathryn did the same. Smokey's mom said, "Come visit us at Easter." Smokey could tell his mother was a bit lonely at times. He promised he would take the bus up to see them as soon as he could save thirty dollars for the trip.

The winter months passed. Smokey was good to his word and made a trip up to see his parents in March. During the winter months, Smokey sat on his cushion regularly. It was no longer as difficult to sit. He actually found himself needing to sit on a regular basis. Smokey couldn't describe what sitting did for him, but he knew it was an important element in his life now.

It was a warm spring day when Smokey received a call from Ross. "How would you like to spend the weekend at the cabin?" Ross asked.

Smokey said, "I was hoping for a chance to go up there."

"I'll pick you up tomorrow morning," Ross said.

Ross picked Smokey up at 6:00 A.M. the next morning and they headed for the cabin. It felt good to gradually rid oneself of the city stresses. As the landscape changed from industrial grey to farm red soil, then to an evergreen tree line, Smokey felt excitement build in his bones. They arrived at the cabin in the early afternoon. Tim and David were there, and Brad was expected shortly.

When all had arrived, they decided to go for a hike through the Algonquin Park. It was too early for bugs of any kind, so it was a real treat to be outside. They climbed steadily for about an hour until they reached a lookout. Smokey gazed out at the forest. He thought he saw an eagle circling in the distance. This was God's country! Smokey noticed a sign. He went over to it and checked it out. CANOE THE MADAWASKA RAPIDS. WEEKEND RATES AS LOW AS $300.

Smokey knew he had a new dream—something he could work toward. He could save about twenty dollars a month, and he could start working out. He needed to get in shape. He could see himself canoeing the Madawaska Rapids in no time at all. Maybe he could even hire on as a naturalist-canoeist. Anything was possible. Smokey kept his dreams to himself, but he was very excited.

That evening the men sat out under the stars. Brad brought out his telescope. It was a great way to end the day. The day had brought some life back into Smokey. He had friends. He had goals and dreams. Life was really worth living. Not only that, his fellowship among Zen Buddhist had renewed his convictions. Before the evening ended, Smokey wrote in his diary with the aid of a flashlight. "My dreams are smaller, but I will canoe the Madawaska Rapids, and when I don't understand a God who can create such suffering, I shall count my breath. When at the end of a day I have been blessed with true friendships and yet still I feel an emptiness within, I shall count my breath! And when the voices in my head cause me to cry out, 'Stop! Stop!' I shall sit and count my breath."

Smokey pulled out his cushion in the dark and placed it two feet from the cabin wall. He sat down. He began to count his breath.